MESSAGES

David Cunningham

*To Henry —
So nice to meet you.
Keep writing, and
stay creative!

David Cunningham*

AmErica House
Baltimore

First printing

On the Cover: "Romantic Day" by Jim Warren is used with gracious permission of the artist. Mr. Warren won a Grammy Award for his cover art on Bob Seger's hit album "Against the Wind," and his work has appeared on more than 100 other book covers. His fine art studio in Clearwater, Florida, can be contacted through www.jimwarren.com.

ISBN: 1-58851-179-0
PUBLISHED BY AMERICA HOUSE BOOK PUBLISHERS
www.publishamerica.com
Baltimore

Printed in the United States of America

For Debra, who is love in its purest form.

And for Tara and Brad, the lighthouses of my life.

ACKNOWLEDGMENTS

You wouldn't be reading this if not for Debra Sack. She encouraged me to quit a perfectly good career, load everything I own onto a truck, drive across the entire country, and then sit in front of a computer until a book appeared. She believed it would happen. I believed she was crazy.

A book did appear. I leave it for you to decide if it has any value, but this much I do know – it's much better now than it was before I joined the Fiction Writers Discussion Group, which meets every Tuesday night at the Borders bookstore in Brea, California. My sincere thanks to everyone in the group who lovingly lambasted my humble effort, chapter by chapter. Because of them, this work is readable.

I'm also grateful to AmErica House Book Publishers, who put this book in your hands and had the guts to say they want to see my next one, too.

Oh, and Debra Sack is now Debra Cunningham. I'm grateful for that, too. Happy endings all around.

TABLE OF CONTENTS

Prologue

Something magical happened in the autumn of 2000. As word spreads, eventually it may come to be seen as the dawn of a new age for mankind. How can we ever be the same, now that Jewel and Dakin Caravans have opened the door for us? They've given us definitive answers to two of life's greatest questions, once thought unanswerable:

Is there life after death?

Why are we here?

I could be wrong. I'm a writer admittedly given to occasional flights of imagination. I look for deep meanings and happy endings. I'm captivated by the mysterious and beautiful. And this story has all those elements. I sensed it immediately when I read that first newspaper article on the death of Dakin Caravans.

It wasn't a major event. Few people had ever heard of him, although Caravans had been a newspaper sportswriter, a drummer for minor rock bands, and a modestly talented artist who sold celebrity portraits.

Until October of 2000, his main distinction was having been witness to history. As a news, sports and entertainment reporter, he met three U.S. Presidents, countless stars from Bob Hope to Tom Hanks, Aretha Franklin to Heather Locklear, plus every major sports figure of the last 30 years, from Muhammad Ali to Michael Jordan and, yes, O.J. Simpson.

Despite his fascination with the Simpson case, Dakin Caravans was no murderer and he did not commit suicide, no matter what the police may think. He could no more have killed his wife than he could have spread his arms and flown to the moon.

Actually, it's more likely that Dakin Caravans could have flown to the moon than kill another human being. He definitely flew somewhere, and he did it under his own power. He was shown the way by his remarkable wife, Jewel, who left this realm of existence exactly one month before Dakin did.

There's no doubt in my mind that they're still together, watching us and waiting for others to discover what they have: we are not yet fully evolved. There is a higher reality. In researching the Caravans case, I have come to believe that.

What will you believe? Here's the evidence. Make up your own mind. I begin with a copy of the police report on Dakin Caravans' death.

---------◇---------

City of Greentree Police Department
Incident report

Date: 10/29/2000
Greentree PD Case Number: 71000719-00

INCIDENT DATA
Incident type: SUSPICIOUS DEATH; POSSIBLE SUICIDE
Address of occurrence: 401 AVENIDA DE LA LUZ
Originally received as: REPORT OF DEAD BODY
Type of premise: POLICE DEPARTMENT JAIL CELL
Copies to: INTERNAL AFFAIRS
Date reported: 10/28/2000
Time reported: 2235 HRS
Weapons or objects used: UNKNOWN
Reporting officer: SGT. BUSSIERE
Processed by: L. PARKER

VICTIM
Name: DAKIN CARAVANS
Sex: MALE
Race: CAUCASIAN
Age: 47
Date of birth: 1/5/53
Home address: 19 SANTA BELLA RD, IRVINE, CA.
Occupation: RETIRED SPORTSWRITER
Business address: N/A
Place of birth: PASADENA, CA.
Marital status: WIDOWER

NARRATIVE
    Subject DAKIN CARAVANS was arrested on 10/28/2000 at 1033 HRS and was being held at the Greentree PD pending indictment for first-degree murder in the death of his wife, JEWEL CARAVANS, which occurred on 9/28/00 in a motor home parked within the Greentree city limits (See GPD report 71000413-00). Subject DAKIN CARAVANS was cooperative and had been interviewed by LT. DICK NAJERA shortly after booking. CARAVANS was being held in Cell No. 1 and was last seen alive by LORRAINE PARKER, a civilian clerk with GPD, at approximately 2015

HRS, when she passed through the cell area and saw him sitting in a cross-legged position, apparently meditating. This was an activity he was known to practice. I entered the cell area at approximately 2235 HRS and found subject CARAVANS lying in a supine position, motionless and apparently not breathing. There were no signs of trauma or visible injuries. Subject had no pulse or respiration. GFD paramedics were summoned. Efforts to revive the subject were unsuccessful. Subject CARAVANS was pronounced dead on arrival at Torrance Memorial Hospital.

Subject CARAVANS did not display any signs of illness during his interview with LT. NAJERA. During the booking procedure, subject CARAVANS stated that he was not taking medication for any condition. Subject CARAVANS appeared to be in good health. He appeared physically fit, with normal skin color, clear eyes and a calm demeanor.

SUPPLEMENTAL
Date: 11/04/2000
Greentree PD case number: 71000719-00

On 11/1/00, I received a phone call from CASEY CARAVANS, 18, son of the deceased. He reported that in examining the personal effects of his father, he discovered numerous email messages on DAKIN CARAVANS' computer hard drive which the son thought might clear his father's name in the death of his wife and possibly explain his father's own death. LT. NAJERA recovered the computer and its peripherals and booked them into evidence.

While at the Caravans residence, LT. NAJERA also discovered two additional computers, a laptop and a PC, which apparently had belonged to JEWEL CARAVANS, deceased wife of DAKIN CARAVANS. They were also booked into evidence.

Reporting officer: SGT. BERK BUSSIERE
Supervising officer: LT. DICK NAJERA

--------◇--------

What you are about to read are the actual email messages from the computers of Dakin Caravans and his wife Jewel, as recovered by the Greentree PD.

The messages from Dakin Caravans' computer are unedited and reprinted in chronological order, covering the events of the 30 days between his wife's death and his own. It will become clear that Dakin Caravans underwent a life-changing transformation during that time.

Messages from the computers of Jewel Halpern-Caravans are inserted as alternating chapters to provide perspective and background. Her messages were written from Jan. 14, 1999, to Sept. 28, 2000 – the day she died. During this period, Jewel Halpern entered a Narcotics Anonymous 12-step program and began her correspondence with God. Many of her messages are written to Dr. Sara Lyman, a psychologist who was working with her during her time with NA.

The subtitles of each chapter are maxims that Dakin Caravans liked and used as headings for various passages in his personal journal, which was found by his son, Casey. Those sayings prophetically match with events in the final weeks of his life.

Many of Dakin Caravans' emails were sent to Corena Bissett, a friend and family counseling therapist he met while living in Arizona. It is in these frank, heartfelt and sometimes bizarre messages to their own personal counselors and friends that Jewel and Dakin Caravans reveal two sides of what began as a captivating story of love and life and ended in mystery – and, just possibly, the greatest revelation of the last 2,000 years.

David Cunningham
Jan. 19, 2001

Chapter One: Dakin

Laughter may not be the best medicine,
but it's better than a spinal tap

Background: In the aftermath of his wife's mysterious death, Dakin Caravans wrote her often, sending pained emails into cyberspace. He believed no one would ever read them. Jewel Halpern-Caravans' personal computer sat untouched in a dark corner of their condominium.

Dr. Corena Bissett, Dakin's witty and irreverent friend from Arizona, is an unconventional family therapist who may seem in these emails to have little regard for Dakin's feelings at his time of personal loss. But she told me later that she was just trying to nudge him back into reality with humor.

In my interviews with Lt. Dick Najera, a detective with the Greentree Police Department, I asked why he exchanged email with Dakin, rather than conduct what appeared to be official police business by phone or in person. His reply:

"This guy emailed everybody. That's how he communicated. He didn't like talking on the phone – at least, not to us. I figured it might have something to do with his grief. It frustrated me at times, because he was tough to reach on the phone and didn't always return messages, but he checked his email all the time and responded promptly, so I ended up communicating that way with him a lot. More than I liked, really."

If nothing else, it left a path easy to follow.

–David Cunningham

--------<>--------

Subject: Angels
Date: Wed, 04 Oct 2000 11:18:39
From: Dakin Caravans
To: Jewel Halpern-Caravans

Hello Supergirl,

This may be the last message I ever send you. I hope so. Because that would mean I'm finally starting to become a little more normal. Writing emails to dead people might be therapeutic, but after a while it gets creepy. I know you believed you would be able to look down on me and interact with my life after you were gone, and I wish I could share that belief, but I don't.

All I know is that you're dead and gone and I'm getting no signs, no messages that you are anywhere except in the ashes we scattered yesterday. Did you know your mom was there and how she cried? Did you see your brother? Did you see how lost and confused he looked? And your little nephew, too young to understand what was happening, not fully realizing he will never see his aunt again? And me? Did you see me? Do you have any idea how hard it was just to stand? Do you know how much I wanted to lie down and die, in hopes there really IS some kind of afterlife where you are waiting for me, and that I could join you right there and then?

God, I miss you. Tell me how this is fair. Tell me how we can go through so much and come so far as a couple, only to have this happen. We were so perfect together. We had the kind of love others only dream of. People saw it in our eyes, the way we looked at each other, the way we touched. We had found it. We had such a blissful life to look forward to. And now, for no reason I can decipher, it's gone...

```
    * . *(\ *** /) * . *
       * (\(_)/) *
    . * . (_/ll\_) . * .
         /___\
        * .. *
```

A friend emailed this picture to me, and I thought you'd like it. If there really are such things as angels, what do they look like? And are you one?

I will love you forever,
Dakin

--------<>--------

Subject: Jewel!
Date: Wed, 04 Oct 2000 11:45:02
From: Spider Juncal
To: Dakin Caravans

Dude!

Praise Jewel! You MUST let me come worship her in your presence! You're stuck in time and space, and you don't understand that you were chosen! This is so BIG, man! Let your head open up and be warmed by The Light! Someday the whole wide world will know that Jewel Halpern-Caravans – your WIFE! – was the Second Coming, that the Daughter of God has walked among us, and that She is Risen! You and I both know the miracle that occurred on the night she died! And it is my mission to be her disciple and spread the word! I have to capture her words, her thoughts, her being! I am to be her scribe! The scribe of her life and times, dude! The New Good News Testament will be written by ME! Do not fight this! I will call you again tomorrow. Please take my call this time.

In Jewel's name, we pray.

Spider Juncal
The Disciple

"... and they said to the woman, now we believe, not because of thy speaking: for we have heard for ourselves, and know that this is indeed the Savior of the world." (John 4:42)

"Find a release from your cares. Have a good time." (Peking Noodle Co.)

--------◇--------

Subject: SNAP OUT OF IT!
Date: Wed, 04 Oct 2000 11:48:38
From: Corena Bissett
To: Dakin Caravans

OK, MISTER, talk to me. Ya can't hold this inside forever. Life goes on. I wanna help. Use me. Beat me. Whip me. (Sorry, got carried away there). If nothing else, talk to me. Give me a call. You know the number. I know you better than you think, and I know you'll curl up into a fetal position for the rest of your life if you don't let someone reach you and prod you back into a meaningful existence. You have too much to offer to just waste away. Jewel would've felt the same way, and you know it. So call me. I can help. I'm not just your friend. I am a licensed, practicing family counselor, in case you forgot.

OK, time to cheer ya up a little. You talked about writing a book someday? This was emailed to me by one of my crazy friends on the humor web ring:

TOP 15 CHILDREN'S BOOK TITLES REJECTED BY PUBLISHERS

1. You Are Different and That's Bad
2. Dad's New Wife Robert
3. Curious George and the High-Powered Fence
4. Some Kittens Can Fly
5. The Pop-Up Book of Human Anatomy
6. The Magic World Inside the Abandoned Refrigerator
7. Grandpa Gets a Casket
8. You Were an Accident
9. The Kids' Guide to Hitchhiking
10. Kathy Was So Bad Her Mom Stopped Loving Her
11. Green Eggs and Crack
12. Things Rich Kids Have, But You Never Will
13. Your Nightmares Are Real
14. Pop! Goes the Hamster And Other Great Microwave Games
15. Daddy Drinks Because You Cry

Call me, OK?
Corena

--------<>--------

Subject: Sorry
Date: Thu, 05 Oct 2000 12:09:02
From: Dakin Caravans
To: Jewel Halpern-Caravans

My Darling Jewel,

OK, I lied. Here I am again, writing to a person who doesn't exist anymore. Someday, I'll get over you. No, strike that. I will never get over you. But maybe I'll be strong enough to carry on with my life and put on some kind of facade that makes people believe I'm somewhere within the parameters of normal. Do you see how you've cursed me? I could never kiss another woman again. How could I ever hold anyone else in my arms, look into her eyes, make love with her? It's impossible. Completely out of the question. You are the last woman I will ever love, and I will keep on loving you as long as I can draw a breath.

Even though I rejected you and kicked you out and broke up with you eight times, we always found our way back into each other's arms, where we were meant to be. Our journey took us in so many different directions over so many years, together, apart, then together again, and finally, it all clicked. And then you had to disappear. Just expire, like God was calling you home or something. No illness, no accident, no heart attack, no nothing. Just dead. A smile, a few mysterious words, and then the lights go out forever. How is that possible? What does that mean? Please, Jewel, if you really are still hanging around, as a spirit or a butterfly or a silicon chip or whatever, tell me. Send me a reply to this email.

Love,
Your lost man

--------<>--------

Subject: Sweety :)~
Date: 10/05/00 12:46:03
From: TheTruOne
BCC: Dakin Caravans

You're so sweet ... I'd LOVE to be with you! Did I mention ... This was made specifically for you! Hot! Tight! CLICK HERE TO ENTER > (Adults only)

--------<>--------

Subject: Thank you
Date: Thu, 05 Oct 2000 14:29:11
From: Lt. Dick Najera, Greentree PD
To: Dakin Caravans

Dear Mr. Caravans:

As you requested, I'm sending you a message rather than phoning. Thank you for coming in again yesterday to discuss the case. We appreciate your cooperation at this difficult time. As you know, your wife's death leaves a lot of questions unanswered, and since you were the last one to see her alive, any information you can give us is important. In reviewing your statement, we have come up with a few more questions that we would like to ask you in person. We will be calling you in the next day or two to set up a time when you can come back in.

Thank you,
Lt. Dick Najera, Greentree PD

--------<>--------

Subject: miss you
Date: Thu, 05 Oct 2000 22:01:09
From: Dakin Caravans
To: Jewel Halpern-Caravans

My lost Jewel,

Hi, it's me again. I guess I won't ever let you rest in peace. Today was a tough one. Can't seem to get you out of my mind. What would you want me to do? Become a totally helpless pile of heaving, sobbing protoplasm, or pick myself up, dust myself off and start all over again? We were so close to some of the answers to those big questions. Why are we here? What really matters? How should the fully evolved life be lived? We had all the tools and all the motivation. We were getting there. Then you had to tap into some other worldly realm that wouldn't let you come back. Or maybe you didn't want to come back. Maybe you evolved into some higher form of consciousness. Maybe you found the ultimate answer, after all. But why couldn't you take me along?

Ah, but I may as well try to catch the wind ...

PS: Remember Tommy Lasorda? The old Dodgers' manager? I introduced you at the All-Star Game party. He sent a sympathy message. The baseball writers are setting up a scholarship fund in your name.

Oh yeah, I almost forgot. I'm starting to get the feeling that a detective, Lt. Najera, thinks I had something to do with your death. If he only knew. He's this intimidating, big bull of a man with thinning hair, bushy mustache and cold, killer eyes that stare right through you. He says pleasant, courteous words, but his face shows no warmth. I think he must have been beaten mercilessly as a child. Why do those types always go into law enforcement?

--------<>--------

Subject: You see?
Date: Fri, 06 Oct 2000 01:00:00
From: Spider Juncal
To: Dakin Caravans

Dude!

I can't believe you hung up on me! You gotta talk to me, man! Like the Greatest Story Ever Told is happening right here, and you're right in the middle of it, and here I am, sent on a mission to Spread the Good Word, and you won't even talk to me, dude! Think about it! Jewel was born to a mother who could not have children! The lady had adopted two other kids, man! Then, boom! She has a kid by NATURAL childbirth? You don't think that's a SIGN? Jewel goes out into the world on her own at 17 years old, man! She does all this great stuff, even becomes a cop for a while! She was born Jewish, but she wanders away from the faith, and then what happens as an adult? She finds God! She writes letters to God, and He answers her back, man! You have the letters yourself! And I've seen them! Then she quits her job and starts to write a SELF-HELP book, dude! Don't you get it? That's the 21st Century version of the Gospel! She was SUPPOSED to write that book for All Mankind! You're sitting on the new Bible, and you won't even TALK to me, man! I can't believe this! But I really can't believe that the biggest sign of ALL has escaped you, man! Her resurrection! You and I both know she didn't die for any reason other than the Father calling her home! It was beautiful, man, a genuine miracle! You know it, and I know it! Let me help! Let me do what I was put on this earth to do!

Spider Juncal
The Apostle

"A soft answer turns away wrath, but a harsh word stirs up anger." (Proverbs 15:1)

"That's the way it is ..." (Walter Cronkite)

--------<>--------

Subject: music of my heart
Date: Fri, 06 Oct 2000 06:28:01
From: Dakin Caravans
To: Jewel Halpern-Caravans

My Supergirl,

Hello, it's me. Not much, how about you? But there's a warm wind blowing the stars around, and I'd really love to see you tonight ...

Can you come back? Just for a little while? I sit here listening to music, and lyrics float into my head that make me fight to hold back tears.

Jewel, someday I'm going to walk over to your computer and turn it on, go online and get your email messages and find all the pain I sent to you over the last week. I don't really know why I'm writing these, except that it makes me feel like I'm still talking to you. Like you're still here. Like you might walk through that door in the next 30 seconds and give me a big hug and kiss. I miss you so much.

You know, you'll never really die as long as I'm alive. You're still here in my head, my thoughts, my heart, my emotions. You are still loved.

What good does it do to have a million dollars if I don't have you to spend it with? You used to talk about the freedom that your inheritance would give us. We would retire and drive around the country in our motor home, helping people and volunteering and seeing the hinterlands. We would LIVE every day. And it was coming true. We were on our way.

And now you're gone. I am lost.

Reach down from heaven and touch me. I need you.

Your Dakin

PS: That nut-case you met at Narcotics Anonymous keeps bugging me. He insists you were the Second Coming. If he weren't such a whacko, I might actually believe him.

--------<>--------

Subject: Searching?
Date: Fri, 06 Oct 2000 09:33:11
From: ANSWERS6590
To: Dakin Caravans

Hello DAKIN!

CLICK HERE to start your NEW LIFE today!

Make big money in your spare time with this unique HOME-BASED business opportunity! FREE! We GUARANTEE you will be able to retire within 6 months!

--------◇--------

Subject: OK, you win!
Date: Fri, 06 Oct 2000 10:59:01
From: Dakin Caravans
To: Corena Bissett

Hello Dr. Corena,

'Twas good to talk to you last night. You always have a way of cutting through the crap and getting right to the heart of the matter. But then, that's your job, isn't it? You realize, of course, if I tell you all the things you want to know in a professional setting, it would cost me every cent I have even if you gave me a discount rate. And there's no guarantee you could cure me. I don't even know if I want to be cured. Or, if there's anything wrong with me at all. And I refuse to lie on a couch.

But OK, you asked, so here's the whole Dakin Caravans story. It's going to have to be told in installments, because I could never get it down in one email. I don't think the server memory could handle it. But mine can. Almost everything from this relationship is burned into my synapses, and they won't stop flashing. I see her when I'm dreaming, when I'm awake, when I'm playing drums, when I'm taking a shower, when I'm painting ... her face never leaves me. The episodes of our lives keep playing in my head like a videotape loop that won't stop.

I first laid eyes on Jewel during a cool clear Halloween Night in the L.A. suburb of Greentree. I was 16 years old, she was 15. Over the years, I always thought we were impossibly young to experience what we did. I don't care how young Romeo and Juliet were supposed to be, this was 1969, and kids like us weren't mature enough to fall in love. That's what I thought when I looked back on it long after we had gone our separate ways... and before our unexpected rebirth as a couple.

Anyway, it was the most electric, unbelievably vivid moment of my entire life. She was supposed to be dressed as a hobo or something, raggedly clothes and no makeup, and I was just dressed all in black, because we were too old to be out trick-or-treating anyway, so we were just out on the streets with our friends goofing around.

I didn't know her, never heard of her. At the top of the hill on my street, in the glow of moonlight, our two groups met. Some of my friends knew some of hers. They started talking. I eased toward the front of the group to see who these people were. And there she was. Jewel Halpern. The most beautiful creature I'd ever seen and would ever see in my life. Absolutely exquisite. I can't put into words the feeling that rushed through me. It wasn't just her long blond hair and cute little figure. It was everything. The spark in her eyes, the way she moved, the way she talked. I was instantly drawn to her. I may have romanticized that moment in my mind over the years. Maybe I've made it into a much bigger deal than it really was at the time. But I don't think so.

She had this unusual speaking pattern, a very flirtatious, soft voice and a coy way of moving her head and eyes as she spoke, like she was interested in you but too shy to really say anything about it. She would look at me, then look away as she started to smile. Green eyes with long lashes, the face of an angel, perfect, natural blonde hair, a big dimple in her chin, and this certain indescribable something that made her more desirable than any woman I would ever see again.

I was hit by the proverbial thunderbolt. One look, and my world changed forever. I didn't even know for sure what I was feeling. I was so young and naive. But I'll never forget that moment. Oddly enough, I did nothing about it for the next eight months.

I was too shy and immature. Oh, I'd had girlfriends before, but they were all this innocent going-steady kind of thing. We even did some kissy-face stuff, and I was pretty taken with one of them, a cute girl with big doe eyes and great lips, but I didn't really know what I was doing.

So after I met Jewel, all I did was think about her. I asked about her at school, I looked for her in the halls, I made note of what she wore (everything about her was perfect, including her short skirts and satin blouses and big sweaters. She looked great in everything). But I was too terrified to speak to her. I was afraid I'd turn hot crimson (I embarrassed very easily back then) and trip over my tongue and make a fool of myself.

Finally, on the last day of school, I mustered the courage to ask her to sign my yearbook, and she gave me hers to sign. I wrote something about how special I thought she was, and she wrote that if I was ever "unbusy" I should give her a call, and she wrote down her phone number. I called her that night, and we talked for two hours. We spent that whole summer together, almost every day.

As you can see, I can get carried away when I talk about Jewel. I'll write more later. If there are specific things you want to know about, ask.

And remember, I'm not paying for this, and you're not my therapist. You're a friend. And a very good one.

Later,
Dakin

--------◇--------

Subject: what is real?
Date: Fri, 06 Oct 2000 16:28:01
From: Dakin Caravans
To: Jewel Halpern-Caravans

Hi Supergirl,

I'm sitting here wondering if you're real, if you still exist in some way, and then I think, what IS real, anyway? This email? It doesn't exist at all. It's not like a letter on paper that you can hold in your hands and touch and maybe even smell. What is an electronic message, anyway? It's nothing. I type on the keyboard, and letters dance on the screen in front of me. They're not really there. It's just some kind of electronic representation. No ink, no tangible, lasting imprint. If I turn off the computer, they disappear. Where did they go? Nowhere. Because they never really existed. It's just a microscopic bit of digital code on a hard drive. It doesn't make any sense to anybody unless the program that can decode it is used to bring it back to life.

Bring it back to life ... And what of you, my beloved Jewel? Are you a microscopic bit of digital code somewhere in this universe, waiting to be unscrambled? Will the Master Program bring you back as a puppy or a butterfly?

You still exist in my head, but the monitor has gone dark. I can't see you anymore. But somehow, I know you are still a real entity. There is life in what you wrote, who you touched, who you loved. You can never really die.
I love you.
I miss you.
Your Dakin

--------<>--------

Subject: !!!!!!!!!!!
Date: Fri, 06 Oct 2000 23:56:10
From: Spider Juncal
To: Dakin Caravans

Danakin Skyfaker Jr., you are a fool! I am your father, Luke! I am your son! I am your mother! I am your future, your past, your present tense! Hear me! See me! Touch me! Feel Me! Forgive him, Father, for he knows not what he does! LISTEN! Two thousand years ago, God gave us His only begotten Son. Exactly two thousand years later, He gave us His only begotten daughter. Jewel Halpern Caravans died for your sins! And still you commit them! Open your eyes that you might be saved!

Tomorrow I will come to you, Dakin Caravans. Do not forsake me. Hear me, or face the wrath of God!

Sincerely yours,
Spider Juncal
The Apostle

"Behold, the day of Jehovah cometh, cruel, with wrath and fierce anger; to make the land a desolation, and destroy the sinners thereof out of it." (Isaiah 13:9)

"A Jedi must have the deepest commitment, the most serious mind." (Yoda)

--------◇--------

Chapter Two: Dakin
Nobody can bring you peace but yourself

Background: Spider Juncal, who now owns and operates a profitable web site shrine dedicated to Jewel Halpern-Caravans, agreed to be interviewed for this book. A tall, skinny man with wild eyes, prominent cheekbones, pock-marked complexion and long, stringy, black hair, Juncal can be unnerving in a Charles Manson sort of way.

He insists to this day that he "committed no crimes. I am about love and peace, man."

In this chapter, Dakin corresponds with his two children from a prior marriage, Heather and Casey, who were both college students when these emails were written. He also writes to a longtime friend, Steve "Pig" Logan, and an attractive divorcee he dated briefly between marriages named Jeri Starrette.

–David Cunningham

--------◇--------

Subject: possible harassment
Date: Sat, 07 Oct 2000 09:18:39
From: Dakin Caravans
To: Lt. Dick Najera, Greentree PD

Dear Lt. Najera:

I don't want to overreact to this, but I thought I should notify somebody, and your name came to mind, since you're the only police official I know at the moment.

Since the death of my wife I've been contacted numerous times via both telephone and email by an individual who knew my wife through Narcotics Anonymous. His name is Spider Juncal; I don't know where the "Spider" comes from, although it wouldn't surprise me if it's because he sucks the life juices out of his victims. His most recent email to me sounded like a vague threat of some kind, and he has always struck me as an unstable individual. I'm forwarding a copy of his email so you can judge for yourself.

I don't know if any police action is warranted at this time, but in case something were to happen in the future, I wanted some kind of record that this man has been harassing me.

Thank you for your time,
Dakin Caravans

--------<>--------

Subject: Thanks
Date: Sat, 07 Oct 2000, 10:22:56
From: Dakin Caravans
To: Pig Logan

Hey Pig,

Just wanted to say thanks for all you did through this very difficult week. I may have seemed somewhat composed, but inside, I was a mess, and I don't know how I could have gotten though it without you and Cari. In answer to your question, I really don't know what I'm going to do now. Can't sit around and listen to Sinatra records for the rest of my life. I sent a couple resumes out. Maybe a real job will get me back into the swing of things and get my mind off my grief. I don't see how I could play drums in a band anymore. Just doesn't seem right. The painting was going pretty well, made me a few bucks, and I could lose myself in artwork, which was good for a while, but I think I have to start getting out with real people pretty soon. Maybe I'll go back to writing, but not sports. It's time to grow up. I'm 47, after all.

Anyway, thanks again for being there. You guys are what friends are supposed to be. You're the best.

Dakin

--------<>--------

Subject: Are you motivated?
Date: Sat, 7 Oct 11:19:35
From: BlastOff4120
To: Dakin Caravans

Hello,

This is not for everyone, so if you are not a motivated, goal-oriented person with a desire to be successful and wealthy, please delete this message now and go back to your miserable little life.

But if you have reached the point in your life where you are ready to have FREEDOM and a real opportunity to retire in 2-3 years, CLICK HERE>

---------◇---------

Subject: i'm here
Date: Sat, 07 Oct 2000 12:16:22
From: Jeri Starrette
To: Dakin Caravans

hi dakin,

i want you to know that if you ever need anything at all, i'm here. don't be shy ;-)

here's a picture for you. i remember how you said you liked these typing pictures. you are my knight in shining armor.

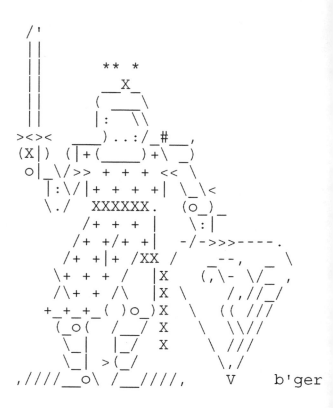

your friend always,
jeri

ps – back when we were dating, you told me something i forget. did you like
me better in the blue halter-top or the black bare midriff?

--------◇--------

Subject: why didn't you call?
Date: Sat, 07 Oct 2000 13:34:41
From: Kitty C.
To: Dakin Caravans

You know you want it! These are the HOTTEST pix on the net! VERY young girls! Celebrities! Pamela Anderson ... Heather Locklear ... Sandra Bullock ... even Dr. Laura Schlessinger! (OK, so she's not young, but she WAS when these pictures were taken!)

Click here> You must be at least 18 years old to enter this site.

--------<>---------

Subject: Hi Dad
Date: Sat, 07 Oct 2000 14:22:13
From: Heather Caravans
To: Dakin Caravans

Hi Dad,

So how are you doing? How was the memorial service for Jewel? Sorry I couldn't be there. Couldn't get a flight.

Just wanted to see how things were going. I'm all settled into my new apartment. It's great and my roommates seem wonderful. And if they aren't, it's only for six months. Can't believe I'm actually graduating in June! I talked with Casey today, and he seems to be doing fine. You don't have to worry about him. He's a great kid (really, he's not a kid anymore. He's an 18-year-old man. He's changed so much in the last couple years. But how could he be anything else? He's your son). Anyway, I think it's good that you let him move out on his own. He'll be fine. And if anything happens, Mom is just a half-hour away. Don't worry.

Love,
Heather

--------<>---------

31

Subject: Re: Hi Dad
Date: Sat, 07 Oct 2000 14:59:01
From: Dakin Caravans
To: Heather Caravans

Hi Heather,

I'm doing fine, and the service went as well as could be expected. The death of a loved one is something we all have to face at some point in our lives, and I hope you don't have to experience it for another 60 years, when I finally die at the ripe old age of 107. Maybe someday I can tell you what Jewel meant to me. I know I never talked a lot about us, but that was because I didn't want to confuse you or make you feel bad because I wasn't with your mom. In truth, I would still be married to your mom today if she would've had me. You know I didn't want the divorce. I always loved that family life we had, with the nice house and the dog and the mini-van and Little League and dance lessons and the American Dream. I looked forward to you and Casey growing up and having families and coming back to the house to visit with kids of your own. But Mom did her middle-age crazy thing, and even though I would've forgiven her (or at least I said I was willing to try), she wasn't turning back. I hope it doesn't hurt you to hear this, but in the end, my life was better for it. I never would've found Jewel again if Mom hadn't done what she did. Yes, Jewel and I had a rocky relationship for a while, but during the last year, I was happier than I ever dreamed possible. Someday maybe I will tell you all about it.

Have fun, study hard, and make me proud (you always do),

love,
Dad

--------<>--------

Subject: You
Date: Sat, 07 Oct 2000 15:00:20
From: Dakin Caravans
To: Casey Caravans

Hi Casey,

Just got an email from Heather, and she assures me you're old enough and mature enough to be on your own. I hope she's right. I'm concerned that you'll get in over your head, but I know you're a lot more responsible and level-headed than most kids your age, so go for it, but be careful. It's not easy balancing a full-time job and college classes. I know. I did it myself.

Now that I'm back in California, I'll always be nearby, and you can also call Mom if you ever need anything.

love,
Dad

PS: Every time I boot up my computer, it gives me a message that says "bad command or file name," but then it continues to boot up, and everything works fine. But it still bothers me. How can I fix that?

--------<>--------

Subject: virus
Date: Sat, 07 Oct 2000 15:15:03
From: Casey Caravans
To: Dakin Caravans

Hi Dad,

It's easy. Click on Start, click on "Help," type in startup, then click on "commands, confirming" and follow the directions.

Did you get the HotZone virus? It started eating my hard drive, but I caught it and wiped it out. Let me know if you get any emails from a sender called HotZone. I can clean it up for you.

Don't worry about me, Dad. Everything's under control.

Casey

PS – can you loan me $50 until payday? Thanks.

--------◇--------

Subject: A voice from the past
Date: Sat, 07 Oct 2000 15:33:54
From: Dakin Caravans
To: Jeri Starrette

Hi Jeri,

Thanks for the message. I don't really know where my head is at right now, but I appreciate your contact.

What's going on with you? Married yet? In love? How are the kids? I'll never forget the time we spent together, and if Jewel hadn't come back into my life, or if she never existed, maybe things could have been different for you and me. Or maybe not. I mean, you know I couldn't get used to the idea of being a step-dad. But I almost took that plunge, and it's because you are a very special person, a good, sweet person who deserves the best life has to offer.

Be well.
Dakin

--------◇--------

Subject: us
Date: Sat, 07 Oct 2000 18:21:16
From: Jeri Starrette
To: Dakin Caravans

hey there,

no, I'm not married yet, no plans at the moment, thank you. not in love, either. the kids are fine. jimi threw a rock threw a window at school, so the teacher wants to increase his ritalin, but i don't want to do it. guess i will, though. he really does seem to do better on it. janis has been a little moody lately. she spent last weekend at her dad's, and i think she might have gotten the belt. she had this mark on her butt, but i couldn't be sure.

you don't need to say anything about not wanting to be a stepdad. i KNOW that. all i ever wanted was for you to be happy. and with jewel gone now, i wanted to check and make sure you were doing ok. i will always love you, and like i said, it there's ever anything i can do, just ask. if you want to talk to somebody, i'm here. and don't take this the wrong way, but if you ever have any other needs that aren't being met, i'm available for that, too. ;-)

love,
jeri

ps: do you have that love positions picture book I bought? I can't find it anywhere. here's me, eyes closed, dreaming of you ...

```
                        @@@@
                     @@@@@@@
                  -   @@@@
                 '_   @@@
                   _\@  \@
        _\\   (/  )  @\_/)
       |(__/ /        /|
       \___/  " " " " " _|
          , x       * (
          |x          \
          |x           )
          |/\_____    |
          |      / /
          |     /  (
          |   /\__ \
          (__\|   |
          |   |[*  |
        [* |  |,   \
      ,   \ /|/ b'ger
        ,__ /|/
```

-------- <> --------

Subject: Re: Thank you
Date: Sat, 07 Oct 2000, 20:22:56
From: Pig Logan
To: Dakin Caravans

Dakin,

Hey, most of the guys from the old softball team were thinking about going to a UCLA football game and wondered which one you might be able to make. The Bruins look pretty good this year. Coz might even come down from Oregon. Toppy will be there for sure, and his brother, plus Smutley, Butt-breath, Fish, Cut, Buck and Scuz. Hard to believe it's been more than 10 years since the Blue Spirit played together. We sure had some great times with that team, didn't we?

Hey, you said you wanted to write a book someday, maybe you could write about the slow-pitch team. How many guys play together in the same league for 16 years? You could tell a lot of great stories from those years. Lotta memories, lotta championships, lotta ups and downs for everybody. We went through all kinds of changes in our lives, but there was always that Thursday night softball game to keep us together.

Well, pick a UCLA game, and we'll get the tickets ... unless you still have friends in the PR department and can get us some good seats. Go Bruins!

Steve (Pig)

--------<>--------

Subject: Fear
Date: Sat, 07 Oct 2000 22:00:19
From: Dakin Caravans
To: Lt. Dick Najera, Greentree PD

Dear Lt. Najera:

If you have read my email from earlier today, you will know what this is about. The man I wrote to you about confronted me this evening.

Around 6 p.m., I left my condo to go to the store. I opened the automatic garage door, got into my car, then turned to look as I backed up out of the garage. There, sitting in the back seat, was the crazy man, Spider Juncal. I was suddenly nose to nose with him.

I have no idea how he got inside the locked garage, but once he did that, he easily could have gotten into my car, because I never lock it when it's inside the garage.

This is a scary guy. He's in his mid-40s, but he seems to be some kind of drugged-out derelict from The Sixties or a Jesus freak or something. I know he had substance abuse problems because he met my late wife in a counseling workshop that was set up by Narc Anonymous. I don't know his address, but I believe he lives in Laguna Beach.

He told me that my late wife was the savior or the second coming of Jesus or something like that. He said that she was writing the new gospel, and that it was his job to spread that word, her word, to the entire world. Jewel had been keeping a journal of her thoughts for about a year or so and had written some letters to God in that journal, which I think might be an exercise for people in a 12-step recovery program. This whacked-out Spider guy seems to be under the delusion that God actually wrote her back, and that her journal is a holy book of some kind.

I yelled at him to get out, to leave me alone, and to stop phoning me and emailing me. He said he would "do what God sent me to do, and no one will stop me. Not even you, who shared the flesh of Jewel Halpern-Caravans, the new messiah."

I don't know if this man truly is dangerous or not, but I believe it is a crime to enter someone's locked garage, get in their vehicle and lie in wait for them. I fear that next time, he might be waiting with a knife to wield in his delusional holy fervor. He seems to be an intelligent man, but very off-balance.

I eventually convinced him to leave, but not before he vowed to get what he came for, sooner or later. I didn't report the incident to my local police department. Since your department has jurisdiction over the case of my wife's death, and this man is somehow connected to her, I thought you should know about the incident.

Let me know if I can help you in any way.

Dakin Caravans

--------<>--------

Subject: INTERNET SNOOP
Date: Sat, 07 Oct 00 22:05:23
From: spyguy29
To: Friend@public.com

CONFIDENTIAL INFORMATION YOU WANT TO KNOW.

"The Internet Snoop" shows you how to get all the hidden facts on anyone
simply by using the Internet.

This is the software they want banned from the INTERNET!

Click Here> for details.
//
One time mailing, no need for removal.
//

--------<>--------

Subject: My story, Part II
Date: Sun, 08 Oct 2000 10:19:09
From: Dakin Caravans
To: Corena Bissett

Hi Dr. (Bones) Bissett –

It's been a very earth-shattering week (at least for the earth as I know it),
and I need to talk. Remind me to tell you later about the crazy man who is
stalking me.

I will pick up my story with Jewel where we last left off. Feel free to
write back with your analysis at any time (if you decide I need to be
committed, I will gladly consent.)

Actually, before I return to "Dakin and Jewel, the Early Years," I want
to go back a little earlier than that. What was the greatest period of your life,
when you were happier than any other time? Is it now? If so, consider
yourself one of the fortunate few. I think most people are like me; they
remember some time in their distant past, when the sun shone a little

brighter, the food tasted a little better, and your friends really were your friends.

For me, it was the summer of 1965, when I was 12 years old. Girls were starting to become an interest, but they still were just pretty, soft things in the distance, fascinating to look at, but completely out of reach. None of them had hurt me yet, so I still had this innocent, abstract, idealized view of them. What really mattered was baseball. Sandy Koufax was pitching for the Dodgers, and they were winning pennants and World Series. I saw every game through the word-pictures of Vin Scully on the radio, I played baseball in the street with my friends, and I pitched an endless number of championship games, striking out fearsome imaginary hitters with a tennis ball hurled against our garage door.

We played entire seasons of a baseball fantasy game we called "spinner," because it involved cardboard disks representing real players, which were placed on a spinner. I think the original version of the game was called Strat-o-Matic, but we improved upon it by creating cards of all-time great players like Babe Ruth and Ty Cobb that Strat-o-Matic didn't manufacture back then, and we made up our own rules. We had trades and a league commissioner and scoresheets and printed schedules. We even designed our own boxes to hold the cards of the players on our teams, and I would draw on my box to make it look like a stadium, complete with a "Players Only" entrance. God, we loved that game.

My older brother invented an electronic spinner, so instead of flicking the arrow-pointer with his finger (which sometimes created bloody injuries, so often did we play this game), now all he had to do was flip a switch, and the spinner spun. My best friend, Coz (not his real name; nobody I grew up with was called by their given name), took the game more seriously than anybody. Once he put in Vernon Law as a reliever, and after Law gave up a game-winning home run in our World Series, Coz took a match to the card and burned Law's "arm" off. But Coz felt bad about it later, and he fixed the card by taping new cardboard over the burned area and drawing in the numbers that had gone up in smoke. It was the first reconstructive surgery in spinner history, and Law lived to pitch another day.

I became hooked on baseball. When Roger Maris hit 61 home runs in 1961, an 8-year-old left-handed boy named Dakin first noticed America's national pastime. The idyll lasted through 1966, when I turned 13 and started into puberty. Until then, the world consisted of baseball, beaches, Sandy Koufax, the Beatles, my drum set, hiking in the canyon and catching lizards. In 1966, Sandy Koufax retired, the Beatles stopped touring, and for the first time, I realized I'd never have the talent to become a major-league baseball player. The age of innocence was over.

But at 12, I was still good enough to dream. When we weren't playing baseball or spinner, we were down at the beach body surfing, playing a gruesome game of tag by pulling sea slugs out of the tidepools and throwing them at each other, or just lying around on the sand and watching girls in bikinis. It was the greatest time to be alive. It was only later, when we had to start thinking about actually approaching those girls with crude pickup lines, that our world started to get complicated. But fears, insecurities and rejections were not yet a reality in 1965.

Let me fast-forward now to the summer of 1969, before anybody knew what fast-forward meant, and when Jewel Halpern had become my first real girlfriend. Mostly, we were doing kid stuff – going to the movies, hanging out at her house or swimming in her pool, going for walks and drives. I was in love. Like I said, it happened from that first thunderbolt, and it grew rapidly. I've thought a lot about it in the years since, and I don't really know if it was a healthy love back then. I was totally blinded to anything and everything else. There was just Jewel.

There was no real sex – I was 16, she was 15. But there was a lot of kissing – the deepest and most sensual I had ever experienced. She was the first girl to kiss my neck and ears, I was the first boy to fondle her breasts and tease her between her legs. It was way more exciting than later years with bolder women who rolled over so easily. She was a goddess to me. And that's probably why I started to go crazy.

I remember one night when she was a volunteer curtain-puller for the high school theater production. I decided to surprise her by sneaking backstage to say hi. Standing in the darkness, I saw her playing little flirty games with another boy, stupid little touchy-feely games, complete with giggling and hair tossing. Nothing that you'd call cheating on a boyfriend, but my vision clouded, and my head seemed to implode. Clearly, this love was not healthy, but I was so naive. I walked up to her, interrupted her little flirtation and said, "Hi, Jewel. I just wanted to tell you I'm going to kill myself."

With that, I turned and fled. I fully intended to run straight to the beach, dive through the waves and drown myself. I was a classic case of adolescent love-struck insanity. But I ran for less than a mile, stopped in exhaustion, and allowed my head to clear. Then I walked home. The next day, I called her house, and her dad answered. I asked for Jewel and after a few moments her dad came back on the line and said Jewel didn't want to speak with me. I had ruined everything.

Or so I thought. Within a week, Jewel was speaking to me again, and we were dating again. I was happy, but stupid. I really HAD ruined everything. Jewel's dad got involved with her love life at that point and found out about my silly little suicide threat. He didn't think it was so silly. He thought I was a nut case, and he didn't want his precious and beautiful daughter hanging around with me. It wasn't long after that when Jewel said she had to talk with me, and we took a drive. We parked at one of our favorite make-out places overlooking the city lights of Los Angeles, and she told me her dad would not let us see each other any more. We talked, we cried, we hugged, and we sat in silence for the longest time. Then I took her home. I was a lost little boy, still so far from learning what it meant to be a man. But my heart was broken for the first time in my life, and it hurt. It physically hurt.

I kept a journal during high school. Actually, I started the journal as an English class assignment, but I kept writing it through the years and even now still make an occasional entry in it, usually when I'm depressed. Why do we become most creative when we're troubled? Anyway, I just picked up that journal and turned back to the "Jewel Halpern Early Years" entries. Here is one from an 18-year-old Dakin Caravans, written more than a year after we broke up:

Why Jewel Halpern Bugs the Hell Out of Me

All she has to do is sit there, not even say anything, and I feel as if a rat is gnawing its way out of my stomach. If she opens her mouth and starts to say the funny-sad things in the funny-sad way she always has, it's even worse. No one in the world can touch her now. She has gone. I don't like her very much. I love her. She seems more attractive every time I see her. I've taken her to lunch a couple of times since the end. Very strange. I sit uneasy, she makes me uncomfortable without trying. I want to touch her, to kiss her and tell her, but I can't. It's strange. To relieve myself, I stay away from her as much as possible and pretend I could still have her. I'll take out another girl and feel empty. Last year I would walk at school and stare empty-minded through the faces. Suddenly I'd see the familiar one that stands out like a moon against the stars. And I'd look disinterested and pretend my pulse hadn't quickened.

Two years later, at the age of 19, Jewel Halpern was on the cover of *Playboy* Magazine. I told you she was gorgeous, and I wasn't the only one who could see it. Her hairdresser knew a *Playboy* photographer and got her a test shoot, but Jewel was nervous about it. She came from a religious Jewish family, and posing nude wasn't on their list of acceptable activities. Even though Jewel was a Jew in name only, she didn't want to offend her family. Still, it was a lot of money, and she was always a bit of a rebel. She did it, but she used a fake name. I'd heard rumors of all this, but Jewel and I had drifted apart since high school. When I saw the cover photo, I froze. Ohmigod, that's Jewel! I looked for the cover credits and saw that the model's name was Bambi Berger. Yeah, right. That girl on the cover who was tearing the tight pants off her own butt was Jewel Halpern. Now the whole world could see her naked body, and I, who had loved her more than life itself, was seeing that naked body for the first time. It wasn't the way I had wanted it to happen.

Well, Dr. B., this is great therapy for me, writing about how I came to be such a messed up adult, and if I'm boring you, hit the delete key every time you see one of my emails. I'm on a roll now. I'll write more tomorrow. Maybe we can talk on the phone soon, and you can tell me how screwed up I am.

So how's the weather in Phoenix? Let me guess: Temp in the high 90s, cactus and retirees everywhere, and not one single elevated consciousness outside of your own home.

I miss your brilliant repartee.

Later,
Dakin

---------◇---------

Subject: Try the phone
Date: Sun, 08 Oct 2000 12:59:11
From: Lt. Dick Najera, Greentree PD
To: Dakin Caravans

Dear Mr. Caravans,

I got your email messages about the person whom you suspect might pose a potential danger to you, and I just left a message on your answering machine. Have you ever thought of actually picking up the phone and calling when something like that happens? Not everybody checks his email messages three times a day. Do you have any reason to believe he could have had something to do with your wife's death? We have run preliminary checks, but have not found a Spider Juncal in any database yet. We will continue to search for subjects named Juncal to see if we can find a match to your suspect. Perhaps your late wife left paperwork that might further identify him.

If you encounter him again and there is any potentially criminal activity, please call our office immediately, or call your own local police department.

Sincerely,
Lt. Dick Najera, Greentree PD

---------◇---------

Subject: Ranting and raving
Date: Sun, 08 Oct 2000 23:34:19
From: Dakin Caravans
To: Corena Bissett

Hey Dr. Demento,

Sorry to write you twice in one day. I'm feeling more than a little crazy right now. This will probably be a venting and ranting, and please don't hold it against me. Let me rip away, and then you can hit delete and we'll both forget about it.

44

I'm feeling absolutely bottled up and ready to explode. My brain can't handle all this anymore. I've spent my whole adult life trying to be a man, stoic and in control. I can handle anything. So what if my dad beats up my mom and they get divorced? I can handle it. So what if my mom turns lesbian? I can handle it. So what if both my parents were alcoholics? I can handle it. So what if my first wife cheats on me, and then my second wife does the same? I can handle it. So what if my dog dies, someone crashes into me on the freeway, I was born color blind and left-handed and I'm nearly blind without contacts? I can handle it. So what if my appendix bursts? I can handle it. So what if my company is sold to a new owner and they cut everybody's pay by 25 percent? I can handle it. So what if the love of my life finally re-enters my world and gives me a glimpse of bliss, and then she dies? I can handle it.

I CAN'T handle it. I feel like crying. The man in me is trying to prevent it, but I feel like collapsing into a big, heaving, pathetic ball of sobbing distress. I wish I could say I'm mad as hell and won't take it anymore, but I can't even do that. I'm giving up inside. I've taken all I care to take, and I don't want to take any more. I've paid all the dues I want to pay. Somebody show me the door. I believe this is my stop.

AAAHHH! Well, I feel a little better now. Just had to get that off my chest. I suppose everybody needs a primal scream once in a while, don't they? Sniff. No, please, I'm fine. Let me take a moment to compose myself. There. Much better.

Thank you. We'll talk again later.

Your humble servant,
Dakin

--------<>--------

Subject: Sorry, dude!
Date: Sun, 08 Oct 2000 23:59:02
From: Spider Juncal
To: Dakin Caravans

Hey, brother, that was SO wrong of me to hole up in your car! Very sorry! I didn't mean to stalk you or scare you, dude! (I was in there TWO HOURS, man, you'd think I would have sobered up and realized my approach was all wrong at some point during that time!) But you have to understand that something much bigger than ALL of us is happening! You're going down in history, man! You and Jewel and me and her letters from God! This is a train that's not stopping, dude!

You don't know this – NOBODY does, yet – but God appeared before me and spoke to me and TOLD me what my mission in life is! I am to chronicle the life of Jewel Halpern-Caravans and publish her letters to and from God and show the world who she was, that she was here and God spoke to her and through her, that she has a message for all of us! And that she is risen, dude! You don't have to lead, you don't have to follow, but for God's sake, step aside! I am coming!

Spider
"He that believeth and is baptized shall be saved; but he that disbelieveth shall be condemned." (Mark 16:16)

"Life goes by so fast. Stop for a moment and take a look at it." (Polaroid Cameras)

--------◇--------

Chapter Three: Jewel

*Happy relationships depend not on finding the right
person, but being the right person*

Background: Jewel and Dakin's romance survived no less than eight breakups before they finally married. Jewel's messages begin during a period of separation. At the time, she and Dakin both thought it was over.

Jewel's addiction to painkillers grew out of treatment for a back injury, and she was arrested twice for driving under the influence of a controlled substance. The turmoil in her personal life led Jewel to start seeing a psychiatrist, Dr. Sara Lyman, who suggested she keep a personal journal. Portions of that deeply introspective journal ended up in several of her emails.

–David Cunningham

--------<>--------

Subject: It's me
Date: Thu, 14 Jan 1999 10:13:55
From: Jewel Halpern
To: Vivienne Myers

Hey Viv –

Remember me? Sorry I've been out of touch so long. Dakin and I broke up again, only this time I think it's permanent, and I haven't felt like talking much. I moved from Arizona back to California and am looking for a job. Boy, a lot sure has happened to me since I left you and my friends in Vermont, huh? Was it just four years ago? Seems like a lifetime.

Dakin and I actually bought a marriage license in Phoenix a couple months ago but never quite made it to the altar. Eighty bucks down the drain. Well, I did keep the license. Part of me says it's for the best, and I need to start my life over and go in a new, better direction. But another part of me feels like we are soulmates who were meant for each other, no matter what. In many ways, I blame myself for the breakup. I was so lost in Phoenix. He had his baseball writing job and his travel and familiar routine, and I floundered. I didn't get a job like I should have. I just laid around getting a tan and waited for Dakin to come home so we could go out and play. I didn't have a real purpose.

Now I'm going back into the dating scene full throttle, but so far not finding what I want. I hate to admit it, but every guy I dance with only reminds me that he is not Dakin. I will press on. Life is what you make it, and it's about time I started making something of mine.

All those years in Vermont when we would walk and talk and complain about men and work and life – I never realized how important those times were for my soul until they were gone. I miss you. I hope your life has been going at least a little better than mine has.

Call you soon.

Jewel

--------<>--------

Subject: Per your request
Date: Thu, 28 Jan 1999 18:44:16
From: Jewel Halpern
To: Dr. Sara Lyman

Hi Dr. Lyman:

I'm taking your advice from our session last week and will write a journal of my thoughts and experiences for you. I'll try to give you some more of my background, so you'll have a clearer idea of where I'm coming from. I'm typing the journal entries on the computer because it's much easier and faster for me. Here's the first one, which I clipped and pasted from the word program where I'm keeping the journal:

I don't know what point there is to existence without love. Without a deep, committed relationship, someone to care for and hold and love, I don't see any meaning in getting up, going to work, coming home, exercising, eating, going to bed and then doing it all over again.

I'm beginning to believe that Dakin and I were meant for each other, and I want to find a way for us to get back together. Our love spanned decades, starting when we were teens. We broke up, went our separate ways, married other people and lived different lifetimes, then eventually found our way back together. Our relationship since then has been a roller coaster. Sometimes it was the most intense and beautiful thing I could imagine. Other times, it was filled with friction and misunderstandings, to put it mildly.

I'll never forget the Halloween Night we met. When I saw Dakin for the first time, I actually said, "Oh, you're cute," but I was shy and said it too softly for him to hear. We talked a little, and I wanted to talk to him a lot more, but we drifted our separate ways that night, and for most of the rest of that year at school, we just said hi to each other passing in the hall. I wanted to get to know him better, but he didn't seem too interested. I found out later it was because he was just as shy as I was.

We started dating that summer. He was the first guy I ever fell in love with, and even though I married someone else several years later, I still believe I never really loved any man except Dakin. We did so many things together that I had never done before. He was artistic like me and took me to art shows, and one weekend we drained my family swimming pool and painted a huge sea serpent on the bottom. It looked so cool when we filled up the pool again. He also played drums for a rock band, so we went to a lot of dances and concerts, some to watch other groups, and some when his own band was playing. He had just gotten his license and had a car, so he was the first guy who actually took me places, and he was such an interesting guy with such eclectic tastes that I loved every minute we spent together. He took me from being a little girl to being a young woman in just 18 months. That's all the time we had together that first time around.

It all started to change the night he came to see me backstage at the high school theater when I was working the curtain. I guess he saw me talking to one of my friends there, a guy. Dakin's an incredibly jealous man and always has been. In some ways, he's very insecure. When he flipped out and said he was going to kill himself, I didn't know what to do. He ran off, but I couldn't leave. I never really believed he'd do it, but I couldn't be sure, and I didn't hear from him until the next afternoon. I was so upset about the whole thing that I didn't want to talk to him.

Even though we patched things up the following week and everything was fine as far as I was concerned, my dad decided Dakin and I were getting too close at too young an age. He started finding ways to keep us apart. Dad thought Dakin was a little odd, and that was absolutely true. Dakin never fit in with other people. He had his own unique way of looking at the world, and nobody else seemed to see things the same way. Later I came to see him as a tortured soul, someone who saw and thought and felt more deeply than others, and that left him vulnerable. But what Dad didn't know at the time was that I was even more out-of-step with the rest of the world than Dakin was. I think that's one of the things that attracted me to him. Oh, and there's the physical thing, too. Back then, he was thin and gangly, a prototypical adolescent boy with puppy-dog hands and feet. He also had puppy-dog eyes, pale blue and penetrating. But there was a fire in his eyes that made you realize he was different. He also had those All-American-boy good looks that I've always liked: strong, square features and thick brown hair that got wavy and almost curly when he grew it longer, which he did a lot back then. He later filled out into a well-built, intelligent man with wise eyes and a sweet, sensitive streak, but back then, I just saw cute and interesting. Dad, however, began to see an oddball. Finally, he told me I had to break up with him. Dakin was hurt terribly. We both cried that night.

It was a bigger loss for me than I realized at the time. I've always been the kind of girl who could turn men's heads, and as soon as it was known that Dakin and I weren't going steady anymore, a lot of guys started asking me out, and I was having a pretty good time.

Then came the night when a boy who was 20 – three years older than me – took me out to a nice dinner, and then he parked on a hill overlooking the city, and we started kissing. It was the sort of thing Dakin and I had done hundreds of times, but with us, it was always safe and fun. Neither of us had ever had sex before, and we knew we weren't ready. But this wasn't Dakin. This guy started pushing me to go further, and when I resisted, he got rough. I yelled at him to take me home, and he put his hand over my mouth and turned into some kind of animal. He said he'd hurt me if I didn't be quiet. Then he pinned me down and raped me.

For a long time, I was in a state of disbelief that it had happened. I told no one. Then one day I ran into Dakin at school, and he asked how I was doing and if I was seeing anybody. It started as a casual conversation

50

between two old friends, but Dakin and I were soulmates even then, and I asked him what he thought a girl should do when a guy won't take no for an answer.

"Has that ever happened to you?" he asked.
"Yes."
"What did you do?"
"I couldn't do much of anything."

He didn't push for details, and I was glad. It was the closest I ever came to telling anyone I'd been raped, but the fear I felt that night will stay with me forever.

It was also the end of my innocence. I started moving into a different world. I was raised Jewish, but in the 1960s and early '70s, we were turning our backs on everything, and that included religion. I drifted away from Judaism, drifted away from school, drifted away from my friends. I wonder sometimes how much the rape had to do with my disenchantment with everything.

God, this sounds so cliché, but it's true – I had an unhappy childhood. Everything was fine until I was 8, when I saw Mom smash Daddy in the face with a fire poker during an argument. She punched and battered him a lot, and he left her three times, but he kept coming back. Whenever he left, he took us kids with him. It was always Daddy, Alvin and Sandy (my adopted brother and sister) and me, the miracle baby that doctors said my mom couldn't have.

We sometimes stayed in Salvation Army shelters, and the experience left me with emotional scars, trite as that may sound. Dad was not a strong-willed person, and I remember at age nine, when he seemed hopeless and despondent, I told him, "Don't worry, Daddy. I'll take care of you." It was true. The nine-year-old little girl had to give strength to the grown man. I never had a childhood after that. I had to be the responsible one. After the divorce, we moved around a lot as Dad looked for work in the packaging business. It wasn't until I met Dakin at age 15 that I started to feel rooted. He was only one year older, but he seemed much more together than I was. I was leaning on him as a father figure or solid big brother (my real big brother reacted to our family instability by becoming a reckless rebel, complete with drugs and petty crimes, so he wasn't a particularly good role model at that time). Maybe that's why I grew so emotionally attached to Dakin. I wonder sometimes how things might have been different if Daddy hadn't forced me to break up with Dakin way back then.

After high school, I got a job and started dating my hairdresser, a man eight years older than I. He had a friend who was a photographer for *Playboy* magazine and thought I could be a Playmate of the Year. After a lot of soul searching, I decided to go for the photo shoot, which was a test. It turned out they liked the test shots, and I did several shoots for the magazine. My pictures were used in three different pictorials, and I ended up on the cover of one issue. It was all very tastefully done, and I was never shown full frontal nude, but there's no getting around the fact that my breasts and buttocks are still out there in magazines all over the world for men to masturbate to. I've found that the passing years don't really make it go away. In some ways, I'm glad I did it, but in others, I wish I hadn't. And again, I wonder sometimes how being raped might have changed my outlook on things.

Anyway, my brother eventually introduced me to a very different and interesting man, Red Bjerke, who was almost 13 years older than I, and we began what became a very long on-again, off-again relationship, one that actually spanned almost 17 years. He was even more of a father figure than Dakin, but he had another aspect to his personality that Dakin did not – he was extremely sexual. I think now that he actually was addicted to sex. He masturbated five to 10 times a day. He collected porn books and videos. He talked about sex, joked about sex, thought about sex and pursued sex all the time. He liked to try new, sometimes deviant sex acts. He was always experimenting. After I became attached to Red, I began to equate my self-worth with my sexual attractiveness. He wanted me as a sexual vessel, and because his attention made me feel wanted, I tried to please him whenever possible. After all, I had been on the cover of *Playboy*. The only thing I was good for was satisfying the sexual urges of men, right?

Red and I moved to a little town in Vermont, where I entered college and eventually got my BA degree in sociology (So Dr. Sara, be careful using psychobabble on me, because I've heard most of it before). I worked in advertising for a few years, then somehow got the idea that all I ever really wanted to do was be a police officer. After almost two years of trying, I finally got accepted into the Brattleboro, Vermont, police department. The academy was rough, especially for a good-looking young woman, but by then, I was starting to get a very tough exterior. When I want to, I can be very focused and determined.

I finished the academy and started working patrol, but they gave me the worst possible shifts, all-nighters, with mandatory overtime, and since nothing very exciting ever happened in Brattleboro, I grew bored very quickly. Most of my time was spent picking deer carcasses off the road, breaking up marital fights and letting speeders go with warnings. I wonder sometimes if my need to be a cop had something to do with being raped or watching my mom assault my dad with a fire poker. Maybe I had a need to right wrongs and punish the wicked.

And so I quit the police department and got myself a steady job. I went back into advertising, where my long blond hair and cute figure seemed less out of place. Red and I lived together two different times, but we kept breaking up. He didn't seem to have the same priorities as I. But we had become such a part of each other that I finally agreed to marry him. Actually, I think it was my idea. By that time, I was nearly 38, and I didn't want to spend my whole life drifting away from projects that I started. My life was an unfinished symphony. I wanted to complete something. So we got married, a quick civil ceremony. It lasted two years (the marriage, not the ceremony). I knew it was a mistake within two months.

As my marriage was breaking apart, Dad retired from the packaging business – his health wasn't too great – and I decided to move back home to Greentree in sunny, warm, beautiful Southern California. I was always close to Daddy, and I thought he might need me nearby. Red was not invited to join me. He was crushed by the divorce, and that almost made me reconsider, but something was missing, and I didn't want to spend the rest of my life wondering what it was.

Little did I know that this move would bring me face-to-face with Dakin Caravans. It had been more than 20 years since the last time I'd seen him or even heard his name.

That's all I wrote, Dr. Sara. I guess that's plenty, huh? I'll see you at our usual Wednesday session.

Jewel

--------<>--------

Subject: Dear God letter
Date: Wed, 03 Feb 1999 21:29:48
From: Dr. Sara Lyman
To: Jewel Halpern

Dear Jewel,

Just a quick note to say I think you are making remarkable progress, and after several sessions with you, I think you're an extraordinary woman. And if I ever slip into "psychobabble," feel free to snap me out of it.

I want to remind you to try the method of "corresponding" with your God. Sometimes a dialogue with yourself, under the guise of addressing your highest authority, can be very enlightening and helpful.

See you next week,

Dr. Lyman

--------<>--------

Subject: Dear God letter
Date: Thu, 04 Feb 1999 19:12:25
From: Jewel Halpern
To: Dr. Sara Lyman

Hi Dr. Lyman,

Here's my first letter to God. Is this what you had in mind?

Dear God,

I'm sorry I have been away so long.

Really, I think I've been away from you my whole life. What do you want me to do? How can I serve you now? I am in your hands. Mold me. Sometimes I think you have had a plan for me all along, and everything that ever happened to me has happened exactly as you wanted it to. I believe in

54

fate. Sometimes I feel powerless, and all the good and bad that has happened in my life is serving your higher purpose. I look for signs from you, God.

I'm on your side now. And I know you'll be on my side. In *Les Miserables*, they sing, "To love another person is to see the face of God," and I believe that. Love is the answer. What do you have in store for me? Will I ever find that kind of love I had with Dakin again? Is he the one? What can I do to win him back?

I know now that I had to stop taking Vicodin to gain clarity and see you. The pain pills played a big role in my breakup with Dakin. I couldn't control it. It was stronger than anything, even my love for Dakin. For someone like me, who needs to be in total control of my surroundings, it was inconceivable that anything could be stronger than my will. But those little pills were. For so long, I refused to accept it, but the painkillers were stronger than I was.

When Dakin called off our wedding, it should have been a wake-up call for me, but I ignored it. I had to hit rock bottom – arrested twice for driving under the influence of a controlled substance – and even then, I didn't care. My first few mandatory classes with Narcotics Anonymous were taken very stubbornly. But slowly I began to wake up. I felt welcome. These people accepted me for me, with all my human frailties. They didn't judge me for the drug abuse. Dakin always made me feel weak for making mistakes. Here was a place I could go where nobody put me down or made me feel inferior. It was all about love. And it led me back to you, God. I'm a child, just now beginning to understand what unconditional love is all about. But I'm beginning to feel so much stronger. I haven't taken a pill in 10 days, and every night, I awaken in a sweat and feel the toxins oozing out of my skin. Every day I feel better and better. And every day I feel closer and closer to you.

I am your humble servant. Do with me what you will.

Jewel

--------◇--------

Subject: Follow-up on your court case
Date: Fri, 05 Feb 1999 09:31:21
From: Schermerhorn Brothers, Attorneys at Law
To: Jewel Halpern

Hi Jewel,

Your case will be heard in Riverside County court next week, and I remain hopeful that we can avoid jail time, but it is likely you will have to continue with the Narcotics Anonymous classes, pay a fine and have your driver's license suspended. Continuing the therapy sessions with Dr. Sara Lyman is very important, too. We'll talk before your appearance in court so I can brief you on a few pointers.

Talk to you soon,
Barry Schermerhorn

--------<>--------

Subject: Dear God letter
Date: Fri, 05 Feb 1999 18:17:12
From: Jewel Halpern
To: Dr. Sara Lyman

Dear God,

Why have I been lost for so long? Where do you want me to go now? How can I be the best of all possible daughters for you? I open my heart and mind to you.

I wonder sometimes why I never did drugs in all those teen years or in my 20s, when everybody else did. It seemed so wrong to me. Such a waste of time. My brother and sister smoked pot and ditched school and got drunk, but I was always so straight and narrow. I even became a cop, and when they were teaching us in the academy about drugs, it seemed so funny when they lit some marijuana so we could all get familiar with the smell. I had smelled it countless times coming from my sister's room. I tried to be so strong and tough and rigid. It's funny, but someone else might have looked at me during those years and thought I was already a faithful servant of God and truth and righteousness. But I was so screwed up, so repressed, so unsure of myself. I just hid it well. It wasn't until after I started abusing painkillers in my early 40's and became addicted and got arrested twice that I finally became a halfway decent servant of God. You work in mysterious ways, indeed.

I want to ask you a question, God. Can I ever recapture that spark of love with Dakin? We're very different, but we mesh in ways I can't even articulate. I want to call him, even though I know he's been dating other people. I still have this overwhelming feeling that Dakin and I are meant to be together. Can you give me some sign, some direction? If I'm meant to take another path, I'll do it. If I'm meant never to see Dakin again, I'll do it. I'm tired of fighting fate and destiny. I am in your hands, God.

Jewel

--------<>--------

Subject: God's letter to me
Date: Fri, 05 Feb 1999 19:02:21
From: Jewel Halpern
To: Dr. Sara Lyman

Dear Jewel,

I am so proud of you. After so many falls, you keep getting up. You are on the right path.
God

--------<>--------

Chapter Four: Dakin
Defeat isn't bitter if you don't swallow it

Background: Dr. Corena Bissett uses piercing, pale-blue eyes to cut into your soul, and her sarcastic wit can do the same. She met Dakin Caravans on a blind date after he and Jewel broke up in January 1999. Although romance never bloomed, they became close friends. An intelligent, independent woman, Dr. Bissett graciously offered me information and insight during research for this book.
–David Cunningham

--------<>--------

Subject: Go with that
Date: Mon, 09 Oct. 2000 10:14:33
From: Corena Bissett
To: Dakin Caravans

Hi Dakin,

Well, I'm beginning to understand now why you had this obsession with Ms. Jewel, but are you sure it wasn't just because she was a *Playboy* bunny? You never talked much about her with me before, but I'll chalk that up to the fact that you and I had two casual dates while you were between stormy, torrid affairs. I'm sure you didn't want to be so gauche as to talk about a former (and, who knew, maybe a future) love. Why did I have to be the brainy type, when all you wanted was big boobs?

Just kidding! No, I do not think you need to be committed to the funny farm ... yet. I'll need a little more information first. You DID say you were married for 17 years, and it was NOT to Ms. Jewel. Why not the all-consuming, passionate lifelong love with the mother of your children? You made two babies with that woman, no? Were you carrying an Olympic torch for Jewel the whole time you were married to Amanda?

Feel free to write (if that's better therapy for you) or call. I'll be home around 7:30 tonight.

Your friend always,
Corena

--------<>--------

Subject: Be a man!
Date: 10/09/00 11:15:38
From: The Medicine Cabinet
To: Dakin Caravans

Dear Dakin,

GET VIAGRA TODAY! GET PROPECIA TODAY! GET XENICAL TODAY!
STOP paying a doctor's fee every time you need a refill. We give ALL our customers UNLIMITED REFILLS on just one consultation fee. No consultation – just a consultation fee! To get your medication today, Click Here>

--------<>--------

Subject: My story, Part XXXVIII
Date: Mon, 09 Oct 2000 12:48:01
From: Dakin Caravans
To: Corena Bissett

Dear Dr. Freud,

You women can be SO shallow sometimes. No, the attraction was NOT big boobs, although Jewel most definitely was adequate in that category. Is there a French word to describe a person's "everything?" I was drawn to Jewel's everything. I loved her *je ne sais quois*, as you French might say. From her long blond hair to her painted toenails, she was everything I could imagine the perfect woman to be. And no matter what you cynics say, my love for her went far deeper than her perfect skin.

As for the mother of my children – I loved her, too. For the entire time I was married to Amanda, Jewel Halpern was no more than a distant memory. That's my story, and I'm sticking to it.

Maybe you'll understand as I return to the Dakin Caravans Story, episode thirty-eight, in which we meet the witch Amanda.

What you don't know yet is that Jewel actually was my third wife. When we last left our story, I was stunned at seeing Jewel Halpern's perfect body on the cover of *Playboy* magazine. I had recently graduated from high school. In that same year, my parents got divorced, I moved into an apartment with a buddy, and I got a job as sports editor of a local bi-weekly newspaper. Sports editor, hell, I was the entire sports department, as well as the chief news photographer, typesetter, ambulance chaser, police reporter and paste-up artist. It was a small outfit, but a great place to learn the newspaper business from the ground up. I was 19 years old, going to college part-time, morning and evening classes, and supporting myself with a full-time job. If it was hard work, I didn't notice, because I loved every minute of it.

During my first year there, the paper hired a high school senior to work part-time as a receptionist. She had a cute face with a little turned-up nose that she wrinkled like a bunny whenever I told a bad joke, which was often. Her long, straight brown hair hung almost to the top of her buttocks, and she had legs that were perfectly suited for the era of hot pants, which this most fortunately was. I have never seen, before or since, more sexy legs, and with hot pants, she could bare them almost all the way up to Never Land. My attraction to Jewel was never purely physical, but my attraction to this girl, I'm ashamed to admit, was. Triniti and I began dating almost immediately after she started working there.

As it turned out, she was a ripe virgin aching to lose that distinction, and I was happy to oblige. During the next year, we had sex in every conceivable position and locale. She was far more adventurous than I was, and, quite frankly, she almost wore me out. But at that age of incredible stupidity (naiveté, you shrinks might say gently), I thought it was love. When she went away to college the next year, we talked on the phone every night. One evening when she admitted she was stressed out from classes and a male friend gave her a massage that "made me feel so good," I went a little crazy. I jumped in my car, drove 100 miles to her school, knocked on her dorm door and asked her to marry me. I didn't want to lose my sex kitten.

She quit school and got a job, we had a big church wedding with the families and friends, and in less than two years, I came to realize that Triniti was a sex addict. I had married her because she liked to have sex anytime and anyplace, but I didn't realize that she also liked to have sex with any*body*.

I filed for divorce less than a week after she admitted her infidelity.

For the next four years, I did the single bachelor thing. I'd never really done much of that before, because I went straight from an intense adolescent relationship with Jewel to a series of casual girlfriends and then right into a premature marriage with Le Sex Machine.

To make a long story short (too late for that, huh?), I started to grow weary of the chase. It was the time of loud disco bars, too much drinking, too much dancing, too much meaningless sex. I decided it was time to get serious about my life. My career was moving along well – I had progressed to larger newspapers and was getting to cover important events. Now I wanted a family. That's when Amanda entered, stage left. I met her in the lobby of a movie theatre and was immediately struck by her poise, sense of humor, beautiful eyes and Ann-Margaret looks (the young Ann-Margaret). She was only 19.

I was five years older, but our maturity levels were just about the same. She, too, was ready to pursue the American Dream, which for both of us meant a house in the suburbs, a white picket fence, a dog, a mini-van and 2.5 kids.

Following in the footsteps of mom and grandmother, Amanda got married at 20 and was pregnant just a few months later. We were very happy. She wanted to stay home and raise the kids, and I think I was the last American male who thought that was a good idea and had the financial wherewithal to pull it off. There is no doubt in my mind I loved her very much, and I loved being a father.

We had Heather in 1979, which is easy for me to remember, because that was the first year the California Angels went to the playoffs. I was covering the Angels at the time. Although the demands of being a baseball writer kept me on the road a lot, I also got to be home when other fathers couldn't. I had winters off, and during the summer, when the kids were out of school, I was home until 3 p.m., when I would leave for the ballpark. So

I got to see most of the dance recitals and Little League games and birthday parties.

Do I sound a little defensive? I'm not surprised. I do regret the time spent away from home, and I wonder sometimes how it affected what eventually happened. Amanda was starting to get moody and distant within our first three years of marriage, and although she admitted she wasn't happy, she couldn't, or wouldn't, say why. When she got pregnant a second time, I was hopeful we would return to the same blissful existence we enjoyed during her first pregnancy, when she was so thrilled with the idea of being a mother for the first time. Unfortunately, she was sick throughout the entire second pregnancy, stricken with asthma so severe it put her in the hospital for much of the nine months.

When Casey was born, I again looked forward to a return to happiness and normalcy. But her asthma hung on for another five years, diminishing only gradually as time went by. What happened to us as a couple was predictable, don't you think, Ms. Family Counselor? We focused all our attention on the children. We were great parents, or at least as great as we could be. I married her because I knew she would be good mother material, and she was. You couldn't imagine a better mom. I admired and loved her for it. But the intimacy between us gradually disappeared. I didn't like it but didn't know how to fix it. I asked if she wanted to see someone like you, a family therapist. We could go together or separately, whichever she preferred, but she kept saying it was her own problem, and she wanted to handle it her own way. She kept saying she had no complaint or problem with me. She said I was a good husband and father. Despite all my traveling, I had never been unfaithful to her, and I was never the kind who went on hunting vacations with the guys or demanded a weekly poker night. Whatever time was not spent on the job, I devoted to my family.

Defensive again? Yeah, I know. I feel bad about how we drifted apart, and I suppose it's natural for me to want to lay all the blame on her. In truth, I don't really know what went wrong. But at some point, we stopped saying "I love you" to each other, stopped cuddling on the couch, stopped almost all intimacy. I'm embarrassed to admit that during one particular year, we had sex just once, not that I didn't try about a hundred times to get her interested. Big warning flag, huh?

But she seemed as happy being a mom as I was being a dad, and since I took my comfort in the family life, I assumed she did, too. How little I knew about the needs of women. I shouldn't have been surprised, but I was, when I found out that after 17 years of marriage, she was having an affair. He was 10 years younger than she, a man I knew, and I saw it for what it was – he just wanted the thrill of illicit sex. But she thought he loved her and that if she divorced me, he would stay.

Corena, I was devastated. This was not like my 20-year-old nymphomaniac sleeping with the truck driver who lived in the next apartment. That divorce was like breaking up with a girlfriend. But this was the mother of my children, the woman I wanted to grow old with, the one I had built my life around. Well, maybe if I really HAD built my life around her, she wouldn't have strayed.

I'll get back to my narrative in the next email, but I want to say a few things about how I felt during the divorce, and maybe when we talk on the phone tomorrow, you can help me through that. Because even now, after I reunited with Jewel and we experienced such bliss, and even after Jewel's death, I still feel heartache when I think back to the time of my divorce from Amanda.

So much is made in this society of the dirty, cheating, rotten man who can cavalierly jump into bed with any little tramp and not even feel like he is breaking his marital vows. And the woman is held up as the champion of home and hearth, the faithful spouse who is so often wronged and therefore deserves to get the house and the kids and half of his money for the rest of his miserable, cheating life.

Maybe that was true once. Maybe to some extent, it's still true today. But now I hear a lot more about men whose wives cheated on them than the other way around.

And I'm here to tell you it's no fun. The lies, the sneaking around, the mental imagery of your wife in bed with another man ... it gave me the dry heaves. I drove around sobbing so hard I couldn't see. I finally had to pull over and collapse. I was a pitiful wreck. Our kids were 16 and 13 years old at the time. For all the misery I went though, it had to be even tougher on them.

Shut up! Pull yourself together! (I can't. I'm such a weakling.) Stop that whining! Act like a man! (I am so confused. Where is truth? What is love?)

Your 50 minutes are up.

Thank you,
Dakin

--------◇--------

Subject: you
Date: Mon, 09 Oct 2000 19:23:56
From: Jeri Starrette
To: Dakin Caravans

hi dakin,

hi there hey there ho there, are you as happy as can be? no i guess not, but not to worry. it's a great big beautiful tomorrow, and guess what? i got a job down in orange county! at that big amusement park near you? now i won't be an hour away anymore. just a few minutes, probably.

dakin, they want me to start in two weeks! there's so much to do, but i'm so excited. you can be my tour guide and show me around orange county. i can't wait.

love,
jeri

ps -- it may take a while to find a good place to live. do you mind if we stay with you for a while until i can get settled? i don't think it will take us long, and i promise we won't be any inconvenience. i can even earn my keep by cooking and cleaning for you. remember how much you loved my lasagna?

oh, here's your picture of the day ... it's me, admiring you ...

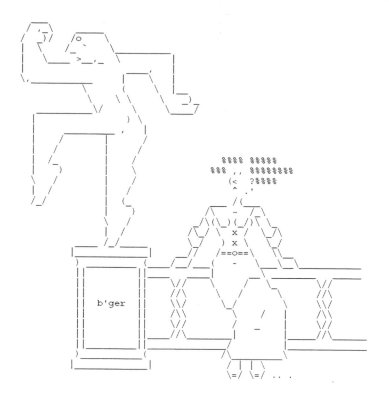

- - - - - - -<>- - - - - - - -

Subject: Sounds of silence
Date: Mon, 09 Oct 2000 23:11:55
From: Dakin Caravans
To: Jewel Halpern

My missing Jewel,

Hello darkness, my old friend. I've come to talk with you again.

That Paul Simon line has always haunted me and, at the same time, comforted me over the years. I'm back sending emails to the Spirit of Jewel Past. I hope you're listening or watching or reading over my shoulder or intercepting the transmission on the phone line. How do spirits work, exactly?

I've been pouring out my heart, soul and life story to Corena Bissett, the family counselor from Phoenix I met before you and I got back together. It makes me feel better, but it also makes me uneasy. I don't know where any of this will lead. All I know is I love you and miss you and don't really know what to do with myself now that you're gone.

Here's what I do know: You and I were the happiest couple I could ever imagine, and then you died for no apparent reason or cause. The Greentree cops think I may have murdered you. A crazy ex-druggie thinks you were the Second Coming, and he'll probably kill me if I don't let him publish your journals and letters to God as some kind of new bible. Jeri Starrette, the girl I dated for a while before you and I reunited, wants to minister to my physical needs.

And my creative spark has flickered out. I have no desire to paint, play music or write. All I want to do is find a way to go back in time, choose one perfect day and night with you, and stay there for eternity.

Reach out and touch somebody's hand. Make this world a better place if you can.

Adieu, my Supergirl. My love for you will never die, but I fear I am crippling myself by dwelling on the emptiness you have left inside of me. No more emails to the dead. You will always be in my heart.

Your Dakin

--------<>--------

Subject: FYI
Date: Tue, 10 Oct 2000 11:15:33
From: Lt. Dick Najera, Greentree PD
To: Dakin Caravans

Dear Mr. Caravans,

I will be calling you later today, but since you seem to be more responsive to email than phone messages, I decided to write, as well.

We have identified Spider Juncal as one Erasmus Timothy Juncal III, 48, an artist who does, indeed, live and work in Laguna Beach. He has three prior arrests, but none involving violence.

If you choose to press charges, I can talk to a friend of mine with the Irvine PD. In the meantime, keep us posted if he makes any more threats, veiled or otherwise.

Lt. Dick Najera, Greentree PD

--------<>--------

Subject: Burglary
Date: Tue, 10 Oct, 2000 20:46:22
From: Dakin Caravans
To: Lt. Dick Najera, Greentree PD

Lt. Najera:

I called and reported this to the Irvine Police Department, and they are on their way to take the report, but I thought I should notify you, too.

When I got home this evening, I found my condo had been broken into. The front door handle was sheared off, and the door was ajar. My place had been ransacked. It's a horrible feeling of personal violation, as I'm sure other victims have told you. I'm guessing it was this Spider Juncal character, although I have no reason to say that other than he is the only person I can think of who might have a motive. Everything was thrown all over the place, as if the burglar were hunting for something. My guess, if it actually was Juncal, was that he was looking for my late wife's journals and letters. They're still here, but maybe he just couldn't find them.

On the other hand, maybe it wasn't Juncal at all. The burglar did take a blue plastic piggy bank of pennies and my camcorder, so maybe it was just a kid looking for a thrill and a little loot. The piggy bank was a silly little thing. The pig tipped his hat every time you dropped a coin in. There couldn't have been more than $25 in that pig. But none of my other electronic equipment was touched – stereo, TVs, VCRs, computers, etc.

The Irvine police just pulled up. I'll call you soon.

Dakin

---------◇---------

Subject: Burglary
Date: Tue, 10 Oct 2000 23:31:16
From: Dakin Caravans
To: Lt. Dick Najera, Greentree PD

Lt. Najera:

About an hour after the Irvine police officer left and I started to clean up, I noticed one more thing that was missing in the burglary. The thief took a framed photograph of me and Jewel.
Dakin

---------◇---------

Chapter Five: Jewel
Every ending is a new beginning

Background: Jewel's therapist, Dr. Sara Lyman, would not consent to be interviewed for this book. All emails to and from Dr. Lyman were copied from the files of Jewel's own personal computer.
–David Cunningham

--------◇--------

Subject: My journal
Date: Fri, 12 Feb 1999 17:18:21
From: Jewel Halpern
To: Dr. Sara Lyman

Hi Dr. Lyman:

Here's more of my journal, as you requested. These are so long. I wonder sometimes if you actually read them. Or is it just supposed to be therapy for me to write them, and you don't really care what it says? Anyway, the latest chapter:

I returned to Southern California in '96 after 17 years in Vermont. I was helping take care of my dad, who wasn't well, while I looked for a job. I also started dating as a way to leave Red Bjerke and my abortive marriage behind. Dating might not be the right word for it. This was an obsession. I started calling ads in the singles section of the Orange County Register and setting up meetings. I was very scientific about it. I'd screen the ads for men with the right qualities, then call and listen to their taped messages. I was shopping for a mate, and I was very picky. I called over 100 ads, and in a span of three weeks, I met 30 of these guys, often two or three in a single day. It would be a casual, afternoon meeting at a coffee house at first, and if they passed that test, I'd agree to a dinner date. I was having a pretty good time, because even at 40, I was pretty damn attractive, if I do say so myself, so I found myself showered with attention, not to mention a lot of free meals. (I needed the free meals, because my phone bill with all those 1-900 calls to the singles line was astronomical.)

71

None of these guys quite measured up to my impossibly high standards, however. I kept thinking something better was just around the next corner, but I also was beginning to wonder if I was destined to be unfulfilled my entire life. Nothing ever made me truly happy.

Posing for *Playboy* made me feel empty, and the money didn't make it go away. Moving to Vermont seemed like a great adventure, but it was too cold for me. Red Bjerke seemed like an exciting and different guy, but in the end, I couldn't agree with his values. Working as a cop seemed like the perfect job – no dresses and nylons, no deskwork, and the power to let loose my control-freak personality. But it turned out to be monotonous and boring, and I felt so isolated. I could never be part of that good-old-boy cop camaraderie. Working in advertising led me to some wonderful friendships, especially with Vivienne, with whom I will always be close, but I still felt like I was spinning my wheels. Something was missing, even if I didn't know what it was.

And now as I searched for a lifemate through the classified ads, that same feeling came over me. Is this the way it's supposed to be?

Then, completely out of the blue, Dakin Caravans re-entered my life.

He'd been married himself, for almost 17 years, and was the father of two teenaged kids, a boy and a girl. But he and his wife had been divorced for a while when Dakin tracked me down. Although I'd changed my name from Halpern to Bjerke when I got married, Dakin got the help of an investigative reporter at his newspaper, and they were able to find an email address for my sister in Indiana. Dakin sent her a message saying he was trying to find me, and my sister emailed him my phone number in California.

He called and left a voice message for me. It was so strange. After hearing all these different guys from the singles connection on my message machine, here was a familiar voice out of the past. I hadn't heard that voice since the early 1970's. So much had happened to me since then, and certainly the same was true of him. Were we completely different people now? How could it be otherwise?

I wondered what he wanted. At that point, I knew nothing of his marriage, his kids, his divorce, his life. I had heard long ago that he had become a successful newspaper writer, but during all my years in Vermont, he was just a distant memory. I called him back.

"Dakin, this is Jewel," I said when I heard his voice.

"No way!" he shouted with an obvious smile in his voice. "Jewel Halpern?"

"Well, I'm Jewel Bjerke now, but that's in the process of changing."

"You're married?"

"Getting divorced. I'm surprised you were able to track me down. I've been in Vermont for a long time. I came back out here after filing for divorce."

There was a long silence on his end. I was the one to finally break it.

"So Dakin, you must be married, then, right?" I asked, feeling a little tense.

"Actually, divorced, too. About nine months ago. I have to admit, that's why I tried to find you. We had such a special relationship way back then, and there's this old song by the Moody Blues where they sing, 'I know you're out there somewhere.' Every time I heard it, I thought of you. I just wondered where you were, what you were doing, how your life had gone. All the years I was married, I could only wonder. Now that I'm single again, I figured, why not try to find out? I hope you don't feel like I'm some old stalker or anything, and if you're uncomfortable with it, this will be our only conversation. But I just wanted to know you were still alive and kicking."

"No, I'm not uncomfortable with it. Still alive. Still very much kicking."

We talked for about 30 minutes, catching up on each other's lives. He seemed so much more mature than the boy I once knew, but I guess I should have expected that. He was very different, but also, in some very important ways, the same. He was still the thinker, the questioner, the rebel, the guy who was into meditation and Eastern philosophy. He still hated the idea of wearing a necktie and going into an office. He never wanted to grow up, and covering sports for most of his life had enabled him to keep a very youthful attitude. But he also seemed to have the maturity and wisdom of a man who had helped raise two children, who tried to be a good husband and father, and who took his responsibilities seriously. It seemed like Dakin Caravans had turned into a good man. I was interested.

"Can I call you again sometime?" he asked. "Just to talk?"

Of course I said yes.

That was the beginning of a wild roller coaster ride.

I agreed to meet him at a coffee shop, just like one of my guys from the newspaper singles connection. He was number 33 on my list. I kept score on everybody – looks, personality, compatibility, etc. I gave points for the good qualities, took points away for the negatives, such as having small children from a prior marriage. I never had kids. I felt they got in the way of a good relationship. I had seen so many couples lose their intimacy because of children. Plus, if I dated a guy with kids, he would be forever tied to his ex-wife through the kids. If I married again, I didn't want to marry into someone else's family, complete with kids and a bitchy ex-wife hanging in the background. Dakin had kids, which cost him some points, but they were teenagers, so it wasn't as demanding a situation as if they were toddlers.

Dakin got to the coffee shop before me and was waiting in the parking lot, standing next to his car. My first reaction was, "Good, he didn't let himself go. He's still fit and has all his hair." As I walked toward him and he took off his sunglasses, I blurted out, "Oh, you're cute!"

It was the exact same thing I said when I first met him back in 1969. Only this time, I said it loud enough for him to hear. "Thank you. So are you," he replied with a grin. I kept my sunglasses on. I was a little insecure.

Dr. Lyman, that's all I wrote this week. I'll see you on Wednesday, and I'll write more in the journal. There's so much to tell. We got together, broke up, then got back together again ... we actually broke up several times before he finally kicked me out for good. In a way, our relationship was like it was back when we were teenagers – too intense, too good, too bad, too everything.

Later,
Jewel

--------<>--------

Subject: Dear God letter
Date: Tue, 16 Feb 1999 20:19:34
From: Jewel Halpern
To: Dr. Sara Lyman

Dear God:

Sometimes I feel so lost, and sometimes I feel so found. You are the light, and I must follow you, but I waver almost daily. I ask questions.

As you know, my father is very ill. I pray for him, but it appears he won't last out the week. Nobody knew he had any heart problems. Then he has a sudden, massive heart attack, and two days later in the hospital, he suffers a stroke. I don't know what your plan is for him or me, and I won't try to pretend I can figure it out. You'll do what must be done. I would love someday to sit at your feet and learn what this is all about. Why is my father dying? Why did he live? Was there a purpose to his existence? Could it be that I, his only natural-born daughter, am part of his purpose? Or is that too self-centered? When I think of his legacy to me, I am at a loss. He has always been a soft, spineless man – gentle and kind, but wholly unqualified to be a parent. As a child, I never had rules or restrictions. I could do whatever I wanted. When childhood friends asked me to stay out late or do something a little naughty, I told them my parents wouldn't allow me to do it, even though that wasn't true. I became my own disciplinarian. I invented my own imaginary parents.

So what does my father leave me with? It's good that I'll never be a parent, because I didn't learn good parenting skills from him. I don't know for sure, but I believe he'll leave me close to $1 million in his will. Maybe that's his gift to me – financial freedom. But what is that, really? Does that provide happiness? Does it fill the soul? I can't buy love. I can't buy Dakin back for my own.

I know one thing I got from my dad: the stereotypical Jewish tightness with money. He's a millionaire who lives like a pauper. All those years we lived modestly, he was socking away money from his packaging business, investing it in stocks and real estate and letting it grow. He never touched it. I had to badger and humiliate him into giving me money for college, for crying out loud. I never knew, until the last few months, that he had so much money saved away. And I'm just like him. Every week, I stashed away money from my paychecks, and even though I clip coupons and pick up pennies from the ground, I have almost $100,000 in savings. It sounds like a lot of money to me, but when my dad goes, I'll have 10 times that much, and I don't think it will make me any less unhappy.

God, I pray to you to watch over my father. He's not perfect, but he's a good man. He has a good heart, at least emotionally, if not physically. Let him live, if it's your will. I love him. But if it's his time to join you, I pray you give me some insight, some direction. I haven't been a follower of yours for many years, so I have much to learn, but I'm ready now. I've always been a believer. Show me the way.

I've been telling the story of my life and loves to Dr. Lyman, and it's been very good therapy for me. Thank you for sending her to me. I'll try to be the kind of daughter you want and will be proud of. I realize that I'm powerless to change so many things – that so much of it is in your hands, God – and knowing that gives me a kind of peace I've never known before.

With love in my heart,
Jewel

--------<>--------

Subject: God's letter to me
Date: Wed, 17 Feb 1999 18:40:12
From: Jewel Halpern
To: Dr. Sara Lyman

Dear Jewel,

Your father will die tonight. Please do not despair. It will be exactly as it was supposed to be.

Dying is as natural as being born. It happens to every living thing. Every death is by natural causes, no matter how it occurs. All life has a destiny, and that destiny is to be returned to the earth. So when your father dies tonight, he will be fulfilling the destiny that was written for him before he was born. There is a death waiting for you, for Dakin, for your mother, and for everyone else you know. Believe me when I say there is nothing to be afraid of. Pain, anguish, suffering – all the sensations that often accompany death are temporary. Compared to eternity, they are as insignificant as one grain of sand to all the beaches of the world.

But don't let you father's passing go unheeded. There are lessons the living can learn from every death. Allow the experience to widen your horizons. Let the feelings of mortality enter you. The world will never be quite the same after tonight. Your father is gone. But you are not, and the man he was will live in your heart. Let his passing give you strength. Resolve that your own death will not come without you being prepared. If you live your life to the fullest every day, if you love freely and honestly, if you always strive to be the best Jewel you can possibly be, then death can never rob you.

I am with you.
God

--------◇--------

Subject: Hello!
Date: Thu, 18 Feb 1999 11:06:22
From: Spider Juncal
To: Jewel Halpern

Hi Jewel!

I hope you don't mind, but I got your email address off the Narc Anon list. You are one amazing woman! I loved what you said at the meeting last night!

Oh, in case you don't remember, I'm the guy who hugged you afterward! Remember the guy named Spider? Most people don't forget that name! You spoke so eloquently, so passionately, I couldn't take my eyes off you! There's something about you that seems so special! Anyway, I just wanted to tell you that and let you know that if you ever need anything – a shoulder to cry on, a friend to talk to, whatever – I'm your guy! Believe me, I know what it's about! I've been down this road too many times, with the cocaine and other stuff, but mostly coke, and it sucks, man! Sometime soon, I'd like to talk to you about an answer that I think is better than all the drugs and pills in the world – Jesus! I could tell you were a spiritual person, and I felt you would be open to this! I will pray for you!

Until we meet again (next week's class!),
Spider Juncal

"...and the unclean spirit, tearing him and crying with a loud voice, came out of him." (Mark 1:26)

"Crystal wings and powdered dreamflakes dust my path with sweet delusions." (Larry Hama)

--------<>--------

Subject: You're weird
Date: Mon, 22 Feb 1999 19:10:57
From: Jewel Halpern
To: Spider Juncal

Hi Spider,

Yes, I remember you. You're weird, but strangely sincere. I welcome your offer of friendship and help, but if you're thinking I might be eligible for dating, forget it. That's not where my head is at right now.

See you at the meeting,
Jewel

--------<>--------

Subject: My father
Date: Tue, 23 Feb 1999 17:38:44
From: Jewel Halpern
To: Dakin Caravans

Hi Dakin,

I thought you might want to know that my father died Friday night. He had a heart attack, then a stroke after he was hospitalized. I know you really didn't want to talk to me and hear from me after we broke up, and I apologize if you really didn't want any messages from me, but you knew my dad and I think you liked him (I know he liked you), so I thought you'd want to know.

I hope all is well with you.

Jewel

--------<>--------

Subject: Please come back!
Date: Fri, 26 Feb 1999 10:46:12
From: Jewel Halpern
To: Dr. Sara Lyman

Dr. Lyman,

If you ever take another Thursday off, I'm going to skip my session rather than go to your partner, Dr. Eggers. Either that, or I will have to slit my wrists. How could you work with that guy? He's either senile or an Alzheimer's victim or completely nuts. Do people with real problems come to him for HELP? I will never see him again.

Here's how our session went:

Dr. Eggers: "So, Jewel, how do you feel about your father? Were you close? I was very close to my father. He died when I was nine years old. I still see him sometimes. I see his face. I see it in the window. I see it in the cathedral ceiling. I count." (He stares out the window silently for a very long time.)

Me: "You count? What do you count?
"One ... two ... three ... four ... five ... six ... seven ... eight ..."
"What are you counting?"
"Faces. His faces. I count. And then I touch his nose."

Then he throws back his head and looks like he is laughing, but no sound comes out. He did that several times. He would laugh completely out of context.

Me: "I've had some severe problems with addiction, and I've hurt myself and a lot of other people because of it."

Dr. Eggers throws back his head and laughs his silent laugh.

He cried twice, both times while talking about his father. I told him our family moved around a lot when I was young.

Dr. Eggers: "We moved around a lot, too. In second and third grade, I was at Washington Elementary ... In fourth and fifth grade, I was at Hamilton ... In sixth and seventh grade, I was at Starr King ...Eighth grade, I was at Jefferson. ... First two years of high school, I went to Williamsport ... Second two years– "

Me: "OK! I get the point."

He stared into space a lot. He occasionally farted out loud and acted like it didn't happen. He didn't listen to my answers. He repeated a lot of his questions. He told me he was looking for his father's ashes. He said he went back to the cemetery in Ohio looking for them. Three times.

Me: "Is there a headstone for him there?"

Dr. Eggers: "No."

"So what makes you think his ashes are there?"

He throws back his head and laughs his silent laugh.

Dr. Eggers: "I told my wife I'm having hallucinations again."

Me: (getting more nervous by the minute): "What does she say?"

"She says to close my eyes."

"Listen, my time is up."

"This boyfriend of yours, were you intimate with him?"

"I really have to go."

"How intimate?"

"I'm going now."

A few minutes later, when I was out talking to your receptionist, Dr. Eggers comes out to get some coffee, sees me, acts surprised and says, "Hi Jewel!" like he was seeing an old friend for the first time in years. If I were one of your more disturbed patients, I might have jumped out the window.

Can't wait til you get back,

Jewel

--------<>--------

Subject: Your father's will
Date: Fri, 26 Feb 1999 18:40:12
From: Schermerhorn Brothers, Attorneys at Law
To: Jewel Halpern

Hi Jewel,

Per your request from our meeting earlier this week, I have confirmed that your father's will provides you with an estate worth about $900,000, most of it in real estate holdings, mutual funds and life insurance. A like amount is to be distributed to your brother and sister. As executor of the estate, you will be required to handle a lot of the paperwork. We can discuss all that at our appointment next week.

Sincerely,
Barry Schermerhorn

--------<>--------

Chapter Six: Dakin
The impossible is the untried

Background: Large portions of the police reports on the deaths of Dakin and Jewel Caravans have been sealed away from public scrutiny. This chapter includes the only known record, in Dakin Caravan's own words, of what happened the night Jewel died.

   –David Cunningham

--------◇--------

Subject: OK, besides that, what's new?
Date: Wed, 11 Oct 2000 17:23:56
From: Corena Bissett
To: Dakin Caravans

Hi Dakin,

Your life just never seems to get boring, does it? You find your childhood sweetheart after a 20-plus-year separation, she inherits $1 million, you marry her, she dies, the cops think you killed her, one of her odd friends decides she was Jesus Christ's superstar sister, and now someone burglarizes your condo. Call me when something really interesting happens, will you?

Seriously, let me know if they get any leads on your burglar. I hope it really was just some troubled teens and not your born-again stalker.

I need to ask you something. You never told me much about how Jewel died, other than to say she just stopped breathing. And now you tell me the police believe you had something to do with it. Do they have any evidence that would incriminate you? Did you have means, motive and opportunity?

Please understand, I am not suggesting for a moment that I believe you might have had something to do with Jewel's death, no matter how it happened. But in addition to being a sounding board for you, I'm actually trying to help you through what is obviously a very challenging time for you. I'm professionally qualified to do that, and as your good friend, I'm very motivated to do that. But you have to help me. Tell me what happened that night. Leave nothing out. And if you really DID kill her, you can rest easy in

knowing that ours is a patient-doctor relationship, and I cannot be compelled to testify to any of this.
KIDDING! Just kidding!

Look forward to hearing from you, Dakin.

Your friend always,
Corena (Dr. Bissett to you)

--------<>--------

Subject: What do you mean?
Date: Wed, 11 Oct 2000 19:19:09
From: Dakin Caravans
To: Corena Bissett

Dear Dr. Watson,

Don't beat around the bush, lady. Just come right out and say it: did I kill Jewel? The answer is no. As for the O.J. Simpson qualifications, yes, I did have the opportunity, because I was the only one there, but I did not have motive or means. Well, Lt. Dick (Inspector Clouseau) Najera of the Greentree PD might disagree with that.

She DID have $1 million, and I suppose a cynical person would say that if I killed her, I would have all that money to myself, and that would be motive. But that cynical person could not possibly know me, because money has never been the motivating force in my life, and I loved Jewel more than anything. I didn't become a baseball writer for money; I loved the game, and I loved writing. I didn't become an artist because of the money; lord knows, there wasn't much to be had in painting portraits, but I loved the creative feeling it gave me. I didn't become a drummer because I wanted to be a rich rock star. I just loved being part of the creation of music. No, money alone never made my heart flutter. As long as I had enough to pay the bills, I was happy.

So opportunity and motive, maybe, but I wonder where Lt. Najera gets the idea that I had the means to kill Jewel. She didn't have her throat cut like Nicole Simpson. She wasn't poisoned. She wasn't bludgeoned. She just stopped breathing. The coroner's office said there was no sign of foul play. The only reason it was listed as a suspicious death is because Jewel was 46 years old and in perfect health. She didn't have a heart attack or an aneurysm or asthma attack or anything else they could find. She just stopped living. How could I do that to anyone, let alone Jewel? What are the means for that?

First, some background. I haven't told you much about my meditation, self-hypnosis and out-of-body adventures, so it may sound like nut-case stuff to you, but I swear this is all true.

I've been exploring altered states of consciousness since I was 15. It started with typical drug experimentation in the late 1960's, when everybody was playing that game. Then I read Aldous Huxley's essay, <u>The Doors of Perception</u>, and started getting into all kinds of trippy stuff, from Transcendental Meditation to astral projection. It wasn't a fad for me, although each level of experimentation might be termed a phase. They were progressive stages. As I grew into adulthood, my journeys into inner space were not tossed out along with my water pipe and bellbottoms. It became a secret part of me, something I told very few about, because I didn't expect anybody to understand.

Here's something I wrote in my journal when I was 17 years old:

"I begin the voyage. The lights are dim. It is blue. The music is soft. It is classical. Some Moody Blues, too. Background noise. I am calm, relaxed. Every muscle releases its tension. The neck, the spine, the arms, legs, each toe and finger, my eyelids. The jaw loosens slightly. A deep breath, and oxygen is rushed to the brain. Each sense has its moment: touch, hear, smell. The sounds and sights dance as visions. I leave the body and the room. The program, set before departure, begins. I am lost in it. A myriad of colors. High play. Optimums of truth and beauty. Ecstasy without. Is the mind secreting drugs that catalyze the same reactions caused by LSD, hashish, or cannabis? Shut off. Better breathe and move slowly. Relaxed. It's getting better all the time."

I've been reading my old journal a lot lately. It seems to be giving me clues as to what really happened with Jewel, which is very bizarre, because many of those entries were written 30 years ago. Here's another one from 1971:

"Man is always seeking pleasure. But there are more than one or two kinds of pleasure. Physical pleasures are only part of it. Pleasure, as desired by most, is flimsy and fleeting. The pleasure I seek is forever, a state of being, a stream of consciousness, a way of life. I am finding it. I have a grasp, a glimpse of it. I will have it all. I'm not greedy. I just want what I came here for. And when I have it all, when I reach Nirvana, the absolute bliss consciousness, the heaven that is there for anyone who wishes to take it, then I will want not. I will BE. Hurt, jealousy, anger, pain, fear and all the rest will be past. What a trip! Without the benefit of organized religion I have found the gates of heaven. I am at the threshold of heaven, and I know what few Catholics, Jews or Muslims know. Heaven is not dying. It is living."

You see, Corena, this is what we were seeking, Jewel and I. When I was a teenager, I felt I was so very close to it. At 47, I'm still stuck in that purgatory phase. My heaven is experienced in glimpses, moments, transitory feelings. I can't hold it and live inside it all the time. After Jewel and I reconnected and married, I taught her meditation, and together we continued to read about and research altered states and absolute bliss. She had a knack for it that was natural and beautiful. She instantly mastered techniques that took me years of practice. I think it was because Jewel was one of those people who are naturally high all the time. Her head was already living in a different place.

So, back to the night of Sept. 28.

As you know, Jewel and I had been traveling around the country in our motor home. It was a journey of the mind, as well as our bodies. We were searching for answers. How do we achieve the perfect relationship? Why are we here? How should the fully evolved life be lived? Her inheritance enabled us to search on a full-time basis. We had many adventures, met many fascinating people and teachers, and felt we were making progress in all our pursuits. Jewel was becoming very good and very daring in her meditation and out-of-body travel. She came back telling fantastic tales. I envied her. I had spent so many years climbing toward the level she achieved so quickly and easily.

We had returned to the area where we grew up, Greentree, a beautiful little jewel (if I may use that word) of a community in the hills overlooking Los Angeles. We pulled our motor home onto a bluff overlooking the ocean, sat outside and watched the sun set. We talked of many things, big and small. We were naturally high, so happy to be with each other, so happy to feel close to finding real meaning in our lives. We watched the stars come out, and I pointed out some of the constellations and planets. I've always loved astronomy. Looking into the heavens always gives me deep feelings. It makes me feel insignificant, certainly, but it also makes me feel like I'm part of something infinitely magnificent.

When it grew too chilly, we went inside the motor home and decided to meditate. I call it transcension, since what I do is my own invention, a little different from meditation or self-hypnosis, but similar to both. Jewel didn't even have a name for what she practiced, but it was deep, meaningful, relaxing and always very moving for her. We were lying side by side on the large bed in the back of the motor home. After about 20 minutes, I slowly brought myself back to a waking consciousness. As always, I felt refreshed, happy, relaxed and alert. Jewel's eyes were still closed, but under her eyelids, I could see she was in some kind of strange rapid-eye-movement phase. Her eyelids were fluttering like crazy. As always, I left her alone. At that point, I had no reason to be fearful. I put on a coat and went outside to look for shooting stars.

After a little more than an hour, I came back inside, and Jewel was still out. I figured she had simply fallen asleep, which wasn't unusual. I was standing several feet away, looking in her direction, when she called out my name.

I gently moved to her side. Her eyes were still closed. "Dakin," she said. "It's so beautiful. So beautiful. So warm and wonderful."

I said nothing. I couldn't tell if she was talking in her sleep or actually having some kind of experience with her meditation. She began to hum very softly, a low monotone, sort of like a mantra. Then the "mmmmmm" sound became a soft "aaaahhhhhhh." I couldn't wait for her to bring herself around and tell me what she had experienced. Then she became very still and quiet. Too still. For the first time, I felt a flicker of worry inside my gut. I had to address that worry. "Jewel?" I said, knowing it would break her reverie.

She moved her head slightly, and she was smiling, but her eyes were still closed. I will never forget her next words, spoken with quiet love and wonderment in her voice:

"It is here ... It is love ... we are one ... you can come ..."

What do the words mean? I can't say. I can guess, but I will never know, because she never spoke again. She continued to smile, so I assumed all was well. That smile never left her lips. I think she stopped living just seconds after her mysterious statement, because she never moved another muscle. But because of that smile, I left her alone. I will always regret that. Maybe if I had checked and been able to give her CPR immediately or called 911 or kissed her and breathed life back into her body, she would still be with me today. Instead, I sat there and watched her, alone with my thoughts, for another 30 minutes. Finally concluding she was asleep, I got ready for bed myself, curled up next to my Jewel, and moved to gently kiss her lips. They were cold. So was her body. I tried to awaken her. She was limp and lifeless. I immediately got to the cell phone and called 911, then spent the next 20 minutes trying to get her to breathe. I'm trained in CPR, but I never had to use it, and I couldn't remember how many breaths I was supposed to give, how many chest compressions, or how hard I was supposed to push. I just kept calling her name and worked over her body until I was drenched in sweat and the paramedics arrived. They couldn't do anything to help her, either.

Corena, she just died on her own. She didn't have any history of any medical conditions. She was a health nut who exercised more and ate better than I did. Most people thought she was in her early 30s, not her mid-40s. She wasn't taking any medication. The coroner's office can't explain it any better than I can.

If she used her mind to travel to some other kind of existence, where she lives as a spirit or angel or god or something, then maybe you can say I killed her, because I introduced her to the kind of mind games we were playing. But did I kill her in the traditional sense, with poison or a gun or a knife or the pipe in the kitchen with Col. Mustard? No, I did not.

If I have any clue as to what happened, it might be from this journal entry I wrote 26 years ago:

"Well, I'm glad that's over. What a frightening feeling! I still haven't come completely down from it. I've been trying to get into this out-of-body travel business, which I wasn't sure I really believed in. I can meditate freely and use self-hypnosis to accomplish plenty, but out-of-body travel sounded a little too bizarre. Two other times I tried it, and by wiping the slate of my brain completely clean, I was able to get this feeling of drifting away. It was very strange. But tonight, it was actually scary. I completely lost the umbilical cord to myself. I felt myself float above my body, and I could see myself lying there below me. I floated through the ceiling and out into the night sky. I started sailing higher and higher, farther and farther away from my body, and I got the strangest feeling, like I was actually leaving my body behind. This was not an imaginary journey in my head, like I was just conjuring up pictures. It felt like it was actually happening. My mind or spirit or consciousness or whatever you want to call it was moving faster and faster, always upward, and everything was a blur. I began to feel a sense of fear, like my body was in trouble, and I was too far away from it. I had to concentrate hard on getting back to my body. I had to will it to happen. And it did, like a lightning flash, but as soon as I was zapped back into my body, I took a huge, gasping breath, and my heart started pounding furiously. I have no idea what actually happened there, but it was deep and frightening, and I don't care to go back there again. I think I need to stick with mellow thoughts of meditation and stay away from this astral projection stuff. Some say the devil can inhabit your body if your spirit leaves it through astral projection. I don't believe anybody in this world has any evidence to suggest that's true, but why take a chance, you know?"

Corena, ever since that day long ago, I've believed that out-of-body travel was possible. I know of no other explanation for what happened to Jewel. I think she left her body behind and went somewhere else.

All right, there it is. NOW you can send the men with the white coats to get me.

Dakin

--------<>--------

Subject: That's not what you said before
Date: 10/11/00 23:34:07
From: WANDAXXX
BCC: Dakin Caravans

The adventure of a lifetime! Pure excellence can be yours! XXX Click
Here>

--------<>--------

Subject: speak to me
Date: Thu, 12 Oct 2000 10:31:49
From: Dakin Caravans
To: Jewel Halpern

Hello Supergirl,

My world is spinning out of control, and I can't seem to stop it. Can you help me? Are you there? I don't know whom else to turn to but you. Real human beings don't have any answers for me. But you are immortal now, and you have joined with the Almighty. Surely you know some secret that can help me. If you won't reach down and touch your soulmate, then what good is Absolute Knowledge?

I am still talking and writing to Corena Bissett, the counselor. I've told her many things I would tell no one else. My deepest thoughts and emotions are meant only for you and I, but you're not here anymore, and I need to talk to someone.

Sometimes I feel fine, like I'm in total control, and everything will be OK. Life is always worth living, no matter what challenges present themselves. I'd rather be a bum riding the rails than be dead. I'd rather be a beggar than fertilizer in the earth. But other times, I feel like I'm slipping away. I had this dream last night where I was sailing a boat on a bright, sunny day, and then the wheel started spinning out of control. It was spinning so fast, I couldn't grab it and stop it. And the boat was starting to tip over, and it moved toward this black wall, like I was sailing off the edge of the flat earth. I woke up breathing heavy. If dreams mean anything, was this a metaphor for my life? Again, I turn to you, living in the supernatural world, for answers.

And I hear nothing. To tell you the truth, I don't think you exist at all anymore. I think you're fertilizer. I think you abandoned me.

Goodbye, Jewel.
Dakin

--------◇--------

Subject: You're wrong!
Date: Thu, 12 Oct 2000 12:59:52
From: Spider Juncal
To: Dakin Caravans

Bad Dakin!

I just spent two hours in the police station, man! You have any idea why? Because of you! Someone breaks into your home, and you automatically think it's me! I told them the same thing I tell you now – I didn't take your damn piggy bank, and I didn't break into your home!

You need to get one thing straight, man! I'm no thug! I AM THE LIGHT! I am here to spread the gospel of Jewel, and that is the gospel of peace and love! So get off my back, dude!

Sincerely,
Spider Juncal

"Open your hearts to us: we wronged no man, we corrupted no man, we took advantage of no man." (2nd Corinthians, 7:2)

"When a small man casts a long shadow, the sundown is near." (Vietnamese saying)

--------◇--------

Subject: Just wondering
Date: Thu, 12 Oct 2000 14:27:03
From: Dakin Caravans
To: Spider Juncal

Mr. Juncal:

How did you know that a piggy bank was stolen from my home? I called Lt. Najera, and he says you were never told what items were taken in the burglary.

Dakin

--------◇--------

Chapter Seven: Jewel
No man is free who is not master of himself

Background: While in recovery for her addiction to the painkiller Vicodin, Jewel kept a personal journal and began her strange correspondence to God. Curiously, the actual letters have never been found.

Versions of the letters and journal were believed to exist on Jewel's computer hard drive – Dakin referred to them in his emails – but those are also missing, according to Lt. Dick Najera. However, Casey Caravans discovered the journal notebook, itself, in Jewel and Dakin's strongbox. He graciously allowed me to review it, and I confirmed that the journal entries sent via email to Dr. Sara Lyman were verbatim copies of those in the notebook.

Fortunately, Jewel copied many of her letters to God onto emails and sent them to Dr. Lyman, so those, too, were recovered from Jewel's computer.

–David Cunningham

--------<>--------

Subject: My journal
Date: Tue, 2 Mar 1999 18:32:57
From: Jewel Halpern
To: Dr. Sara Lyman

Hi Dr. Lyman:

OK, now we get to the good stuff. Hold onto your seat, and keep your arms and legs inside the car at all times. In my last journal entry, Dakin and I had just met again, after more than 20 years apart. Here's what I wrote yesterday in my journal:

I guess I should have expected that any relationship between Dakin and I would be rocky, but I didn't. I think I was just remembering all the good times back when we were teenagers, and here was this grown man inside the Dakin Caravans shell, telling me how much he missed me and how he thought of me all those years and wondered where I was and what I was doing. It seemed so deliciously romantic.

The fact is, even when we were teenagers, it wasn't so rosy and perfect. He was SO jealous. I'd forgotten about that. And he was SO completely into me that he didn't see anything else, barely thought of anything else. At 16, I thought it was wonderful, even if it was a little suffocating at times. But in my 40s, I could look back at that and realize it was kind of dysfunctional. If my dad hadn't forced us to break up, I doubt that the relationship would have been a keeper. We were very different people, but we seemed to fit together. Where I zigged, he zagged. Alone, we were probably neurotic and needy kids. Together, we seemed to feed off one another and make each other stronger.

So at the age of 42, Dakin reintroduced himself to me as a changed man. Our first meeting in the coffee shop led to a dinner date, and we had so much to catch up on, we couldn't stop talking. Although we had led completely different kinds of lives, we had this strong common background – where we had grown up, who we had known, and those crazy times in The Sixties that we shared.

He was a baseball writer, so he had winters off, and it was in late October that we reconnected. He had plenty of time. I did, too, because I'd just moved back to Southern California, and I hadn't found a job yet. Dad was helping while I got back on my feet after my divorce from Red the Jerk. Dakin and I got together almost every night, having romantic dinners, listening to live music, going to stage plays and comedy clubs and movies. It was one of the greatest periods of my life.

I could tell he was falling for me all over again, and although I resisted a little, I knew it was happening to me, too. One night during dinner at a nice Mexican restaurant, sitting outdoors under the moonlight while mariachis played, I gave him one of those romantic cards that told him how much he meant to me. But I didn't use the word "love" anywhere. It was too soon for me. Apparently, it wasn't too soon for Dakin. After he read it and paid the bill, we started to walk to the car. He stopped, gently turned me toward him by the shoulders, then gave me a deep, sensuous kiss, the kind that make your head swirl. I haven't had too many of those kisses in my lifetime. It instantly made me remember how great a kisser he was. He pulled away very slowly, just a few inches from my face, looked into my eyes and said, "I love you, Jewel."

I was shell-shocked, to tell the truth. Yes, we had this history together, but that was so long ago. He was moving a little too fast for me. We'd only been seeing each other for three weeks. I don't remember what I said to him that night, but it wasn't "I love you." That came about a week later. So I guess it wasn't all that soon for me, after all.

After the first few weeks, we stopped dating anybody but each other. I didn't know where this was headed, but it felt good. And remember what we said in The Sixties: if it feels good, do it. He gave me a sense of wonder about the world, because that's something Dakin always had. He sees everything as if he were looking through the eyes of a child. Everything is always fresh and new to him and filled with beauty. He sees little things the rest of us don't. Maybe that's why he became a writer. He doesn't just see, he observes and studies. He's fascinated by everything. I would drive by a park and look right past it. Dakin would see what kind of trees were there and what kind of birds lived in them. He knew what the blooming flowers smelled like and what games the children were playing.

Oh, his children. I met Heather and Casey when we all went to the San Diego Zoo one Sunday afternoon. I had a lot of apprehension about it. I never wanted to have children. Sometimes, frankly, I consider them a nuisance – mewling and puking and disrupting any chance at intimacy between the parents. But his kids were almost adults.

Dakin had dated a few other women after his divorce but didn't introduce any of them to his kids because he didn't want to confuse them. He knew that the deepest wish of any kid in a divorce is that their parents will remarry, and he didn't see any reason to keep smashing down those wishes by bringing around all his casual dates. So I guess I graduated from being a casual date to a serious one when he finally let me meet Heather and Casey. I wanted them to like me. I guess they did.

It wasn't long after that when Dakin started wondering whether or not HE liked me anymore. I had begun working at an advertising agency, and because I was still technically single, still good looking and in a new work environment, I attracted a lot of attention. I have to admit I liked it. And I felt a little cheated because after that long relationship with Red in Vermont, I never really got to stretch my wings as a single woman. At 41, my time to do that was running short. Falling into Dakin's arms so quickly after returning to California had constricted me. So I flirted a little at work, innocent stuff, but I did go to lunch with a few men and was being asked out for dinner and drinks. I kept saying no, but I guess not very forcefully. I was confused about what I really wanted, and I really didn't see anything wrong with the flirting and talking. After all, Dakin and I weren't married, or even talking about it at that point.

One of the blessings and curses of our relationship was that we were always honest with each other, sometimes painfully so. I didn't hide anything from him. I think I'd have felt slimy and sneaky if I did. I told him exactly how I felt, and when he asked about my work relationships, I told him. The old jealous dragon inside Dakin reared its ugly head, and we started to clash. He actually broke up with me twice during that phase, but both times, we got back together again within a couple days. I still wasn't sure what I wanted for my life, either in the relationship department or professionally.

It was during this time of minor turbulence between Dakin and I that an episode occurred which triggered the darkest chapter of my life. While driving on the freeway, I was hit from behind by a driver who didn't notice the traffic was backing up. The damage to my car infuriated me – I'm very protective of certain things, and my car is one of them. But the damage to my back was worse. The doctor thought it was muscular and would heal in a few weeks, but the pain was excruciating, especially in the mornings when I would get up from a long sleep. Sometimes the pain would keep me from sleeping more than about four hours, and I got caught in a vicious circle. More sleep – and more time on my back – led to more pain the next day. Less sleep – and less time in a stationary position – eased the back pain somewhat, but left me miserable and cranky. I was going downhill fast, and the only relief I could find was through pills. They not only gave temporary relief from the pain, but also put me in a great, mellow mood. Over time, I grew dependent on that mood, even as the back pain eased. I kept telling the doctor that my back was killing me just so I could get the pills. I took them every day, three and four times a day, and never wanted to stop. If it feels good, do it. That attitude led so many of us astray in The Sixties, and now I was hooked and didn't know it.

I've always prided myself on being in control. When my parents had marital problems, little Jewel was the one who kept her head while everyone around her was losing theirs. I left home at 17 and got an apartment by myself. I bought my own car without help from anybody (that's where my material possessiveness probably comes from; nobody ever gave me anything. I earned it.) I was the cop, always in control of the situation. Maybe because I was raped as a teenager, I never wanted to let anyone control me ever again. That's probably why I kept my heart a little longer than any of the men I dated. They fell in love with me, but I held back. Let THEM get out of control with their emotions. Let Dakin tell me he loves me, but I won't fall so easily. I was in control.

So that's why my addiction to Vicodin snuck up on me. I didn't believe it was possible that a little pill could control me. Despite growing up in The Sixties, I was always steadfastly against drug use. Never touched the stuff. Didn't even drink much. I wonder sometimes if my psychological makeup made me susceptible to addiction, but I honestly think I was pretty screwed up in a few ways even before my accident. I had difficulty making commitments, I never stayed at one job very long, and I think I probably had a deep-seated distrust of men. On a day-to-day basis, I wasn't very happy. Maybe that's another reason I was attracted to Dakin. He was so happy. He could find joy in the simplest things. I wanted that. But during this stage of my life, nothing made me happier than those little pills. It took away my mental pain as well as my physical pain. I felt great in every way. Imagine the world in sharp, crystal clarity under bright lights, where everything is a little overwhelming and makes you want to squint. Sensory overload. Now you take a couple pills, and in a little while, the whole world gets fuzzy at the edges. Nobody speaks too loud, nothing is too bright, nothing is too important. These are great little mood enhancers. No wonder you need a prescription to get them.

After the doctor sensed I was getting out of control with the pills, she refused to prescribe any more for me. But I needed them so desperately I found other ways to get them. I was buying drugs on the black market and not even giving a single thought to what that meant. All I cared about was getting that high, and I'd do whatever I had to do to get it.

In one way, Dakin is a little like my father in that he can be too soft. He's a gentle person, and he doesn't like confrontations. He was pretty sure my fondness of painkillers had grown into an addiction, but he wasn't comfortable coming right out and forcing me to look at it. Not that it would have mattered.

Under the influence of those pills, I started to grow rebellious in the relationship and did some apparently irrational things, like flirting with other men right in front of Dakin. What I really wanted was for Dakin to love me and want me, and in my messed-up condition I thought that making him jealous would force Dakin to realize he wanted to marry me and make me happy the rest of my life. I wanted him to save me. I also started doing something else I never did before – dress like a tramp. I wore tight miniskirts and low-cut blouses and dresses with cutouts on the sides. I showed a lot of skin, a lot of curves. I knew it would turn men's heads. And I only did it when Dakin and I went out together. I wanted him to see other men drooling over me, in hopes that it would increase his desire for me. I realize now how screwed-up that sounds, but I was drugged out most of the time and wasn't able to think straight. Dakin never realized, until I told him much later, how many pills I was taking and how dependent I had become.

Naturally, other men took my slut outfits as advertising. I had something to sell. Plenty of potential clients came around, like moths to a flame. It didn't matter that Dakin was with me. They would slip notes into my hand or wait until Dakin went to the bathroom before approaching. In a strange way, I was captivated by all the attention. Dakin didn't see everything that was happening, but he saw enough of it. We fought bitterly, and we broke up continuously. I don't know why he kept getting back together with me after our fights, but he always did.

Well, almost always. I finally broke his spirit after we moved to Arizona.

Dr. Sara, that's all I wrote yesterday. I'll try to get back to the story next week.

You are so right about this being good therapy for me. Some of these thoughts have never come out of my head before. The incidents have always been out there, but my inner thoughts about what caused them and what was going on inside my head – that's been bottled up. I was in such a drugged-out haze back then. I have you and my friends from Narcotics Anonymous to thank for helping me clear that haze.

Later,
Jewel

--------◇--------

Subject: Beauty!
Date: Thu, 04 Mar 1999 21:02:39
From: Spider Juncal
To: Jewel Halpern

Dear Jewel!

Thank you for sharing with me your letters to God yesterday! They are the most beautiful things I have ever seen outside of the Bible! I believe you are touched by our Creator! There is something so special about you, so perfect! I have never met anyone like you before, and you fill me with such joy! Man, I am SO happy you have kicked your addiction and have moved toward The Light! There is so much to be joyous about, so much to celebrate, and you have so much to offer this world! Don't ever lose sight of that!

I look forward to seeing you at next week's meeting and reading what new revelations you and God have in store for us!

Peace and love,
Spider Juncal

"Jehovah did not set his love upon you, nor choose you, because ye were more in number than any people; for ye were the fewest of all peoples."
(Deuteronomy 7:7)

"If you dress like everybody else, how will anybody know you're different?"
(Cricketeer Clothing)

--------◇--------

Subject: Dear God letter
Date: Tue, 09 Mar 1999 20:19:34
From: Jewel Halpern
To: Dr. Sara Lyman

Dear God:

Help me to understand all that is happening to me and make my life a better service to you and your word.

I'm feeling so much better now that I've found my new friends with Narc Anon, and my life is headed in a better direction than it has ever known. For the first time in my life, I realize I don't need a man to make me feel whole. My relationship with Dakin meant so much to me, and I regret that I threw it all away, but I'm beginning to see that this is how it was supposed to be. I could never have been in a healthy, happy love with him until I got my own problems sorted out. I had to cleanse my body and mind of the drug that was hurting me, and then I had to face my deeper-seated problems head-on with Dr. Lyman, who has helped me so much in these last few weeks. I know I'm headed in the right direction.

Why do you make people who are so screwed up? Do we do it to ourselves? How much control do you really exert over our daily lives? I have so many questions for you, God, and so few answers. But I'm finally beginning to realize that you're not here to provide easy answers for us. We need to find them for ourselves. You give us the tools, and we have to pick them up and use them.

Here are some of the tools I've picked up in the last two weeks. They're words given to me by a sponsor from Narc Anon, but in reality, you, God, have led me to these words, and I will try to take these words to heart:

May you find serenity and tranquillity in a world you may not always understand.

May the pain you have known and the conflict you have experienced give you the strength to walk through life facing each new situation with optimism and courage.

Always know that there are those whose love and understanding will always be there, even when you feel most alone.

May you discover enough goodness in others to believe in a world of peace.

May a kind word, a reassuring touch, a warm smile be yours every day of your life, and may you give these gifts as well as receive them.

Remember the sunshine when the storm seems unending.

Teach love to those who know hate, and let that love embrace you as you go into the world.

May the teaching of those you admire become part of you, so that you may call upon them.

Remember, those whose lives you have touched and who have touched yours are always a part of you, even if the encounters were less than you would have wished.

May you not become too concerned with material matters, but instead place immeasurable value on the goodness in your heart.

Find time in each day to see the beauty and love in the world around you.

Realize that each person has limitless abilities, but each of us is different in our own way.

What you may feel you lack in one regard may be more than compensated for in another.

What you feel you lack in the present may become one of your strengths in the future.

May you see your future as one filled with promise and possibility.

Learn to view everything as a worthwhile experience.

May you find enough inner strength to determine your own worth by yourself and not be dependent on another's judgments of your accomplishments.

May you always feel loved.

Thank you, God.
Jewel

--------◇--------

Subject: Dear God letter
Date: Tue, 09 Mar 1999 21:56:58
From: Jewel Halpern
To: Dr. Sara Lyman

Dear Jewel:

I couldn't have said it better myself.

Love,
God

--------◇--------

Chapter Eight: Dakin
It is better to love than be loved

Background: Dakin and Spider began playing a game of cat-and-mouse about the burglary. Neither of them seemed to be particularly lucid at the time.
–David Cunningham

--------◇--------

Subject: Re: Just wondering
Date: Fri, 13 Oct 2000 16:12:27
From: Spider Juncal
To: Dakin Caravans

Dude, you are so small! You think cops tell the truth? They lie to everybody! Especially you! They told me all about your cute little piggy bank! And they told me about how Jewel's letters and journals were kept on the hard drive of her computer! So shut up! Accuse somebody who is guilty! My conscience is clear!

Sincerely,
Spider Juncal

"And Pilate went out again, and saith unto them, Behold, I bring him out to you, that ye may know that I find no crime in him." (John 19:4)

"As long as Christ knew I wasn't a sissy, I had nothing to fear." (Tiny Tim)

--------◇--------

Subject: I think he did it
Date: Fri, 13 Oct, 2000 20:01:31
From: Dakin Caravans
To: Lt. Dick Najera, Greentree PD

Dear Lt. Najera,

I'm pretty sure now that Spider Juncal is the man who broke into my condo. Remember the email message I told you about on the phone, which he sent me after you questioned him about the burglary? In that message, he said he didn't steal my piggy bank, so I called you and asked how he knew what was stolen. You assured me that you didn't give him ANY information about what was stolen, so I sent Juncal a message asking how he knew about the piggy bank. He claimed you told him after all. I might have believed that, but then he said you also told him that Jewel's letters and journals were kept on the hard drive of her computer. I KNOW I never gave you that information. All I said was that the paper copy of Jewel's journal was untouched. So he couldn't have known about the computer version of her journal and letters unless he went into the computer himself and found them. I'm betting he made copies on diskette, since he wants them for some new-age bible he wants to publish.

I don't know if stealing someone's diary from a computer is a crime, especially since I still have it, but I do know that breaking and entering is a crime, and if you could get this nefarious character off my back, I would greatly appreciate it.

If there's anything more I can do to help, let me know.
Dakin Caravans

--------<>--------

Subject: Us
Date: Sat, 14 Oct 2000 11:16:44
From: Jeri Starrette
To: Dakin Caravans

hi dakin,

hey sweetie, how are ya? you didn't return my call, you bad little boy! but i understand, you've been under a lot of pressure lately. the kids ask about you from time to time, and i'd like to be able to tell them that they can see you sometime soon. they're so excited about moving down to orange county. and you were so good with them when we were dating. janis even called you daddy a few times. i thought that was so cute.

seriously, i'd like to get together with you sometime soon, just to talk. this must be a difficult time for you, and i'm sure you could use a friend to talk to, whether you realize it or not. and, quite frankly, i miss you. i never met a man quite like you, either before or after we were an "item." i think we can help each other a lot. so please give me a call soon. and in case you lost the number, i'll call you. probably tonight.

love,
jeri

ps – i know it's a little early, but do you have any plans for halloween? the kids would love it if you could spend the night with us. and so would i ... :-)
... a halloween picture to remind you ...

```
                                                            *


          *                              *
              *                      *
            )            (\___/)            (
       *  / (            \ (. .)          ) \  *
          # )          c\   >'          ( #
           '            ) - /            '
         \\|,        ___| T__          ,|//
          \ )      (    `   ~    )      ( /
          #\ / /|  .  ' .) \ /#
          | \ / )      ,  / \ / |
           \,/  ;;,,;;;        \,/
            _,#;;;;;;;
          /,i;;;,,,;#,;
          //  %;;;;;;;;;
         ( (     ;#;,;;%;;,,
         _//       ;,;;  ,#;,,
        /_)        #,;        ) )
                  //          \|_
                  \|_         |#\
                   |#\       -"   b'ger
                   _"
```

--------<>--------

Subject: Good riddance
Date: Sat, 14 Oct 2000 13:41:59
From: Dakin Caravans
To: Jewel Halpern

Supergirl? What a stupid nickname for you.

There's nothing super about you. We were supposed to be a team. We were supposed to live the years together. You bailed on me, Jewel. Checked

106

out. Got a better offer. How could you do this to me? You said you loved me more than anything. You said I was the most important thing in your life. You wrote those words in all those romantic cards you gave me. I still have them, just read them all again. It was all a bunch of lies. All you cared about was wandering off into heaven all by yourself. Just left me here to fend for myself. What did I ever do to you? I am abandoned. Left alone. Just like every other woman in my life. Use me for what you want, and then dump me in the garbage. People are no damn good, and women are the worst kind of people of all. You spend your whole life trying to figure them out, and just when you think you have a little bit of a handle on it, they throw a sucker punch and leave you lying on the canvas.

God, I am so alone. This place was never meant for someone as fragile as me.

I hope you're happy in heaven. I hope you can look down and see what a wretched mess I have become because of you. And I hope you're sorry.

D.

--------◇--------

Subject: Are you OK?
Date: Sat, 14 Oct. 2000 14:04:55
From: Corena Bissett
To: Dakin Caravans

Hey you,

Are you sure you're all right? You sounded pretty depressed on the phone last night. I wish you could meet me for a beer at Rustler's Roost. Four hundred miles isn't too far to drive for a good microbrew and even better conversation, is it? Geez, I wish I weren't in Arizona. I didn't like the sound of your voice, and the words weren't that comforting, either.

You've been through a lot, Mr. Caravans, and there's nothing wrong with a good cry to let it all out. Men can do that, you know. Trust me, you'll feel better. OK? That's right, let it out. Don't worry, salt water won't hurt your keyboard. Much. So that's fine, then. Good. Feel better? OK, I'll wait. The tissues are up there on the shelf. There, there.

It's not so bad to be a guy. Here's a little humor to cheer you up, sent to me from my crazy friend on the Internet:

20 Great Reasons To Be A Guy ...

1. Phone conversations are over in 30 seconds flat.

2. A five-day vacation requires only one suitcase.

3. You can open all your own jars.

4. Gas (at either end) is cool.

5. One wallet and one pair of shoes, one color, all seasons.

6. You don't have to shave below your neck.

7. Your pals will never trap you with: "So, notice anything different?"

8. You almost never have strap problems in public.

9. Your underwear is $10 for a three-pack.

10. If you're 34 and single, nobody notices.

11. You can quietly enjoy a car ride from the passenger's seat.

13. You don't have to clean if the meter reader is coming.

14. Car mechanics tell you the truth.

15. You can quietly watch a game with your buddy for hours without ever thinking: "He must be mad at me."

16. You are unable to see wrinkles in your clothes.

17. If another guy shows up at the party in the same outfit, you just might become lifelong friends.

18. You are not expected to know the names of more than five colors.

19. Gray hair and wrinkles only add character.

20. The same hairstyle lasts for years, maybe decades.

--------<>---------

Subject: Back on track
Date: Sat, 14 Oct 2000 21:10:13
From: Dakin Caravans
To: Corena Bissett

Dear Dr. Laura,

Thanks for cheering me up. Laughter may not be the best medicine, but it's better than a spinal tap. OK, so, as we discussed the other night, it's time to get back to my narrative.

When we last left our story, I had just been divorced by my cheating, lying, no-good-for-nuthin' wife Amanda. Sorry, I tend to get carried away with emotional issues. Anyway, the day would come when I would finally realize that Amanda's infidelity and her insistence on divorce were actually among the best things that ever happened to me. They enabled me to reconnect with my once-and-future love, Jewel Halpern.

As I told you before (and why nobody believes me when I say this, I can't fathom), I was completely faithful to my wife for the 17 years we were married. Yes, I traveled all over the country with a bunch of major-league baseball players. Yes, there were young, predatory women around the team at all times. Yes, I probably could have gotten laid many times if I wanted. But believe it or not, I place a high value on my self-esteem, and I'd have a tough time looking in the mirror if the guy staring back at me cheated on his wife and jeopardized the welfare of his family. I never put myself in any compromising positions, never allowed myself to be tempted.

But once the divorce papers were filed and I was kicked out of my own home and forced to leave my children – all because SHE wanted to have her fling (sorry, getting a little crazy again) – anyway, I figured there was no longer any reason to turn away from single women. I was a free agent for the first time in almost two decades. I was 41 years old, but still reasonably good looking and fit. On my first trip of the new baseball season, I flirted with a blond flight attendant about my age, went to have a drink with her after we landed in Toronto, and ended up spending the night in her hotel room. If nothing else, it did wonders for my self-confidence. When your wife rejects you, a man can feel like a worthless piece of crap for a long time, even if he believes he did little or nothing to cause the divorce. At the very least, you feel like nobody would ever want you. If that heartless, old, amoral bitch with the big backside doesn't like you anymore, why would anyone of quality find you attractive?

But it turned out I was somewhat desirable, after all. Several women over the next nine months made that clear to me. But in short order I realized that sexual conquests, while exciting on an animal level, provided no lasting sense of fulfillment. There had to be more to life than that.

I think you know I've always been a searcher. I ask a lot of questions for which there seem to be no answers. I read voraciously, hoping to find the answers in literature. I haven't found them there, or in poetry, popular music (our generation's poetry), or film. You can find clues to answers for the Big Questions in art, music and literature, but nothing concrete, and I believe that's because nobody really knows. Why are we here? What's our purpose? What is good, what is bad, and who decides where the line is drawn? Is there life after birth? And if so, how should it be lived? Is there really a God? And if so, why haven't the Angels ever gone to a World Series?

During that baseball season after my divorce, I went into an airport store during yet another flight delay and picked up a book called "What Really Matters" by Tony Schwartz. It looked like a great concept. This guy was about my age and had spent much of his life searching for the same answers I had. He'd tried a lot of the same things – drugs, meditation, yoga, religion, marriage and family ... he even delved into areas I hadn't, like sensory deprivation, biofeedback, psychotherapy and even (gasp!) tennis. And I figured, from the title of the book, this guy must have finally figured it out.

I expected to get to the end of the book and learn What Really Matters. As it turned out, he didn't know, either.

But if I knew anything, it was that I did not want to spend the rest of my life alone. I wanted to find a lifemate, preferably a soulmate. That didn't seem like an easy task, but it ought to be a little easier than finding the answers to those Big Questions.

The searching was fun but not really going anywhere. Then I took a training course for reporters called "Digging on the Net." It taught us how to use the Internet to get an amazing amount of personal information on people. It also taught us how to find phone numbers and addresses for people when the usual sources (phone book, dialing information) wouldn't work. During the class, the instructor asked if anybody wanted to find somebody. He was going to use his slick Internet tools right in front of us to "pop" that person, as he called it. I raised my hand and blurted out a name I hadn't said in years -- Jewel Halpern. I had thought of her often, but never did my curiosity about my former girlfriend, the first love of my life, go beyond idle thoughts.

As it turned out, I stumped the instructor. I told him I was sure she'd been married long ago, but I had no idea where she was, what her married name was, what line of work she was in. It was a good challenge for an investigative reporter, and he took it as such. Although he failed my test in front of the class, he asked me for more information afterward, because he was going to prove to me that he could find her. Did she have any brothers or sisters? Parents' names? What state was she married in? He pumped me for every scrap of information I knew about her.

Less than 24 hours later, he sent me an email message. He couldn't find Jewel, but he found her sister in Indiana, and she had an email address. I sent her an email saying I was trying to find out if Jewel was still alive and maybe contact her, and I tried my best not to sound like a stalker. After about a week, the sister wrote back, apparently deciding I was a reasonably safe risk. She gave me Jewel's phone number – with a Southern California area code – but no other details about her life. I got the impression Jewel and her sister weren't on particularly good terms.

Filled with apprehension, I called. What if she were married with five kids, fat as a walrus and spiritually brain-dead? What if she told me she hated me, she has always hated me since my suicide threat back in '69, and she would continue to hate me as long as she could draw a breath? What if she were divorced and had been dreaming about me her whole adult life and wanted nothing more than to rush back into my arms? I didn't know if I could handle that, either.

Thankfully, an answering machine with a disembodied digital voice picked up. I identified myself, stated my purpose simply and unemotionally, and left a number "in case you wouldn't mind calling me back."

Another week went by, and then I picked up my phone at work one day and said my usual, "sports department, Dakin Caravans." A sweet, somewhat familiar voice answered, "Hi Dakin, this is Jewel."

I couldn't believe it. Even though I set this whole thing in motion myself, somehow I never believed anything would ever come of it. She would turn out to be dead or never call or who knows what, but the last thing I expected was that her voice would actually be in my phone.

I sounded like a fool. I got tongue-tied and lost all my usual composure. I tried my best to sound casual and ask the kinds of questions one would ask of an old high school classmate they hadn't seen in 20 years – So, what have you been doing with your life? Married? Kids? Where are you living? Man, wasn't that a time we had way back then?

But my heart was racing. We talked for about 20 minutes, and I couldn't tell if there was any connection there or not. She seemed a little shy, a little wary. But it turned out she was recently divorced herself. She'd been in Vermont for years, but now she was back in California. Eventually, we made plans for a casual daytime meeting at a coffee shop. It was to happen in a week. I turned into a silly schoolboy all over again, worrying about what I should wear, whether or not she would like me, how I should act.

At the first meeting, she stunned me by how good she looked. She was not the walrus. Still the same 5-foot-4, 120-pound curvy beauty I remembered, complete with the long, thick, sexy blond hair. She hadn't seemed to age at all in 20 years, except for a few small lines around the eyes. My pulse quickened when she held out her hand for a cool handshake. I never thought I'd see her again, and here I was touching her hand – and she was single.

Corena, this was unlike any other date I'd had since the divorce, including my two dates with you, if you'll pardon the personalization. This was a woman I had a history with, a shared background. In some ways, we grew up together. The years between our last meeting and this one had left both of us deeper, more mature human beings, but inside, I think we both had this feeling of familiarity. It was like going home again. Yes, there were some aches and pains in our past, but they seemed insignificant now.

I wanted to get to know her all over again, see how she had changed. I wanted to see if there was a chance for us. All of that was going through my mind in the first 10 minutes we talked at the coffee shop. I don't think she was on the same wavelength at all. I'm not sure what she was thinking, but I'm sure I started to fall in love with her long before she felt the same way about me. For years, she had literally been my dream girl, a fantasy I never spoke about but never forgot. Over the years, I eventually came to believe that Jewel needed to remain a fantasy for me. She had to remain 16 years old and perfect in my memory.

In some ways, I dreaded meeting her again, because it would spoil that fantasy. Once I saw her at age 41, she could never be that sweet, innocent little girl ever again. But once the meeting because possible, there was no way I could turn down the opportunity.

And if there is a God, he must have loved me very much, because he brought her back to me as the perfect creature she was -- even better than the 16-year-old angel, if that's possible. Since the divorce, I'd been dating girls younger than I, some by as much as 10 years, and although they were attractive, the generation gap led to some awkward conversations. To them, the Kennedy assassination was something out of a history book, not a vivid memory. But here was Jewel, more attractive than any of them, yet with the maturity and wisdom of a woman who had lived and seen and experienced. And we had a connection. We were soulmates. I knew it in my heart. In fact, I'd known it ever since that day when I first saw her.

Over the next several weeks, I eventually convinced Jewel that she loved me, too, and we lived happily ever after, except for the six times we broke up and her drug abuse. Oh, and her mysterious death. That was a bit of a bummer, too.

But I'm fine now. Really. Don't have to worry about me. I'm just dandy. Yessiree. You don't happen to have any Prozac, do you?

Your friend,
R.P. McMurphy

--------<>--------

Subject: Congratulations!
Date: Sun, 15 Oct 2000 12:02:07
From: The Kudos Corporation
To: Dakin Caravans

Dear Dakin,

You were recently selected by The Office of the Managing Director for a free listing on The National Executives Who's Who CD-ROM.

As a highly respected professional in your field of expertise, we believe your contributions merit very serious consideration for inclusion on The National Executives Who's Who CD-ROM.

You can purchase The International Executive Guild's Who's Who CD-ROM, complete with your own personal listing, for a nominal fee. For details, click here>

--------<>--------

Subject: Re: Just wondering
Date: Sun, 15 Oct 2000 14:18:52
From: Spider Juncal
To: Dakin Caravans

Dude, what is wrong with you!? The cops just harassed me again! Were you dropped on your head when you were little? I never said it was the cops from Greentree who told me about the piggy bank and Jewel's journals on her computer! It was the IRVINE police, you weenie! THEY took the report, remember? The Greentree pigs told the Irvine pigs all about your slanderous accusations of me, so they hauled me in for questioning! So get your facts straight before you run off at the mouth, dude! And you were a newspaper reporter? No wonder there are so many mistakes in the newspaper!

Sincerely yours,
Spider

"Consider mine affliction and my travail; And forgive all my sins." (Psalms 25:18)

"If you can take the hot lead enema, then you cast the first stone." (Lenny Bruce)

---------◇---------

Chapter Nine: Jewel
Know thyself

Background: Although Dakin thought Jewel's letters to God were written for her 12-step program with Narcotics Anonymous, they were actually part of therapy designed by Dr. Sara Lyman. Spider Juncal, however, came to believe that Jewel had established a real-life dialogue with the Almighty.
–David Cunningham

--------<>--------

Subject: My journal
Date: Thu, 1 April 1999 19:23:53
From: Jewel Halpern
To: Dr. Sara Lyman

Hi Dr. Lyman,

Well, I did it! I got the job with the greeting card company today. They liked my paintings and sketches, and they're going to use several of them for cards later this year. I'm so happy to finally be doing something creative, something I love, and getting paid for it.

Since coming back from Arizona, I've been floundering a little, not really knowing what I could do with my life. The money I inherited when my dad died actually turned into a curse. Instead of setting me free, it set me adrift. I didn't work for while, just like in Arizona, where I played tennis and golf, laid outside getting a tan, and sat around like a vegetable, waiting for Dakin to come home. It wasn't until long after I got back here to California and was out of that relationship that I realized how self-destructive I was becoming. It doesn't matter how much money a person has, they have to do something meaningful with their life. Now that I've kicked the pain pill habit and have a new job and new friends, I'm feeling healthier than I have in a long, long time.

Well, this was supposed to be another email from my journal, so here it is. This is what I wrote over the last few days, continuing my woeful life story:

Although the pain pills were affecting my personality and somehow killing my inner drive, I was able to function within some broad definition of "normal" in my relationship with Dakin, and he never knew the extent of my problem. He knew I was on pain medication, but for a long time, I don't think he had any idea how addicted I had become. When he accepted a job in Phoenix covering the new baseball team there, the Arizona Diamondbacks, he asked me to come with him.

There was talk of marriage, but nothing really concrete. Not a genuine proposal, and certainly no ring. He said we would live together in Arizona, and after a while, when we were both sure it was what we wanted, we'd get married. He was leery because our "perfect" relationship had hit a few snags, a few breakups, and he was unsure. I was OK with it. I loved him very much. At times, he seemed like the most sane and totally together part of my life. Dakin was a steady, responsible man, a hard worker and a respected writer. We rented a place in Tempe and started living as husband and wife, without the paperwork. His job meant a lot of travel, which is something he was used to. He'd been traveling with the Dodgers and Angels over the last 10 years, and he was very adjusted to the lifestyle: airports, taxicabs, hotels, ballparks, constant travel to big cities. But, it was all new to me. Instead of getting a job, I decided to spend some of my savings and follow Dakin around, traveling wherever he went with the baseball team. It was fun and exciting for a while, but the novelty soon wore off, and it started to bring me down. I didn't have as much time with Dakin as I wanted because his job was very demanding, and I was retreating further and further into my painkiller addiction. I stayed home for the second half of the season and became self-indulgent, doing whatever I wanted whenever I wanted. Sounds great, huh? It's not all it's cracked up to be.

We began to fight more and more. I've always been a forceful, combative person. I stand up for what I think is right. Maybe it's part of my heritage. Jews aren't shy about speaking their minds. Outsiders may see a Jewish couple as quarrelsome, always nagging and picking on each other. But to the couple, it's not like that. It's an important part of the relationship. It's just how they interact. Unfortunately, Dakin isn't Jewish. He didn't get it. Red (my ex) had a Jewish mother and was exactly like me in that regard. We picked on each other all the time, and it was actually a way to show we cared. If we didn't care, it wouldn't be worth the breath to argue about. That's how my parents were, and it's how Red's parents were.

But Dakin preferred quiet over arguing. He was non-confrontational. He would give in on something rather than fight about it. All he wanted was peace. He never got it with me. Maybe he could've gotten a better chance at peace if I wasn't addicted to a mind-altering drug.

We were in Arizona one year. Well, I was in Arizona one year. Dakin stayed – although in another two months he would be coming back to Southern California to try to make a living as a drummer and a portrait painter. We both tried to start new lives. Mine's always been a series of fits and starts. I get into something, then lose interest and move into something else.

Although Dakin was the one who kicked me out, I think I really wanted to force the issue but didn't know how to do it. Instead of telling him I was miserable and wanted something different, I misbehaved and forced his hand. By the end, he knew my problem was an addiction. Twice, he threatened to break up with me if I didn't get help and kick the addiction. Twice, I promised I would. But it never lasted. My first commitment to get help lasted a week, and the second time, just a few days. I couldn't see it through. My addiction was more important than my relationship. It was the only happiness in my life, when that fuzzy, warm feeling would kick in after I took a couple of pills. I didn't know if I was miserable because I hated Arizona and missed my family and friends, or if it was Dakin, or if it was the sin of sloth. But I knew I wasn't happy.

Later, I came to realize that it was the addiction, after all. I didn't hate all that other stuff as much as I hated myself. I knew I was addicted, and I was powerless to do anything about it. I lost all respect for myself. And the only way to make myself feel better about THAT was to blind myself with more drugs.

In Arizona, I reverted to the dysfunctional behavior of trying to keep Dakin interested in me by making him jealous. I would flirt with waiters at restaurants in front of him. Once when he went to the restroom at a tavern that had live music, a man saw me sitting there alone and asked me to dance, and I said yes. Dakin came out of the restroom to find me slow dancing with this stranger. He didn't understand it at all. Can't say that I blame him. He was furious that night. I was blinded to my own behavior because the drug had completely taken over my personality.

Once, under the total influence of medication, I went too far even for Dakin's normally patient demeanor. I had one too many drinks (at least), even though I knew you were not supposed to mix alcohol with my medication. We were dancing and having a wonderful time. But Dakin didn't feel well and around 11 p.m. wanted to go home. I walked to the door with him, and then suddenly said I was staying. He could go if he wanted. He called my bluff and walked out the door, but all he did was go to the car and bring it around to the front. Then he came back inside. I was on a barstool locked in conversation with this young guy. Dakin told me he was giving me one more chance – did I want to stay there or come home with him? I swear I don't know what made me say it, but I told him I was staying. I was so messed up, I thought he was ruining my fun. Maybe I was a little bitter, too, because he was still living with me and enjoying all the benefits of marriage without actually making a commitment to me. Whatever it was, I turned toward the young stud I was talking to and turned my back on the man I loved. Dakin took me at my word and left in a huff.

I took a taxi home about three hours later and found all my clothes and belongings piled in the driveway. He'd kicked me out and chained the door. By this point, I was in some kind of messed-up combination of drunk and high on pills. I begged, cried and pleaded with him to let me inside, and finally – probably because it was 2:30 in the morning and I was making so much noise – he opened the door. But he wouldn't talk with me or touch me. He was done with me. Forever. And I knew I'd done it to myself. I just wasn't sure why.

I think it actually hurt Dakin more than it hurt me, because he was the one who had ached for me all those years after we broke up as teenagers. Once we got back together, I think he saw his chance to settle into the love of his life. That's what he told me. I was overwhelmed by his passion. He loved me so much. More than anyone ever had, more than anyone else ever will. And I threw it away.

But, just like when we were teens, he loved me too much. I was still trying to find myself, and my searching gave him such uneasiness. He's so different from me in so many ways. He's focused, determined, knows what he wants and remains steadfast in going after it. As creative a person as he can be, he's also firmly rooted. His head may be in the stars sometimes, but his feet are always planted. Me, I've got my head in the clouds always, and I'm never really sure where my feet are at any given time. I float. I move with the wind, and I'm hard to pin down. With Dakin, you always know where he stands. While I admired his commitment, I think he envied my ability to flow freely from place to place, idea to idea. I've always been a free spirit, and although Dakin said he loved that about me, I think it also caused him problems. He tried to control that free spirit, and I wouldn't be controlled. Not that any of that excuses my behavior in the nightclubs and taverns. I was under the influence of a powerful drug, and nobody knew how powerful it was, not even me. I didn't start to realize how strong the grip was until I finally got clean, months later, after Dakin was out of my life.

That's all I wrote this week. Sorry if it's a little disjointed. Sometimes I start out with an idea, then go off in another direction. That's just me.

Thanks for listening. Talk to you at my session next week.

Jewel

--------◇--------

Subject: Dear God letter
Date: Fri, 30 April 1999 17:21:40
From: Jewel Halpern
To: Dr. Sara Lyman

Dear God:

Sorry I haven't written lately. Things have been happening in my life. But then, you know that, don't you? I've met a man named Michael who seems to be everything I want: tall, handsome, gentle, very nice and also very well off financially. I'm trying to see signs from you. Is he the one? Is it time for me to move into another phase?

My job is so wonderful, thank you for sending me into this new direction. I love drawing and painting, and I love seeing my work published on the cover of beautiful greeting cards. I love the people I work with, and I love the freedom it provides. I've been drug-free for three months now, and I feel like my head is clearer than it has been in years. The Narc Anon classes have led me to some wonderful friendships and, ultimately, back to you, my God.

Michael takes me to fun places and we have great times together. I don't know where this is leading, so I look for signs from you. You've always helped guide me before. I was lost for a long time, but now I am found. I am your faithful daughter.

Jewel

--------<>--------

Subject: God's letter to me
Date: Sun, 02 May 1999 13:25:41
From: Jewel Halpern
To: Dr. Sara Lyman

Dear Jewel,

Michael is good for you now, so trust him and trust the relationship. But he is not the one.

He will help you and you need it. Be good to him and be kind to him. But most importantly, be good and kind to yourself. Love yourself. You are doing so many things right, after a long, dark winter in your life, but it is not spring yet. You have not yet learned how to love yourself and, until you do that, you will never be fully healed. There is hope for you, but you must feel it and believe it, or it will never happen.

Love,
God

--------<>--------

Subject: Oh, God!!
Date: Thu, 13 May 1999 21:39:10
From: Spider Juncal
To: Jewel Halpern

Jewel, light of all mankind,

Yes, I believe you when you say that God speaks to you! He has spoken to me, too, and shown me The Light! And I believe the letters you showed me have come directly from God's heart! It doesn't matter that your hands typed the letters! He was speaking through you, as He does so often with his children!

You are plugged into the Almighty in a way that no one else I have ever met has been! I believe He has chosen you! I believe everything in your life has had a purpose – your addiction, your breakup with Dakin, your coming back to California and joining our group, and, yes, even meeting me! I think I am supposed to play some role in helping you spread your word! It's wonderful that you're thinking of writing a self-help book, and I'd love to see what you've written so far! I have friends who can help get the word out! Man, I truly think it was destiny that we met!

Sincerely,
Spider

"Verily I say unto you, Wheresoever this gospel shall be preached in the whole world, that also which this woman hath done shall be spoken of for a memorial of her." (Matthew 26:13)

"All I kin say is when you finds yo'self wanderin' in a peach orchard, ya don't go around lookin' for rutabagas." (Kingfish, in Amos and Andy)

---------◇---------

Subject: Re: Oh, God!!
Date: Thu, 20 May 1999 24:57:01
From: Jewel Halpern
To: Spider Juncal

Hi Spider,

I appreciate the kind things you always say about my journal and book and letters, and I also appreciate your advice and help, but I think there's something I should tell you. I may be wrong, and if so, please forgive me, but I have from time to time gotten the impression that your interest in me was more than just as a friend, and I told you before that I wasn't ready for a relationship. That was some time ago. Now I have begun dating a man I met last month. I like him very much and spend most of my social time with him. I just don't want you to be under any wrong impressions about our friendship. I welcome your kindness and words of encouragement, and I hope I can reciprocate in some way. But romantically, my thoughts are elsewhere, and I don't anticipate that changing anytime soon.

Regards,
Jewel

--------<>--------

Subject: Dear God letter
Date: Fri, 16 July 1999 13:25:41
From: Jewel Halpern
To: Dr. Sara Lyman

Dear God,

I'm trying my best to stay with you. I've read "A Return To Love" by Marianne Williamson several times in the last few months, and I've highlighted many passages that seem aimed directly at me. I'm living a good and giving life with my friends and co-workers. I'm donating time to work with the Red Cross and organized a walk to raise money for Cystic Fibrosis research. But I feel like I'm slipping a little.

My relationship with Michael is going very well and I like him very much, but I can't say that I love him. In fact, I'm afraid I'm still in love with Dakin. He awakened feelings in me that I hadn't felt since we were teenagers together, and he made my life brighter and more hopeful than it had ever been before. Then I had to go and screw it up. Part of my inability to completely let go of Dakin is my knowledge that we didn't break up for a good reason. I didn't give him a chance, and I didn't give us a chance. For the entire time in Arizona, I wasn't myself. If he saw me now, he would realize how messed up I was back then. If our love can't grow and thrive in the healthy state that I now find myself in, then fine, I'll accept it and move on, but I feel this strong need to try again with him. And that makes me feel like I'm being unfair to Michael every time we go out. I kiss him and wish he were Dakin.

In the months we have been apart, Dakin and I have talked two or three times on the phone, and I can't really read where his head is at, but I know he has a new girlfriend. I don't want to come between Dakin and his happiness, but I also can't help feeling that I'm where his happiness lies. He knew it long before I did, and we both knew it when I was clean and healthy. It was only when I got hooked on the painkillers that everything started to go haywire on us. So now that I'm back to being Jewel – in fact, I'm healthier than I've been in, well, maybe forever – isn't it right to try again? If I don't, I'll spend the rest of my life wondering.

That's kind of ironic, isn't it? After we broke up as teens, Dakin spent the next two decades wondering. He got married twice, had two kids, lived an entire lifetime apart from me, yet always wondered about me, and I never gave him much thought. Then we reconnected, fell madly in love with each other all over again, and now that we're broken apart, I'm the one who faces a lifetime of wondering, and he seems to have moved on. I think you're telling me, God, that it's my turn. I have to decide what to do with it.

I hope I won't fail you.
Jewel

--------<>--------

125

Subject: So what have you been up to lately?
Date: Fri, 16 July 1999 23:16:58
From: The Hot Zones
To: Jewel Halpern

Have you been naughty this year? Want to be? :) Click here!>

--------◇--------

Chapter Ten: Dakin
It's not whether you won or lost,
but how you played the game

Background: In the final two weeks of his life, Dakin appeared to be drifting dangerously close to insanity. His messages sometimes rambled with out-of-context references from literature, films and song lyrics.
–David Cunningham

--------◇--------

Subject: My (never-ending) story
Date: Mon, 16 Oct 2000 21:53:39
From: Dakin Caravans
To: Corena Bissett

Dear Dr. Jung,

I feel very weird tonight, very stressed and tense. It's like something has been building inside me for a long time, maybe since Jewel's death, maybe before, or maybe just since Spider Juncal ambushed me in the back seat of my car. At any rate, I've got way too much energy right now to be sitting in front of a keyboard, but I promised you on the phone I would write and continue my story, and so I am.

OK, I think I left off with me finally convincing Jewel that she loved me, and us falling into a deep, if somewhat troubled, relationship. Did I say somewhat? It was a f***ing circus. (Can I say f***ing to my therapist?) Never a dull moment with that girl, that's for sure. We loved so much more deeply than I ever imagined was possible, but we also fought bitterly. That's when I started to lose my grip on reality, and I doubt I'll ever get it back.

What are soulmates supposed to be like, Ms. Therapist? Since I never had one besides Jewel, I have no basis for comparison. I thought maybe everything would be beautiful and sweetness and light. We would just walk around smiling at each other all the time, always holding hands and snuggling and kissing and in this perpetual honeymoon. Instead, it was like Gettysburg – all hell breaks loose, then there's an idyllic quiet while

127

everyone reloads and cleans up the dead and wounded, and then the firestorm starts all over again. But I was so attached to this woman, I couldn't have left her if I wanted. The highs were so unbelievably high, I was willing to slog through all the lows, no matter how much despair they brought. Kind of sounds like a heroin addiction, huh? Not that I would know what that's like.

We broke up once because she was regularly meeting a guy at her work for lunch and refused to stop the meetings because that would infringe on her personal freedom (don't confuse the word "meetings" with business; it was strictly social). We broke up another time because she went back to Vermont to visit some of her old friends and, instead of getting a hotel room, decided to stay with her ex-husband – and sleep in his bed. She claimed that he slept on the couch. We broke up another time, and another time, and another time. But they weren't all her fault, no matter how unfairly I try to paint this. I admit I tend to be a little jealous. And after I found out she was staying with her ex in Vermont, I agreed to a business meeting (that's my story, and I'm sticking to it) with a woman who owns a public relations agency. She used to work at my newspaper. And once upon a time she took a run at me, even though I was married at the time (to Amanda, my second wife). I politely deflected her.

But this time, I met her for lunch, and our "meeting" included a bottle of wine. It was very inappropriate, considering the fact that Jewel and I had already begun talking about marriage. I was playing a childish game of payback. We broke up over that, too.

Then there's the Great Painkiller Episode. She was involved in a relatively minor car accident, but she ended up with a lot of back pain, for which she was given a pretty potent, prescription-only drug. She started eating that stuff like candy, and although it didn't produce a high like some other controlled substances I could mention, it definitely altered her personality. You have to understand about Jewel, she didn't react to medication like normal people. Give her a sleeping pill and she was up wide-eyed all night. Coffee made her sleepy. She reacted in the complete opposite way a human is supposed to. Two glasses of wine might make you pretty mellow, but they made Jewel jump up and start performing all the roles in The Sound of Music. I swear if you gave her a birth control pill, she would have dropped a full-term baby on the spot. This woman really WAS from Venus. So when she started taking these pain pills, which were supposed to make one drowsy and maybe feel a little warm and fuzzy, she turned into Kim Basinger in "Blind Date," complete with low-cut dresses, wet hiccups and uncontrollable giggling.

Actually, if it were only that mild, I might have been able to live with it. I could tell you stories. Oh, I guess that's what I'm supposed to be doing, huh? Well, let's just say it wasn't pretty. But the thing is, I didn't realize what effect the pain pills were having on her. She was changing into a she-wolf, but it happened so gradually, I figured this was just a part of Jewel's personality that had emerged over the years, and I simply had to learn how to cope with it. Lord knows, I still loved her very much. But we broke up for what appeared to be the final time over an incident involving pain-pill behavior and a young stud in a very romantic bistro. You may have read about it in the newspapers (I'm kidding. About the newspapers.)

But after several months of separation, we started talking on the phone again, then had a couple of casual meetings. OK, dates. We couldn't leave each other alone. There was a mutual magnetism between us that was simply irresistible. I'm a little edgy right now, so I've been stressing the bad stuff, but there were definitely a lot of magical days and nights together, when everything was better than perfect. Storybook stuff. Kisses so deep and moving that you will remember them for a lifetime. Slow dances where we moved together as if we had one mind. Days and nights together that seemed like we were in heaven. You know that walking-on-air stuff that I think Fred Astaire did in the old movies? We did that. A lot. We both knew that this was a once-in-a-lifetime relationship. I'd been married twice, had lots of girlfriends in between marriages, and honestly felt like I had been in love a few times. But never like this. Jewel said she felt the same way.

Hey, my son's on the phone, gotta go. More later.

Yossarian

--------◇--------

Subject: Us
Date: Tue, 17 Oct 2000 07:28:33
From: Jeri Starrette
To: Dakin Caravans

hi dakin,

thank you SO much for calling. i've missed hearing your voice. i do wish you would reconsider about halloween, though. i think it would be a lot of fun. you sounded a little uptight last night. are you sure everything is ok with you? is there anything i can do for you? anything at all?

i wish we could have gotten together over the weekend while the kids and i were apartment hunting down in your neck of the woods, but i understand. it looks like we'll probably get that place in anaheim and move in next weekend, which means we won't have to impose on you and stay at your place (darn!). anyway, thanks again for the call. i'll talk to you again soon, hopefully.

a friend emailed the following to me when i complained about being stressed out. considering how you have sounded lately, i thought maybe it would help you, too:

"I am hereby officially tendering my resignation as an adult. I have decided I would like to accept the responsibilities of an 8-year-old again. I want to go to McDonald's and think that it's a four-star restaurant. I want to sail sticks across a fresh mud puddle and make a sidewalk with rocks. I want to think M&Ms are better than money because you can eat them. I want to lie under a big oak tree and run a lemonade stand with my friends on a hot summer's day. I want to return to a time when life was simple. When all you knew were colors, multiplication tables and nursery rhymes, but that didn't bother you, because you didn't know what you didn't know, and you didn't care. All you knew was to be happy because you were blissfully unaware of all the things that should make you worried or upset. I want to think the world is fair.

That everyone is honest and good. I want to believe that anything is possible. I want to be oblivious to the complexities of life and be overly excited by the little things again. I want to live simple again.

I don't want my day to consist of computer crashes, mountains of paperwork, depressing news, how to survive more days in the month than there is money in the bank, doctor bills, gossip, illness, and loss of loved ones. I want to believe in the power of smiles, hugs, a kind word, truth, justice, peace, dreams, the imagination, mankind, and making angels in the snow. So ... here's my checkbook and my car keys, my credit card bills and my 401K statements. I am officially resigning from adulthood. And if you want to discuss this further, you'll have to catch me first, 'cause... Tag! You're it!"

isn't that great, dakin? oh, and i can't forget to add a picture for you. it's the child in you, playing drums ...

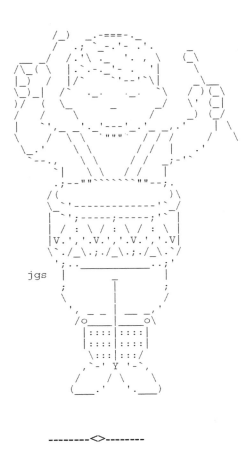

---◇---

Subject: a cry in the dark
Date: Tue, 17 Oct 2000 10:56:17
From: Dakin Caravans
To: Jewel Halpern

Supergirl? You still there?

No, of course not. I'm singing in the darkness. I need to talk. I'm perilously close to insanity right now, and I can think of no one to turn to who would be qualified to counsel me except you, The Dead Artist Formerly Known as Jewel. So much is racing through my cracked-open head. I talked with Jeri last night. She seems so sweet and loving and I know she wants me, and even though I understand it's because she needs/wants a husband and father to complete her family, I can't help feeling attracted. How long is an appropriate time to be lonely and grieving before one jumps back in the saddle?

Ah, what am I saying? Yours is the only saddle I ever wanted for the rest of my life. God, we were so close to so many answers, and life was starting to make a lot of sense. Now, nothing does. All Jeri could ever be is a poor substitute for you, and where's the happiness in that? Where's the happiness in anything? My heart is so empty now, so hungry, hurt, lost and broken. Our motor home sits with spider webs growing around the tires. I haven't stepped inside since the night you left me for another deity. I hope He's good.

I can't even write anymore, which is the one thing I was always able to do. Nothing is falling into line, my head aches almost as painfully as my heart, and my usually rational, logical brain is fried. Short-circuited. Nothing computes. All my life, I've been a follower of the most reasonable path. Sure, I experimented, but I always chose safety over carelessness. My risks were always calculated. I made good choices more often than not. Now I find myself incapable of making any choices, good or otherwise. I sit sit sit and die die die. I c-c-c-can't go on. Jeri makes weird pictures with symbols on her keyboard, while my k-k-k-keyboard, the alleged tool of a writer, produces nothing but mush – which is what my b-b-b-brain look like now, mush. But so what? So what? SO WHAT? That's my philosophy of life now. SO WHAT?

Here I go to no one's difference.
But I am going fast and going strong. Watch my smoke.
What we don't already know, we will learn somehow.
If we don't find it out later, we will find it out now.
I follow the laws I make on my own.
I know it, I know it!
Just shut up, shut up!
Leave me alone!
I can no longer be hurt.
I have reached the breaking point.
I am callused now.
I have subjected myself
And allowed myself to be subjected to
Tortuous pain, mind-rocking.
From now on, I am building a whole
Without a hole to stick suffering.
I can suffer no more. It's all over.

I feel like Dalton Trumbo's Johnny, face and body blown away.

Oh why he thought does a guy have to go through something like this?
He thought why don't they take him out and shoot him while there's still
something in him? He thought everybody has a best friend. Even guys in
penitentiaries have best friends somewhere. But I haven't. He thought why
everybody can find some little spark of self-respect inside himself. Even a
murderer or a thief or a dog or an ant has something that keeps its head up
and going. But I haven't.

i am going to live i am going to live i am going to live i am going to live
please ...

I am tired of people telling me what's best for me. Who knows better
than me what's best for me? I'm Dakin Caravans. No one else is, nor will
they ever be. No one else. Just one. Just me. I have to live only with myself,
no one else. Fools. Let me be me.

Your father is dead. Your mother is dead. Your wife is dead. You are
alone again. Naturally.

133

Hello darkness, my old friend. I've come to talk with you again.

What am I living for? What business do I have using up valuable oxygen?

He lives in the gleam of the evening star, and scarred so deep, he shines for those who gaze from afar.
I can't remember, but I can't forget.

God, I grieve for my sanity. It has died and gone to heaven, joined with Jewel and Johnny who got his gun and everybody else. WHERE ARE ALL OF YOU? WHAT ARE YOU? what am i? who am i?

Don Quixote was right!

"Life as it is? I've lived for over 40 years, and I've seen life as it is – pain, misery, cruelty beyond belief. I've heard all the voices of 'God's noblest creature' – moans from bundles of filth in the street."

We all die despairing, our eyes filled with confusion, questioning why.

"I do not think they were asking why they were dying, but why they had ever lived at all. Life itself seems lunatic. Who knows where madness lies? Perhaps to be too practical is madness, to surrender dreams, this may be madness. To see treasure where there is only trash ... Too much sanity may be madness! And maddest of all, to see life as it is, and not as it should be!"

Chicken Little was right!

With love in my heart and nothing in my head,
D-D-D-Dakin

--------<>--------

Subject: Where were we?
Date: Tue, 17 Oct 2000 13:35:41
From: Dakin Caravans
To: Corena Bissett

Hi Doc Holliday,

Been a very tough day for me, but I think I'm better now. OK, I forget where we were, but I'll just charge right into the next major segment of my life. After a dozen years of covering baseball in Southern California, I was offered a job covering the Arizona Diamondbacks expansion team in Phoenix (hometown of friend and family counselor Corena Bissett, possibly a distant cousin to Jacqueline Bissett, but definitely not mentioned in her will). For some unexplained reason, I took the job. Actually, the reason had something to do with more money and a fresh start. I had managed to piss off several famous people with columns I had written, most notably Mike Piazza, Eric Karros, Bill Russell, Troy Percival, Shaquille O'Neal and even (this took some doing) Wayne Gretzky. The Great One didn't get pissed off easily. It was definitely time to find a new crop of athletes I could alienate.

A word or two thousand about my life as a sportswriter. I loved it. You wouldn't believe the people I interviewed, and any sportswriter who says he doesn't enjoy being friendly with the biggest names in sports is lying. But more than rubbing shoulders with the rich and famous, I loved being witness to history, and I loved being the one to tell people about what happened and what was said about it in the locker room afterward. I was there when Kirk Gibson hit his dramatic home run to win Game One of the 1988 World Series. I actually got goosebumps, so remarkable was that moment. How many people actually know what it feels and sounds like to stand there amid a crowd of 55,000, screaming at the top of their lungs because they just witnessed one of the greatest comebacks and most emotional stories in baseball history? Let me tell you, it was electric. And I was there when Bill Shoemaker rode his last horse race. I interviewed him before and afterward. I covered the Lakers when they had Wilt Chamberlain, Jerry West and Elgin Baylor, and I covered the Lakers when they had Magic Johnson, Kareem Abdul-Jabbar and James Worthy. I talked to these people in locker rooms after they had achieved great feats or suffered crushing losses. My world was filled with highs and lows few people ever experience, and even though I didn't suit up, you really can't say I was living it vicariously. I was there. I saw the tears, and I got champagne in my eyes and on my clothes. I asked them about their innermost thoughts, and I wrote about it. When Mark Langston, who had pitched so brilliantly for so many losing teams in his long career, finally got to a World Series with the San Diego Padres, he and I stood in a corner of the clubhouse, while everyone else was spraying champagne around. We talked about what it meant, after all these years, to finally reach the Promised Land. I was supposed to tell the stories of these men and their feats with detached impartiality, but we all know that's impossible. Langston wept. I didn't just witness these things, I lived them.

I heard the deafening roar of engines at Daytona, I walked with the gallery following Tiger Woods on a pristine golf course, I rocked with the crowd at the Forum when "I Love L.A." blared out of the sound system because Magic had just made a spectacular behind-the-back pass that led to a slam dunk by Kareem. After Super Bowl XVIII, Lyle Alzado came up to me and, with tears of joy and sadness, said he had just played his last football game. He could never top that moment, so why go on? Years later, I felt sickened when I had to write a story about how Alzado died from a cancer most likely caused by all the steroids he took over the years. They were not just stories to me. They were people.

And I sat in the spring sunshine of Vero Beach and talked with an old coach named Sandy Koufax, discussing jazz music because he didn't feel like talking baseball. I wasn't comfortable telling him he was my hero when I was a 10-year-old kid, but the only other interview that thrilled me as much was when I talked with Joe DiMaggio at an old-timers game. The Yankee Clipper didn't give many interviews. I got lucky.

There's an old story about Marilyn Monroe coming back from an overseas trip to entertain U.S. troops and telling her husband, "Joe, you've never heard such cheering." DiMaggio is supposed to have replied, "Yes, I have." Well, in my nearly 30 years as a sportswriter, I heard it, too, even if it wasn't for me. Ten Super Bowls. Countless Rose Bowls. Those wild USC-UCLA football and basketball games, so many World Series games. NBA championships. The Olympic Games. There can't be a better place to be a sportswriter than Southern California. That's one reason it was tough to leave for Arizona, but I was getting older, my newspaper had changed management, and it seemed like a good idea at the time. Plus, I was pretty sure I could get Jewel to come with me.

And she did. It was not the most glorious chapter in either of our lives. I'll tell you about it later. Gotta run.

Thanks for being there.

Dakin

--------◇--------

Subject: Special announcement!
Date: Tue, 17 Oct 2000 22:16:20
From: Spider Juncal
To: <Undisclosed Recipients>

/ / / / / / / / / / / / / / / / / / /

To all Enlightened People on Spider Juncal's mailing list!

/ / / / / / / / / / / / / / / / / / /

I will have a new website up and running within the next week that is of monumental importance! This is the most exciting news of our time! I have come into possession of documents that verify the Second Coming and the miracle that was her life – the Daughter of God! She has walked among us, bringing with her the word of God! She spoke directly with God, and He spoke directly to her! They communicated with messages back and forth, and I will be posting those messages on the website. I also have her story, a complete, new-age bible of her life story, written by the Messiah herself!

Not since the New Testament was written two thousand years ago has such an important document come to light! You will laugh, you will cry, and you will be guided! Soon to be published as a best-selling book! Soon to be a major motion picture! The word of God, delivered directly to our generation from our Creator's daughter! Get a sneak peak at "Jewel of the Universe" – destined to become the gospel of the new millennium!

You will be notified soon with a link to access the website that will change your life.

"And he said unto them, Go ye into all the world, and preach the gospel to the whole creation." (Mark 16:15)

"The whole earth is in jail, and we're plotting this incredible jailbreak." (Wavy Gravy)

--------◇--------

Chapter Eleven: Jewel
Success is a journey, not a destination

Background: In this period, Jewel began a series of rapid transformations as she moved toward spirituality and greater physical health. She also sought reconciliation with Dakin, moving slowly at first, then gradually becoming bolder.
–David Cunningham

--------◇--------

Subject: My journal
Date: Mon, 02 Aug 1999 20:06:15
From: Jewel Halpern
To: Dr. Sara Lyman

Hi Sara,

Guess what? I couldn't wait until our session Wednesday to tell you ... Dakin and I are talking again! In the last 10 days, we've talked on the phone six times, and we really seem to be on a good wavelength. He tells me I sound so much healthier and happier now, and he's right. I have a feeling we might still have a future together after all.

I broke up with Michael. It was during the time when I was making amends to all the people I hurt with my drug addiction. I needed a fresh start with everything, and that included my love life. I actually felt relieved and very good about myself afterward. Michael didn't seem too affected by it, so I guess the relationship wasn't all that important to either one of us – probably just a convenience thing.

The most important person I called during my make-amends period was Dakin. For the first time, I admitted to him that I had been addicted to the painkillers. He already knew that, of course, but it was important for me to come right out and say it. I apologized to him for all the things I did that hurt him. I wasn't doing it in hopes of getting back together with him or anything. I knew he had his girlfriend Jeri. It was really more of an exercise for me, as you said. And after I had made all my calls and apologized to everybody – and prayed, sending a message to my dad in heaven and apologizing to him, as well as to God – I felt like I had been born again. I was cleansed. I've made so much progress since kicking the pill habit, joining Narc Anon and coming to see you.

Well, the phone call to Dakin opened a door. I wasn't playing any more games with him, just being myself, and for the first time in a long while, I was happy with myself. I was the same person he had fallen in love with, and the wheels started to spin again for both of us.

What made me go off the deep end with the pain pills? Why did I become so dependent on them and allow them to change my personality and mess up my life? Was it just a physical addiction or an emotional one? Was I mentally unstable back then? Am I now? So many questions, so few answers.

I wonder sometimes about my motivation for doing things. I think about my childhood, seeing my mom hit my dad in the face with a fire poker, and the constant moving around after my parents divorced. I think about how soft and weak my dad was, and how all that still affects me as an adult. I think about the time I grew up in. The late Sixties seem so exciting and free and liberating when we look back on those times now, but back then, it was just how we lived. We questioned everything. I think of the people whose ideas influenced me, like Germaine Greer, Ayn Rand, Angela Davis, Abbie Hoffman and Jerry Rubin, and wonder how I turned out OK. It was so wild. Everyone was high. Speech and love were free. No one over 30 was trusted. Heck, I didn't ever want to become old. I thought I'd commit suicide when I was 29. I was going to eat a scorpion just to freak out the doctors when they did the autopsy.

Wow, I got off track there for a while, huh? Hey, I just realized, this was like writing in my journal, but instead of typing it out in the journal and then clipping and pasting a copy to you, I just wrote the whole thing directly to you.

Can't wait to talk on Wednesday. I'm feeling so happy and positive about my life's direction now.

Jewel

--------◇---------

Subject: Up in the sky!
Date: Wed, 04 Aug 1999 19:17:38
From: Dakin Caravans
To: Jewel Halpern

Hi Supergirl,

I can't get over how different you sound – and how much better. My nickname for you is coming true again. No matter what obstacles arise, you find a way to toss them aside and fly onward. I truly do admire you for the strength you have shown in the last few months.

As for me, I broke up with Jeri yesterday. Starting to talk with you again had nothing whatsoever to do with it. I've known for quite a while that I couldn't bring myself to take that step to marry her. Her kids are young and a handful, and the thought of becoming a step-dad and helping raise them for the next 10 years or more ... been there, done that. Loved raising my own kids, don't want to do it again with somebody else's, especially not with a wicked ex-husband/abusive father lurking in the background. She's very attractive and sweet, and probably would have been a wonderful wife, but she just isn't what I'm looking for. It was probably the most amicable breakup I've ever had. She wasn't happy about it, but she understood completely. It wasn't exactly a surprise. We had talked at length about all of it before. I was just spinning my wheels for a while, trying to make up my mind once and for all.

And as for you ... I guess we could get together and have a face-to-face talk sometime, now that neither one of us is involved with a significant other. I'll call you soon. Stay as well and happy as you are.

Dakin

--------◇---------

Subject: To the gemstone!
Date: Fri, 05 Aug 1999 21:16:32
From: Spider Juncal
To: Jewel Halpern

Hello my Jewel,

It is such a pleasure to hear you speak in NA! Your letters to God are masterpieces! And his letters to you are a new Gospel! I was honored to take you for coffee afterwards, and I hope we can have such serious and deep talks again sometime ... When you started in this class, I felt I could help you and move you toward a brighter light, but now I feel the tables are turned – you are the healthier one, and now it is you who are helping me!

I was just wondering ... could you bring all your letters and your journal to class next week? I'd like to look at them more deeply and maybe even make copies of them for my own personal salvation!

You friend always,

Spider Juncal

"They change the night into day: The light, say they, is near unto the darkness." (Job 17:12)

"Friend ... GOOD!" (Frankenstein monster)

--------<>--------

Subject: Willing
Date: Tue, 17 Aug 1999 21:23:58
From: Dakin Caravans
To: Jewel Halpern

Hello Supergirl,

Loved spending time with you over the weekend. I can't get over how much better you seem. Totally together, focused, happy and healthy inside and out. It makes you more attractive than ever. Oh, and did I ever tell you what a terrific kisser you are? I cherish our times together, and I hope, as you said, there IS a chance for us. At any rate, I'm ready and willing to explore the possibilities.

I love you,
Dakin

--------◇--------

Subject: Gonna getcha getcha getcha getcha
Date: Fri, 20 Aug 1999 19:17:38
From: Jewel Halpern
To: Dakin Caravans

My precious Dakin,

If I couldn't reach you by phone yesterday, there's always email ... lucky you.

I apologize if I came on too strong the other day ... but I'm not sorry for being me. I feel a lot of passion about a lot of things and about you. I'm not trying to tell you what is right for you.

I am still under construction and always will be ... I'm not perfect and always need to keep learning and try to do better the next time. In my heart, I DO want what's best for you, not just myself. I could never have the best of Dakin if he doesn't make his decisions on his own. I'm fully aware you are an adult man. You're an individual with your own thoughts and ideas, and so am I.

My communication skills aren't perfect, but I'm trying. I'm not responding defensively, only with love for you. I won't always know what to say and what to do, but I'll always think with love for you and try to value your feelings and desires. I'll never treat you disrespectfully, say mean things to you or hurt you ... but I can't promise that I will always say things perfectly. My door and heart are open to you. You can and will do whatever you want ... duh! on my part. I love you and respect you for that. I am so wired, I guess I shouldn't have had that large coffee at 7 p.m. I'm interested in YOU. What do you think this is all about? It's not me. Please continue to tell me how you're feeling and how you feel about what I say ... teach me, help me. Help me to understand and love you right.

One thing I would like from you is the freedom to speak openly about things I think about without necessarily having thought them completely through. That's how we women work ... one thing you can count on is that if a woman has a mind, she has a mind to change. But one thing that will never change is my undying love for you. Sorry, I can't change that unless you change you.

I want to know what you're thinking ... I'm asking you questions. How can I help you with your job search? Is there anything else I can help you with? Above all else, I'm your friend ... what can I do for you? How do you feel about me? About us? What are your fears? What are your doubts? What do you want to see happen? What was our weekend together like for you? What was it like holding me, kissing me, touching me, me touching you, me kissing you, me holding you? What was it like for you when we were making love?

How did you feel sleeping with me, eating with me, sitting next to me in the theater? How did you feel walking beside me, hand in hand? How can I ease any fears, help you in your decision for or against being with me? What do you want from me? I am dedicated to our love working. Tell me what you need. If you don't want to respond to this, don't. I'm asking these questions because I understand that I talk too much about myself and don't spend enough time asking questions about you. Are these the wrong questions? What questions, if any, should I ask next time? I won't know unless you tell me.

Love,
Jewel

--------<>--------

Subject: Re: your queries
Date: Sat, 21 Aug 1999 10:56:02
From: Dakin Caravans
To: Jewel Halpern

Good morning, Supergirl,

So many big questions from such a little girl! Where to begin? Well, let me answer them in order: I am thinking about a lot of things. Our band is recording its CD next week, and I'm nervous about it. I never recorded before, except on tape in a garage band years ago. We're just doing four demo tracks in hopes of getting a contract, but I don't want them to think I'm the weak link in the band. They're pretty good musicians and singers, and I'm just a recycled old surf-rock drummer. I'm also thinking about giving up the painting. It takes too long to turn out anything really good, and it's a lot of work to try to market the paintings. In fact, the drumming is hard work, too. We rehearse a lot and play in small clubs paying very little money. My savings account is dwindling. I probably will have to go back to writing, either sports or freelance features, or maybe back into editing, although I hated that. I'm just not a white-shirt-necktie-9-to-6 kind of guy.

Oh, what am I thinking about US? Is THAT what you meant? (Of course I knew that's what you were asking. I was just stalling). I think we just might have a great future, after all. I love you. I've always loved you, since the day we met. I doubt I could stop loving you no matter how hard I tried. We're soulmates. Yes, I have fears and doubts. Will you get hooked on pain pills again? Will that self-destructive behavior resurface in some ugly way? But as for our weekend together – it was heaven itself. Being with you with total love (and lust!) in our hearts, and being able to express it freely ... it was unbelievably satisfying. Besides, you're kind of cute. Can I call you sometime?
Love,
Dakin

--------<>--------

Subject: Take me, I'm yours
Date: Sun, 22 Aug 1999 09:11:24
From: Jewel Halpern
To: Dakin Caravans

My Dakin,

Thank you for starting to let me in ...

I need you, I want you, I love you ... with all of my heart and soul. We are meant to be together. I want no one else to love for the rest of my life other than you. We can take each other to places we've never been before. Anything is possible!!!

Yours forever faithfully, if you'll have me,
Love,
Your Jewel

--------◇--------

Subject: Dear God letter
Date: Tue, 24 Aug 1999 22:05:43
From: Jewel Halpern
To: Dr. Sara Lyman

Dear God,

My life seems to be coming full circle, and I sit here tonight and wonder, dear God, what you have in store for me. I'm so happy and filled with anticipation. Will Dakin and I get back together for good? Will we be married? Will his band become a big success? Will my artwork win a national award in next month's contest? Will Dakin and I be able to retire with my investments, buy a motor home and travel around the country, as we so often dream about?

One thing I know for sure. I will never get hooked on painkillers or any other kind of drug again. I am clean now and will remain clean for the rest of my life. I'm eating all vegetarian, exercising every day and feeling so much healthier and happier. My sessions with Dr. Lyman have helped me

146

gain so much clarity in my life. My self-esteem problems and insecurities were rooted in my unhappy childhood and the dysfunctional relationship between my mother and father. I've dealt with those issues and am moving past them. Most of all, I have found you, God, and a world of goodness and love and kindness are opening up to me. I see now that it all starts with the self. BE the kind of person you like and respect, GIVE the kind of love you want, expect NOTHING in return. It's all about loving and giving. My problems were all tied up in my ego, which always got in my way. I now understand that there are two ways of seeing – with the ego or with the Holy Spirit. I can choose fear or love ... hell or heaven ... death or life ... damnation or forgiveness ... scarcity or abundance ... time or eternity ... sickness or health ... pain or joy. It's all up to me. You give us all we need, God, and so many of us make the wrong choices. I am with you now, and I choose these things: love, heaven, life, forgiveness, abundance, eternity, health, joy.

I will never turn back. I feel your arms around me, and your love fills me.

Your loving daughter,
Jewel

"The greatness is not in me; I am in the greatness."

--------<>--------

Subject: Really strange news
Date: Wed, 25 Aug 1999 10:13:21
From: The Odd Server
To: Jewel Halpern

Hi Jewel!

As you requested, here are your weekly strange-but-true stories. Click on each headline for the full story:

- Mimes banned for abusive language
- Wife accused of running over her husband after church
- Beer and coffee are good for your heart
- Mega-artichokes to power homes?

·   Man reports wife's death – after game
·   Police kill youth in effort to stop his suicide attempt

--------◇--------

Subject: Are you free? Or at least reasonable?
Date: Thu, 26 Aug 1999 19:27:50
From: Dakin Caravans
To: Jewel Halpern

Hi Supergirl,

Just called and left a message on your machine, not realizing you're probably at your NA meeting. I've been thinking a lot lately about you – and about us. I want to explore some ideas with you this weekend, try some things on for size.

Frankly, I can't get you out of my head. I thought I had gotten over you and was in love with Jeri Starrette, but I realize now that I was just fooling myself. She was some sort of substitute for you, and a poor one at that. There will never be another Jewel, and despite all the ups and downs we had (actually, it's BECAUSE of the ups and IN SPITE OF the downs), I want to take another run at you and I becoming an us. I'd like to take you to Santa Barbara this weekend, just a little getaway so we can walk on the beach, dine in quaint restaurants, visit artsy little shops and fall in love all over again.

Sound OK to you? Call me.

Love,
Dakin

PS: The recording sessions went great, and the songs on CD sound way better than I ever thought possible. But it's still just a plaything for me. I'm sure if the band gets a contract, they'll find a better drummer and let me go, but that's OK. I've fulfilled a childhood fantasy by playing with them and actually going into a recording studio. Anything else now is gravy. In the meantime, I'm starting to send out resumes again for writing and editing jobs.

--------◇--------

Chapter Twelve: Dakin
Everything and everyone around you is your teacher

Background: Dakin's frustrations with Spider and the police mounted, and his fragile psyche continued to wobble.
–David Cunningham

--------◇--------

Subject: alert the authorities
Date: Wed, 18 Oct 2000 08:14:01
From: Dakin Caravans
To: Lt. Dick Najera, Greentree PD

Lt. Najera,

I will call you after you get into the office this morning, but I'm emailing to tell you I am forwarding a notice I got from Spider Juncal. He sent it as a mass emailing to everyone on his address list, and I'm sure he didn't stop to think that I would be on that list, too ... because the message he sent virtually proves he broke into my condo, as far as I'm concerned.

You'll see that he is advertising a new website that he will establish soon. It practically amounts to a confession that he broke into the condo and copied Jewel's files onto disk. He writes: "I have come into possession of documents that verify the Second Coming and the miracle that was her life – the Daughter of God!" He later writes that by going to his website, you can "Get a sneak peak at 'Jewel of the Universe' – destined to become the gospel of the new millennium!" I don't see how it could be any clearer. He's a lunatic obsessed with the delusion that my late wife was a messiah, he broke into my garage and confronted me in the back seat of my car, then broke into my condo, ransacked the place looking for Jewel's diaries and letters, then found a copy of her journals on the computer hard drive, copied it and left. He's a demented criminal, and if you want me to testify to this or anything else, I'll do it. I don't mind telling you that this guy has made me very edgy and unstable at a time when I still haven't fully recovered from my wife's death. Please do your job and arrest this guy. Or notify the Irvine police, and maybe THEY will be willing to do what they are paid to do.

Dakin Caravans

--------◇--------

Subject: hey you!
Date: Wed, 18 Oct 2000 10:11:46
From: Jeri Starrette
To: Dakin Caravans

hi dakin doll,

are you doing better today? i worry about you, love. i will help you any way i can in dealing with the loss of jewel, but you have to understand, everybody dies. we the living must let them go and get on with our own lives. i hope that doesn't sound cold or harsh, but i'm saying it for your own good. you have to move on. think of it like turning a page to a new chapter in your life. the last chapter was good, and the next one might be better. your life didn't end; hers did. it was just her time. now it's your time to do something else. dakin, you have so much to offer this world, i'd hate to see you waste it. you're a talented artist, you've played drums in a really good band, and you're a skilled writer. there are lots of things you can do to make this a better place. just because you inherited all of jewel's money doesn't mean you should sit around and waste away.

now with this picture, i kick you out into the real world so you can face the day!

b'ger

i get most of these pictures off the internet from an artist named b'ger
.... i think they're really cool.

love,
jeri

--------<>--------

Subject: save me
Date: Wed, 18 Oct 2000 12:11:39
From: Dakin Caravans
To: Jewel Halpern

My dear departed Supergirl,

They say Jesus saves, so now I'm wondering if Jewel does, too. You're
the new messiah, right? There's a website going up soon that proclaims you
to be the Second Coming, only this time, God so loved the earth that he sent
it his only begotten DAUGHTER. That's you. So save me. If you don't, I'm
sure to sink in the deep end. Everybody seems to know what's going on but

me. The cops are sure I'm a wolf-crying idiot, jeri (lower-case only) starrette figures I'm too wrapped up in your death and need to let go, and even my friend and counselor, Corena Bissett, seems to think I'm losing my grip. I must be a mushroom, because everybody keeps me in the dark and feeds me bullshit.

Last night, I thought I was having a heart attack. This pressure started to build in my chest, and I felt like the walls were closing in on me. The room started spinning, and I got short of breath. I started hyperventilating. My heart was pounding so hard, I thought it would shoot out of my chest and smack against the wall. I looked around the condo and everywhere saw evidence that you existed, that you lived here and were once a part of me. And all I could think of was that you are gone – forever. I started pacing through the condo, then finally started running, and I ran right out the door, down the stairs and out into the neighborhood. I ran and ran until my body could catch up to my heart and respiration rate. Once it was all pumping at the same level, I gradually slowed down, in hopes that all my parts would slow down in unison. Fortunately, they did. I don't know what's happening to me.

But what a comfort you have been to me, Jewel. Not when you were alive. I mean, now that you're dead. Well, yes, of course you were a great comfort to me while you were alive, but now all you can do is listen, and I like that. You never talk back, never argue, never judge. You simply listen. Everyone should have such a friend.

Until we meet again,
Your Dakin

--------<>--------

Subject: Take me away
Date: Wed, 18 Oct 2000 14:48:03
From: Dakin Caravans
To: Corena Bissett

Dear Dr. Kevorkian,

Won't you please stop by at your convenience and put me out of my misery? I can pay you. A lot. How much do you need?

Sorry, Dr. Corena, but these have not been the best days of my life. In case you want to find out if Jewel truly was the Second Coming or the daughter of God or whatever that screw-loose thinks she was, you'll have a chance to judge for yourself soon, because Mr. Far-Out-Dude! is putting up a website shrine to her sometime in the next week, and I strongly suspect it will include all of Jewel's diaries and letters ... all ripped off from her computer in a burglary that the police don't seem to take seriously, since nothing expensive was stolen. The best they can tell me is, "You know, less than one in 10 of these type burglaries ever ends up with an arrest. It was probably just some kids."

Let's see, where was I? Oh yes, when we last discussed the Rise and Fall of Jewel and Dakin Caravans, they were moving to Arizona. It seemed like a good idea at the time. The newspaper was bigger and healthier than the one I was leaving, and the Diamondbacks represented a fresh start for me. There aren't too many places I would leave Southern California for, but I thought Phoenix would be a fair trade. Beautiful, mild winters, and in the summer, well, OK, it's 140 degrees in the shade, so there's that, but a baseball writer travels half the summer anyway, and the team plays in an air-conditioned, retractable-dome home, so it would be fine. For some reason, it was not so fine with Jewel.

For a while, things were tolerable. We continued to pretend we would be married soon, but she was still eating painkillers like they were popcorn and turning herself into Meg Ryan in "When a Man Loves a Woman." Pretty on the outside, ugly on the inside. She stopped traveling with me, but she didn't use the time to find a job or any useful way to spend her time. She played a little tennis and a little golf, but mostly she laid in The Valley of the Sun and worked on her tan. All she wanted to do was go out dancing and partying all night, and after a while, I was one tired-ass sportswriter. Neither of us was happy, but neither of us really knew why, either. I still loved her, but I wanted to recapture the magic we had back in California, and it wasn't happening. She later admitted that her life would have seemed better if she had gotten a job or volunteered for some charity organization, anything to give her a little meaning. But she was a lost soul at that point.

We put it into cruise control through the end of the baseball season, hoping that when I had more time in the winter, we could reconnect in a more loving way. We tried. God knows we tried. Neither one of us truly was to blame. I knew the medication was messing up her mind, but I had no idea how much she was taking or how all-encompassing her dependence had become. But twice I threatened to break up and kick her out if she didn't get off the painkillers. She agreed twice. Both times, she quickly slipped back into her addiction. Then we had one final blowup that ended it all for me.

There's no point in telling you about the tavern, the guy she picked up, how she told me to go home, and how I dumped everything she owned into the driveway. It wasn't about her and me, anyway. It was always about the drug she was taking. But I gave up. I told her she had to leave, and I meant it. And so she left. Went home to California, was going to spend some time with her dad (who was not well) and find a job out there. Whatever. I didn't care anymore. I was numb. My dream girl had turned into a nightmare, and I just wanted to put it all behind me.

After many weeks of self-pity, I tried my hand at this game of love again. Dated a few women. One of them was you, probably the best friend I ever found in Arizona. And now I need to say a word about that, Dr. Corena Bissett. I'm sorry if, on our blind-date meeting, I offended you by saying I wasn't physically attracted to you. I realize now that was a pretty shallow thing to say. But the fact of the matter is, after a long marriage that ended in divorce, then an intense relationship with Jewel that had just fallen apart, I knew I had to be careful with my heart. I also knew I did not want to spend the rest of my life alone. I may not have discovered the meaning of life, but I knew that a life alone carried no meaning at all. Life without love seemed empty, and I was searching for a lifemate.

Every woman I dated was judged as a potential permanent partner for me, and one of my admittedly shallow requirements was that I needed to like what I saw across the table every day. She didn't have to be Heather Locklear, but I didn't want Roseanne Barr, either. This isn't going very well, is it? See, I'm not saying you're Roseanne Barr – you're a very pleasant-looking woman – but not my type. Gad, I sound like a typical guy, don't I? What I mean to say is that I loved talking with you. You're brilliant, you're witty and funny, and you see things nobody else does. And the only reason I didn't want to keep dating you was that I knew it wasn't the relationship I was looking for. I was being overly picky, I guess. As it turned out, you became the friend I desperately needed, but not (thankfully, for the sake of our friendship) a lover.

Did I wiggle off the hook yet? Sorry. But you don't need to see me squirm. I'm sure you knew all this already, and that's why you have remained my friend. You like crazy people.

So, where was I? OK, I was meeting lots of nice women, including you, and then, after moving back to Southern California, I stumbled across this pretty, sweet young thing who was 13 years my junior, and I asked her out, knowing full well she would reject me with one of those are-you-kidding stares. But I had no pride left to wound, so I tried. And to my great shock, she said yes. The dinner date went spectacularly well, up to the point at the end when she told me that, in addition to being recently divorced, she also had two young children, Jimi and Janis (she seemed too young to like Hendrix and Joplin, but then I learned that her ex was a hard-drinking, blue-collar guy about my own age, so that explained the kids' names). That should have immediately eliminated her from my list of potential lifemates, because I wasn't interested in raising another family. But she was so attractive and sweet that I couldn't walk away (again, you see how the mind of the simpleton male works; he can easily reject the brilliant psychologist on grounds that she isn't attractive enough, but he can't so quickly dispose of the gorgeous girl with the needy kids).

OK, I'm a jerk. I admit it. I may be a slow learner, but at least I'm a learner. I did eventually break up with her, and every step of the way I told her that I wasn't sure the relationship would have a chance to go anywhere because of my reluctance to be a step-father. Oh, forget the excuses. I was a jerk who was being ruled by something other than his brain.

Jeri was more than just a pretty face, and we truly did have a great time together. For more than two months, I allowed myself to toy with the idea of asking her to marry me. I knew she was crazy about me; I just didn't know why. She said she was more comfortable with older men, and of course, I knew that she also saw me as a stable role model for her kids, who didn't have such a good one in their dad.

This relationship, you may recall, was part of my mid-life crisis. I had worked for it, I deserved it, and nobody was going to stop me from having it.

And here's how I eventually came to leave you stranded in the Arizona desert and return home to California:

An old friend from Greentree named Bug Burnett looked me up and asked if I still played drums. He and I played in rock bands when we were in high school and college, but we hadn't seen each other since our 10-year reunion, which was, well, a long time ago. He was still playing guitar and actually making a living at it. He had played some big venues, even some stadium concerts, as the warm-up band for groups like Fleetwood Mac, Heart and the Indigo Girls. Nobody had ever heard of him. He was just the rhythm guitar player in a long series of different bands, but he had gotten pretty good. And he was starting up a new band and needed a drummer. I told him I hadn't even picked up drumsticks in more than a decade, never mind the fact that I was living in Arizona. But I was oddly interested. It would make absolutely no sense to quit a good job covering a major-league baseball team (OK, an expansion team, but still technically major-league) in Phoenix, give up a journalistic career that spanned three decades, and join a fledgling rock band in Southern California. So of course I did it.

I had some money saved that would allow me to coast with little or no income for about eight months. After that, I would be broke. But I decided that I would try to make a living painting portraits by day and playing drums by night, and if it didn't work, so what? My kids were virtually grown (both in college, both in the legal custody of their evil mother), so my biggest responsibilities were behind me. I bought a drum set and started practicing like mad, sometimes eight hours a day. I moved back to Southern California and hooked up with the Bug Burnett Band. They were pretty good. We even recorded several songs for what we hoped would become our first CD. We played a lot of gigs, some of them actually paying decent money. It was fun. And it was a lot of hard work, most of it during rehearsals. I hated it, and I loved it. I couldn't really decide which emotion was stronger. I sold a few paintings and got a lot of positive feedback, but that was even harder work than the drumming, and the money wasn't great. I dated Jeri Starrette, and then broke up with her.

It was right around this time that I started to doubt my sanity and began wondering what line of work I should go into when I grow up. Then I got a phone call out of the blue from Jewel Halpern.

And that's another story for another day.

Thanks for listening,
Dakin

---------<>---------

Subject: Well, that was rude of you
Date: Thu, 19 Oct, 2000 10:15:16
From: Stacy6969
To: Dakin Caravans

Every man's fantasy is two or three women ...

Why does it have to be fantasy? Experience this LIVE...LIVE...LIVE...
CLICK HERE>

---------<>---------

Subject: Re: alert the authorities
Date: Thu, 19 Oct, 2000 11:21:46
From: Lt. Dick Najera, Greentree PD
To: Dakin Caravans

Dear Mr. Caravans,

This is mainly to emphasize what I told you in our phone conversation yesterday afternoon. I informed you that that Mr. Juncal claims to have obtained his copies of the letters and diaries directly from your wife during one of their Narcotics Anonymous meetings many months ago. I have found no evidence to refute his story. We have no evidence that he burglarized your home. Irvine police met with Mr. Juncal last night, and he showed them the photocopies, which are dated from late 1999 and early this year. He does not appear to have any property that was taken during the burglary.

In any case, as I told you, we have no jurisdiction over a burglary in Irvine. Our only interest in the case is whether Mr. Juncal might be a suspect in the death of your wife, which did occur within our city limits. In the last 48 hours, crime lab personnel have uncovered some interesting new facts while studying her autopsy report. These may shed new light on the case.

In short, Mr. Caravans, we now have some doubt whether her death was truly by "natural" causes. I'm sure you will want to review what we have learned. Please call me at your earliest convenience so we can schedule a meeting here at the Greentree PD offices.

Sincerely,
Lt. Dick Najera

---------◇---------

Chapter Thirteen: Jewel
When you rule your mind, you rule your world

Background: Addiction haunted Dakin Caravans' life. His father, mother and sister were alcoholics, his first wife's father needed treatment for cocaine addiction, and Jewel endured her own recurring problems with painkillers.

Dakin never experienced problems in those areas, but his bitter family experiences left him with a cold and unforgiving attitude toward substance abuse.

–David Cunningham

--------<>--------

Subject: One more thing
Date: Sun, 05 Sep 1999 12:28:59
From: Jewel Halpern
To: Dakin Caravans

Hi Dakin –

I loved talking to you last night. I have one more thing to say. I always do.

I know you're concerned about a relapse on my part. Addiction isn't just about me and you and how it affected our relationship. Addiction affects everyone. It's our number one health problem, whether it's nicotine, caffeine, alcohol or pain pills. Addiction – not the drug itself, but addiction – affects everything good in the world. It's a planetary and family disease. No one escapes its grip. Somewhere, somehow, everyone is affected. You sometimes come off sounding holier-than-thou, like you're too strong-willed to fall victim to addiction, and you make it sound as if it's all about weak minds. As you are well aware, alcohol abuse runs rampant in your own family – your father, your mother and your sister. You luckily didn't inherit the physiological makeup to become an alcoholic.

It's not about willpower. Your will may be stronger over other life issues than the will of myself, your mom, dad or sister, but your will is not stronger over addiction than it was for us. Drugs for the addict are very powerful, and the addiction can't be willed away without proper help and treatment. After receiving that help and treatment, and after your head clears, THEN you have a choice and the will not to pop that first pill. But after that first pill, there is no willpower that can stop the addictive response of the body, which becomes an obsession of the mind.

Addiction is a very serious disease and should be treated as such. The drug is not to be feared, nor should the addict be feared. My will is very strong, and I'll use that to never pop that first pill. I have over 40 years ingrained in me of no interest in drugs. Maybe I instinctively knew all the time that I wasn't one of those people who could be a casual user.

I'm writing this to you not just for us, but for your family as well. If I can be of any help to your sister, I want to help a fellow addict. She may never stop drinking, and I can't change or control that. All I can do is reach out to her. And didn't you say your ex-wife's dad had a cocaine problem? It really doesn't matter, because it's in your jeans, I mean genes. (By the way, have I told you how absolutely hot!! fine!! and sexy!! you look in your button-fly Levi's jeans!!?? ... I guess I'm going to have to get rid of my passion and sensuality candles, they're starting to get to me.) Sorry, I got off track as usual, but when I think of your muscular, powerful, manly thighs thrusting down on my body I ... oh, sorry, off track again.

Back to addictions –You're not an alcoholic, but it's still in your genes. My mom isn't an alcoholic, but her dad and brother are. From your own bloodline, your children or grandchildren could be affected. But unlike other diseases, one can prevent addiction from striking with proper education and preventative measures.

Again, this isn't about you and I. Addiction is a family disease. Everyone is affected in some way. I'm very passionate about addiction prevention. I'm not out to save the world, only the small part that I exist in, and if my help reaches out to the world, then I'm blessed and grateful that I, in some small way, helped.

It's your duty and responsibility to yourself and your children and grandchildren to find out what you can about addiction and alcoholism so you can be prepared to help, should it be needed. There are very clear warning signs, and they should be heeded.

Anyway, I love you, Heather, Casey and all of your family. I hope you will let me make a difference in your life and theirs. When I was a kid, if someone asked me, "What do you want to be when you grow up?" I never would have replied, "an addict." Nobody would. Nobody is an addict by choice. That's all I have to say about that.

Now I can step down off my soapbox. I hope I haven't bored you. I know you don't feel the same way as I about many of these things, but I thought it was important that you know where I stand ... where I sit ... where I lie ...

Can't wait to lie with you again.

Love,
Jewel

--------◇--------

Subject: Re: One more thing
Date: Sun, 05 Sep 1999 15:52:22
From: Dakin Caravans
To: Jewel Halpern

My semi-precious Jewel,

You're right – I don't agree with all of what you said about addiction, but a lot of it made sense. I realize that when someone takes heroin or cocaine or even nicotine from cigarettes, the body quickly becomes dependent on the drug. I realize that physical dependence can become stronger than the willpower of the individual to resist taking what he knows is bad for him. But I still believe that those circumstances are the exception, not the rule. I believe that my dad drank because he liked the escape it provided, and if he had been strong enough to deal with the pressures of his life in a healthy and sober manner, he could have stopped drinking in a nanosecond. I see it as a weakness, and in his case, the weakness drove him to an early death. I believe that you used painkillers as an escape, too. You loved the feeling, and you retreated into it. When you were high, you didn't have to cope with anything. You took the easy way out. I believe that the day you stopped taking pills was the day your willpower finally kicked in.

Of course, when I expressed these views to my psychologist friend in Arizona, she said I should immediately enroll in one of those programs for the adult children of alcoholics. She said she didn't even have to ask me if my parents were alcoholics. She could smell it from my hard-line attitude. I guess it's true I'm a little bitter. My dad would still be alive today if he hadn't drunk so much.

As for me, I have nothing against altered states of consciousness. I just prefer to achieve them in natural ways. Meditation. Self-hypnosis. Astral projection. A good 15 minute session of "transcension" – my word for the type of meditation I practice – can take you away from all your problems, lower your blood pressure, calm your nerves, enhance your clarity, clear up your acne, lance your boils, walk your dog and cook your dinner (well, sometimes it burns the garlic bread, but nobody's perfect).
All kidding aside, I'd like to introduce you to some of the techniques I use for meditation. They work for physical pain relief, too. And it's cheaper than going to the Betty Ford Clinic.

Talk to you tonight,

Love,
Dakin

--------◇--------

Subject: Hello from California
Date: Tue, 07 Sep 1999 20:38:56
From: Jewel Halpern
To: Vivienne Myers

Hey Viv!

How's the weather in Vermont? Not 75 degrees and sunny, like it was here today, I'm sure. Tell me all about the marathon you ran. I can't believe you're actually doing that. How in the world does somebody run for 26 miles? I get tired just driving 26 miles.

Well, it's true. Dakin and I are getting back together. We're taking it kind of slow, but it's going to work this time. The only reason it fell apart before was because I couldn't stop taking the pain medication, and it completely changed my personality. I'm clean now and have never felt better in my life. I turned vegetarian, and I exercise religiously. Speaking of religion, I have found it again – but not Judaism. It's more like my own personal relationship with God. You know I always had a tough time embracing that whole Orthodox Jew thing. But if there's one good thing that came out of my addiction, it's the 12-step program and its emphasis on spirituality. I have a very strong feeling of connection to God now, and as part of my rehab, I've been writing letters to God, telling him about my life and thoughts. He writes back and gives me direction. I'm sure our rabbi back in Brattleboro would be thrilled to hear that.

Well, gotta run, but I'll call you again next week. I miss our regular Monday night phone conversations. We should try to talk at least once a month. A friend like you comes along once in a lifetime, and I don't want to let our friendship wither, even though an entire country stands between us.

Dakin and I are talking about buying a motor home after we're married and traveling all over the country, just getting into the essence of what the people and towns of America are all about. When that happens, you can bet we'll be driving into Brattleboro one of these days. See you then.

Your friend always,
Jewel

--------- ◇ ---------

Subject: important words
Date: Thu, 07 Oct 1999 18:45:15
From: Jewel Halpern
To: Spider Juncal

Hi Spider,

Thanks for the scriptures you suggested I read. They were great. I hope you enjoy the Marianne Williamson book I gave you. It's written from a female perspective, but I think it has something for everybody. It's the only book that I can read over and over and get something new and meaningful out of every time.

Here's something else that moved me. Before I got into the program, I might have dismissed this as sappy sentimentality. Now I read it and take every word seriously. It's so true. Erma Bombeck wrote it, and I think she was dying of cancer at the time:

IF I HAD MY LIFE TO LIVE OVER

I would have gone to bed when I was sick instead of pretending the earth would go into a holding pattern if I weren't there for the day.

I would have burned the pink candle sculpted like a rose before it melted in storage.

I would have talked less and listened more.

I would have invited friends over to dinner even if the carpet was stained or the sofa faded.

I would have eaten the popcorn in the "good" living room and worried much less about the dirt when someone wanted to light a fire in the fireplace.

I would have taken the time to listen to my grandfather ramble about his youth.

I would have shared more of the responsibility carried by my husband.

I would never have insisted the car windows be rolled up on a summer day because my hair had just been teased and sprayed.

I would have sat on the lawn with my children and not worried about grass stains.

I would have cried and laughed less while watching television – and more while watching life.

I would never have bought anything just because it was practical, wouldn't show soil, or was guaranteed to last a lifetime.

Instead of wishing away nine months of pregnancy, I'd have cherished every moment and realized that the wonderment growing inside me was the only chance in life to assist God in a miracle.

When my kids kissed me impetuously, I would never have said, "Later. Now go get washed up for dinner."

There would have been more "I love you's"... more "I'm sorry's"

... but ...

mostly, given another shot at life, I would seize every minute ... look at it and really see it ... live it ... and never give it back.

Stop sweating the small stuff. Don't worry about who doesn't like you, who has more, or who's doing what.

Instead, let's cherish the relationships we have with those who do love us. Let's think about what God HAS blessed us with. And what we are doing each day to promote ourselves mentally, physically and emotionally, as well as spiritually.

Life is too short to let it pass you by. We only have one shot at this, and then it's gone.

I hope you all have a blessed day.

---------◇---------

Subject: come back, all is forgiven!
Date: Sun, 31 Oct 1999 11:32:26
From: Spider Juncal
To: Jewel Halpern

Dear Daughter of God,

We miss you so much at our NA meetings! Why have you decided to leave? Just because you've been clean for nine months or so doesn't mean you can't still be of service to your brethren! There is so much for you to share and for you to partake in!

I miss seeing your letters to God and his answers to you! I miss hearing you speak at our meetings! You have a God-given gift to lead and help people! I think you went through your addiction as part of God's purpose for you! You were supposed to live among the fallen so that you could minister to them! Think about this, Jewel! This may be your true calling in life! God has a plan for each of us, and I think his plan for you is much bigger than his plan for the rest of us! You can make a lasting impact on our society! You can be the one who makes a difference! Did Jesus go off and paint pictures for greeting cards when God told him to go out into the world and spread his word? No, he did not! God has told you that you have the power to change people, to make them better! You can lift their eyes up to the Light! You have a pipeline to the Father like no one else has ... use it, Jewel! What is life for, if not to help others? I would gladly lay down all my worldly possessions and become your foot soldier, following you and carrying out your will! Together, we could change the world!

Please write me back or call me and let me know what's going on with you!

Spider

"I therefore, the prisoner in the Lord, beseech you to walk worthily of the calling wherewith ye were called ..." (Ephesians 4:1)

"I was in love with a beautiful blonde once – she drove me to drink. 'Tis the one thing I'm indebted to her for." (W.C. Fields)

--------◇--------

Subject: All of me
Date: Fri, 12 Nov 1999 12:28:59
From: Jewel Halpern
To: Dakin Caravans

Hi Dakin –

I find myself feeling you all around me. I know you're here even when I can't see you or physically feel you. Your essence moves through me and about me. You are with me, you are alive inside of me, you are part of me. My desire for you is great, and that feeling need never be and is no longer numbed away ... your light burns inside of me. I want to taste you and drink in your intoxicating being. The thought of you makes me overwhelmed with love, desire, peace and warmth. These are the feelings I have longed for my whole life. You and I could do great things together and share our love with the world.

Yours eternally,
Jewel

--------◇--------

Subject: moving forward
Date: Sun, 14 Nov 1999 15:52:22
From: Dakin Caravans
To: Jewel Halpern

My Supergirl,

Every day and every night I feel closer and closer to you. I want you, I want us. You're right. Sometimes I'm too careful. What's the worst that could happen? What's the best that could happen? It's worth the risk. If you will be patient with me while I struggle to find myself again (it may take a while for

167

me to discover something I like doing), I will make every effort to put the past behind us and only look forward.

And please, don't feel like you have to play games or avoid talking about how you feel. While it's true that a man in general can lose interest when a woman takes too much control of the relationship, we both need to be ourselves and see where we belong and how we fit together (quite nicely, as I achingly recall)...

Love's not easy. If it were easy, everyone would do it.
Seems to me, nobody does it very well. Do you know ANYBODY who has never been divorced and is clearly very happy and still in love? I didn't think so.

But I remain an optimist.
Have a spectacular day,

Love,
Dakin

--------<>--------

Subject: Never my love
Date: Fri, 19 Nov 1999 20:12:41
From: Jewel Halpern
To: Dakin Caravans

My Dakin,

You ask if there will come a time when I won't desire you ... never ever, my love!! I don't love you for the way that you look or your body (although I do love the way look, and I love your body), your job or what you can do for me ... I only love you for the spirit that is you, which is ageless and all things of beauty.

My feelings are not someone else's 12-step thoughts. This is not a passing fancy, a temporary phase, a cultish notion ... this is a way of life, the only way. For peace and happiness, my attitude can only be one of love, kindness, humility and patience for myself and all others. It is really so simple.

Love is always perfect.

My love for you is never-ending...

Jewel (a.k.a. Supergirl)

--------<>--------

Subject: what to do?
Date: Thu, 16 Dec 1999 20:19:34
From: Jewel Halpern
To: Dr. Sara Lyman

Dear Dr. Lyman:

I needed to talk to you today, but your receptionist wouldn't put me through. I can't afford to wait until our session next week. I'm worried.

I've been taking my pain pills again. Not for pain – for escape. For the feeling it gives me. Sometimes I get so overwhelmed with what's happening in my life, and the only thing that enables me to cope with it all is my medication.

Dakin doesn't know about it. He's so judgmental and rigid sometimes. I know he will think me weak. I don't think I'm addicted again. I'm just using them three or four nights a week, when I need to get away from my problems. I'm so worried about Dakin and I getting back together. I want everything to be perfect, and I don't know what I would do with myself if it didn't work.

I use the pills sometimes before I paint, too, and I find it makes my work more emotional, more moving and subtle. It also helps when Dakin and I go house hunting because there's so much stress to make everything right. We're talking about marriage, but it's still vague. No ring, no date. I'm so nervous. What if he doesn't love me as before? I can't live without him. We are so completely one person, one mind, one love. I need him more than I've ever needed anything.

I would like your advice on what to do. Obviously, I need some help in dealing with certain things. Call me when you can.

Jewel

--------<>--------

Chapter Fourteen: Dakin
Are you part of the problem
or part of the solution?

Background: Dakin's emails sometimes sound like elaborate storytelling, but his friends say that was typical of him. A writer his entire adult life, he relished the written word and seldom used the kind of literary shorthand common in others' emails.
–David Cunningham

--------◇--------

Subject: are you ready?
Date: Fri, 20 Oct 2000 10:31:51
From: Jeri Starrette
To: Dakin Caravans

hello dakin love,

are you ready? i've got a sitter for the kids tonight. can i come over and talk? i really need to see you. and from our last phone conversation, it sounds like you really need to see me, too. Say, 8 p.m.?

i'll bring the wine. you can provide the music.

```
                        | ‾|
                        | +|
                  , , ,  |__|
                  $$$   , ,
                  $$C        >
                  $$$;     _<
            _____/ /_
           |   |__`\~/o\  _,]-]___]-----> 
           |  / \( )  )\/.-//
          _( \  )    / \ |
          //| /    ,/ \ \/
           '/    o  \
          /       o  \
         /_____/\__\
         \      ||  /
          \     ||  /
           \    || /
           /  ) ( \
           |/    \|
           :]    [:
           o|    |o
          /o|    |o\    b'ger
          `_'    `_'
```

i can fix what ails you ...

love,
jeri

--------◇--------

Subject: SEX
Date: Fri, 20 Oct 2000 11:19:18
From: Dakin Caravans
To: Corena Bissett

What's up, doc?

As for me, I just got an open invitation of sex from ex-girlfriend jeri (lower-case) starrette. do you think i'm ready for that, doc?

Maybe it will take my mind off my problems, which don't seem to be getting any better. I can tell you this: the thought that a very pretty young woman wants to share carnal pleasures with me is overwhelmingly enticing right now. My head won't be in it, but this wouldn't be about thought, would it? Just physical sensations. Nothing wrong with that, is there?

I haven't been sleeping much lately, but I don't feel the least bit tired. It's almost like I'm wired on cocaine or something (although I wouldn't really know what that feels like, but I saw "Scarface"). Yet with all my energy and time to think, I haven't figured out which direction my life should take now. And I've become occasionally snappish with friends and family. I'm sure they've noticed I'm not myself. More like Jack Nicholson in "As Good as it Gets."

But enough about me. Let's talk about me and Jewel. Back to the saga – I was playing drums with the Bug Burnett Band and trying to sell my paintings when she called out of the blue. It went something like this:

"Dakin, this is Jewel."
"I'd know that voice anywhere. What's on your mind?"
"I have something I need to tell you. It's not going to be easy."
"What, now your mother died, too? Just send me an email like you did when your father passed away."
"That's not funny, Dakin."
"Sorry. So what is it?"
"God, this is so hard. So, how have you been lately?"
"Jewel!"
"Can't we chat a little bit first? Break the ice?"
"Here, let me break the ice for you. I love you. I've always loved you. I don't think I will ever stop loving you. But you hurt me very badly with all your stunts back in Arizona, especially the last one with the guy in the bar, and I'd prefer to move on. But I won't totally turn my back on you. Ever. So if you need to tell me something, tell me. But don't expect me to be all happy and mushy just because you called for the first time in months. You're with some other guy now, anyway. So just say what you have to say."

"I broke up with Michael."
"That's what you called to tell me?"

"No, but I'm not 'with some other guy.' I'm not with anybody. I actually prefer to be alone now. Makes me feel more sane."

(Long pause on my end...) "So if that's not what you called to tell me, then what is it?"

"How about those Diamondbacks?"

"Jewel!"

"I'm an addict. I was addicted to painkillers."

(Long pause.) "That's it? That's what you called to tell me? Should I alert the media? This is not news to me, Jewel."

"I know, but it's news to me. I had to confront all the things I did while under the influence of my addiction, and I have to talk to all the people I hurt. You're number one on my list. I have to say I'm sorry."

(Long pause.) "I appreciate that."

"I'm sorry, Dakin, so very sorry. I never meant to hurt you. I wasn't myself when I was taking the pills, but that's no excuse. I take full responsibility for my actions. No one did it to me. I did it to myself. And I'm truly sorry for what I put you through. I realize that I messed up our relationship and caused you a lot of pain. It wasn't your fault. It was mine. I'm sorry."

"OK. I'm glad to hear you say that. Not for my sake, but for yours. It sounds like you're finally on the right track now."

That conversation opened a dialogue between us. We started emailing each other and occasionally talking on the phone. At first, it was not about the possibility of us getting back together. That wasn't mentioned. It was about how bad her addiction really was. I had no idea the depths of her dependence until she told me all the stories about buying the pills illegally, hiding them from me, and, after we broke up, her arrests for driving while under the influence. And we talked about her 12-step program, her rediscovery of spiritualism, her psychotherapy and her new, healthy, positive outlook on life. She was a completely different person, Corena. Like the beautiful girl I had fallen in love with, only better. The demons of her childhood, her rape, her sick family and her failed relationships were all flying away. Her head seemed clear and sunny. She was a flower child again.

I broke up with jeri (lower-case) starrette and gradually moved my focus back toward Jewel. You and several of my other friends, of course, cautioned against it. A grown, adult person doesn't change overnight, you said. Be cautious. Be careful. But the lure of a healthy, happy, beautiful, loving Jewel

Halpern was too strong to resist. I came over to her place one Saturday afternoon to talk. She came over to my place one night to talk. We went out to dinner another night. Without realizing it, we were dating again.

Here's another topic I want to address: Jewel's inheritance. After we broke up, her dad died and left her close to $1 million. I had to keep asking myself, am I considering the possibility of getting back together with Jewel because of her money? It was quite a struggle for me. I didn't ever want to believe I would let something like that influence me. Values and ethics were important to me. The fact was, I loved Jewel. I loved her when she had no money, and I even loved her when she had her addiction problems. But once she had money, I almost decided to reject her BECAUSE of it. It was like I couldn't trust myself to make the right decision if money were involved.

Jewel didn't have the kind of hang-up about her money that I did. She put it all in mutual funds and let it grow. She wasn't buying anything, not even a new car. She still rented a studio apartment and worked at her job painting covers for greeting cards. She figured maybe she would retire in 10 years, since she would have plenty of money to last the rest of her life, but she wanted to be sure there was something fulfilling she could do when she retired. Until she figured out what that was, she continued along as if she were a working stiff like everybody else.

Eventually, the fire re-ignited and burned more brightly than ever. Money or no money, I wanted her. I wanted us. I wanted that chance for eternal happiness that seemed so much like a fairy tale to me. Why couldn't it come true? Eventually, we began to talk about marriage again. This time, it was serious. We began looking to buy a condo, and I got a real job. No more drums and artwork. I went back to writing and editing. We figured both of us would retire in a few years, buy a motor home and travel the country. Dreams CAN come true, Corena, even if they don't always turn into happily-ever-after. At least for a while, we found everything we both wanted. We were truly happy.

I have to stop now and cry a little. Self-pity, I suppose. Talk to you later.

Dakin

--------◇--------

Subject: GET A GRIP!
Date: Fri, 20 Oct 2000 13:53:06
From: Corena Bissett
To: Dakin Caravans

Hello Mr. Caravans (I am being formal because I am at the office):

The best advice I can give you – something I tell many of my patients – is GET A GRIP!

You have not sounded particularly well on the phone lately, and no, I do not think meaningless sex with an ex-girlfriend will make you all better. It's been less than a month since Jewel died.

On another subject: do you have any idea what evidence the police are talking about? What could they have discovered that makes them believe Jewel's death was not by natural causes?

As for Spiderman's website, send me the URL and I'll check it out. I wish I could help you with a diagnosis of his personality, but I'd have to actually see him and talk to him. I can't determine if a man is a raving lunatic just based on what you have to say about him. I can, however, make a judgment on you, since I HAVE seen and talked to you. You have a manic disorder. I am dispatching the state mental hospital orderlies immediately, and they will take you someplace where life is beautiful all the time, and you'll be happy to see the nice, young men in their clean white coats. They're coming to take you away, ha ha. (sorry, got carried away again).

But seriously, there is such a thing as bipolar disorder, and I fear you may be showing symptoms of it. Perhaps you should make an appointment to see someone there in Southern California, if you can't come visit me in Phoenix.

Are your mood swings out of proportion or totally unrelated to things going on in your life? Certainly, the death of a spouse can cause severe mood swings and suicidal thoughts, but those will be temporary in most people. Here's what I notice with you, both on the phone and in some of your emails:

176

high, elated and euphoric moods, boundless energy and enthusiasm, decreased need for sleep, erratic behavior, rapid, loud speech that's difficult to interrupt, inflated self-esteem (but then, that's always been a trait of yours), poor judgment, impatience, highly irritable moods.

Those are all symptoms of a manic disorder. Seriously.

Call me tonight.

Your friend and counselor,
Corena

--------<>--------

Subject: Insanity!
Date: Fri, 20 Oct 2000 19:01:56
From: Root Action Group
To: Dakin Caravans

IS IT MADNESS TO SPAM?

Hamlet feigned madness to fight against his powerful, incestuous, murderous uncle and usurper King. The big players on the Internet are powerful & collusively smug. Do you think that they would mourn the death of your free speech on the Net? They would be happy to see free speech killed ... outside of their own realm, of course.

So why don't you people GET WITH THE PROGRAM and pay for your commercials and STOP ALL THIS BULK MAILING CRAP? That's what BIG UNCLE wants ...

But professional bulk advertisers have long since learned to harness the power of mass mailing on the Net. It is very profitable, often amazingly profitable. All you need are the right tools.

Click here to learn about MassEmail, a program than can solve all your advertising problems >

--------<>--------

Subject: Help me, I'm think I'm falling
Date: Sat, 21 Oct 2000 10:53:39
From: Dakin Caravans
To: Jewel Halpern

My dear sweet missing Supergirl,

I need help from The Other Side. Can you reach into the material world and save me?

Yesterday afternoon, I met with Lt. Dick (Columbo) Najera at the Greentree Police Department, and he told me some disturbing facts. There was a toxicology report done during your autopsy, and the results just came back (I guess they send them to Jupiter for processing. You were cremated three weeks ago, and NOW they tell me there's something suspicious going on?). Apparently, there was some kind of "foreign substance" in your system that could have caused heart failure. It also could be considered hallucinogenic. He did not clue me in as to what substance that was. He also asked some very pointed questions, which clearly indicated that he considers me a suspect. Either I gave you some kind of drugs or slipped them into your drink to kill you and inherit all your money, or maybe you took them yourself, but in any case, he suggested I consider getting an attorney because I might be in trouble. So, um, Jewel? Do you know anything about this? Can you shed any Light From Above? I can't imagine that the Second Coming of Jesus Christ would use drugs, let alone overdose on them. Maybe Spider Juncal has all the answers, after all. I suggested that Lt. Najera talk to the DUDE who has an actual history of drug abuse and a clear, established pattern of psychotic obsession with you. He replied, "Yes, well, don't leave town anytime soon. We'll want to talk with you again next week."

T-T-Talk to me! I have meditated on this, even tried the dreaded and feared astral projection. I am becoming a whacked-out New Age freak like yourself, searching for your spirit in some nether world that I know nothing about. I feel like I'm being sucked down a drain.

I don't WANT to get an attorney! I don't WANT to fight anybody! I'll answer any question they want! I'm innocent! I haven't killed anybody! Not really! Hook me up to a lie detector! I'll tell them exactly what happened that night. At least, the part I know. If they REALLY want to know what happened, they'll have to subpoena Jewel Halpern-Caravans and get HER side of the story. She's the only one who knows everything. I just have bits and pieces, quibbles and bits, shards of glass in the eye and arrows piercing my skull. I am a child. I know nothing. Get me out of here! Take me with you! Jewel! JEWEL! I want to come home!

God, I miss my sanity. Where did it go? It was here a minute ago. Just slip-sliding away. Clearly, I must be out of my mind, because a beautiful young woman came over to my home last night and virtually threw herself at me, and I turned her away. Rejected an offer of free, guiltless sex. Or is there such a thing? I told her I needed more time to sort out my mind. Little does she know my mind is so hopelessly shattered, it will never be sorted out. Jeri is truly a good, sweet person, and she seems to care for me. Although, quite frankly, I think she also cares about the $1 million you left me. I would gladly give it to her, or anybody else, if they could give me just one more day and night with you, Jewel. Then I could die happy.
I miss you more than you could ever know.

Love,
Dakin

--------<>--------

A printout of the following email was given to me by Dr. Corena Bissett, albeit somewhat reluctantly. It is inserted here, in its proper chronological place, to provide perspective.
    –David Cunningham

--------<>--------

Subject: follow-up
Date: Sat, 21 Oct 2000 15:46:22
From: Corena Bissett
To: Lt. Dick Najera, Greentree PD

Lt. Najera:

This is a follow-up to our phone conversation of Friday afternoon. As I said, I am not Dakin Caravans' psychotherapist. I am not treating him in any professional way, and we do not have a doctor-patient relationship. We are friends. And I am concerned about him.

I have known Mr. Caravans for more than a year and a half, and in that time, we have had many deep and heartfelt conversations. I have come to know him very well. He is a thoughtful, good, kind and caring person, and among the most interesting men I have ever met. You asked if I thought he was capable of murder, and my answer is most definitely no – assuming he were in his right mind. But my concern now is that Dakin Caravans is teetering on the brink of mental illness. I believe he is suffering from manic disorder. Frankly, I think it has manifested itself as a result of the death of his wife. That would make it highly unlikely that he would have been capable of murdering her. From all that I can determine, I believe he was madly in love with his wife and happier than he had ever been in his entire life. Yes, he was experimenting with altered states of consciousness, but only in a natural way. As far as I know, Dakin hasn't used hallucinogenic drugs since he was a teenager.

Dakin's forays into the field of consciousness were not those of a neophyte explorer. He has been meditating and practicing self-hypnosis for 30 years. He is a knowledgeable and experienced hypnotist, although he preferred to use that discipline on himself rather than as a parlor trick for others. He has studied Zen, yoga and Transcendental Meditation. I know from personal experience – I have seen it – that he can totally control pain with his mind. He can anesthetize any part of his body through simple willpower. I believe he has been toying with some of the more radical and controversial aspects of mind control in recent months, such as astral projection (out-of-body travel). Personally, that's where I parted company with Dakin. I know of no evidence to suggest such a thing is possible. He told me that in his travels around the country with his wife, they sought out fellow mind-travelers and were exposed to "some possibilities that boggle the mind." That's what he said. I don't know exactly what he meant by that.

In any case, I contacted you out of concern for Dakin Caravans' well being, and I trust you will keep our phone conversation and this email in the strictest confidence. My primary concern is that he may be suicidal – it's not uncommon among bipolar disorders – and since I'm in Phoenix, I can't very well take an active, hands-on involvement in his situation. Please contact me at my office or home if there is any way I can be of further assistance.

Sincerely,
Dr. Corena Bissett, Ph.D.

--------<>--------

Chapter Fifteen: Jewel
You're only as good as your word

Background: In January of 2000, Dakin finally proposed to Jewel, and they set a wedding date. Both seemed very happy, but the road was never easy, and the Turn of the Century only changed the nature of their challenges. –David Cunningham

--------◇--------

Subject: A new millennium
Date: Fri, 31 Dec 1999 16:25:39
From: Jewel Halpern
To: Dakin Caravans

Happy New Year, Dakin!

It's the last night of the century, and I won't be with you. Sorry, but I don't like that bar scene anymore, even if your band is playing. I know you guys will put on a good show, but I've heard all those songs a hundred times, and my brother really wanted me to spend New Year's Eve at his house, with his family and their friends. I hope you have fun tonight. It's nice that your band was able to get a good New Year's Eve booking on the last night of the millennium. Something to tell your grandkids, huh? Especially since this is probably your last gig with the Bug Burnett Band. Do they know yet that you accepted a full-time job with the magazine?

I've been thinking a lot today about the turn of the century. I know you don't like to make a big deal about dividing lines between the past and the future, but I think when it comes to something as momentous as this, one should take time for a little reflection. If you can't make resolutions at the turn of the century, when can you?

I've made a lot of mistakes in the 20th century, and I'd like to get a clean slate for the 21st. The past doesn't really exist anyway, right? We spend too much energy fretting over the past and worrying about the future. It keeps us from fully living in the present. I resolve to live each moment as it comes and stop dwelling on things I can't control, like the past. I will "be here now."

Some words to heed on the eve of the new millennium:

"Whatever you can do or dream you can, begin it. Boldness has genius, power and magic in it. Begin it now." – Goethe

"We should have no regrets. The past is finished. There is nothing to be gained by going over it." – Rebecca Beard

"If you don't design your own life plan, chances are you'll fall into someone else's plan. And guess what they have planned for you? Not much." – Jim Rohn

"The highest form of ignorance is when you reject something you don't know anything about." – Wayne Dyer

"Success is simply a matter of luck. Ask any failure." – Unknown

"A free lunch is only found in mousetraps." – John Capuzzi

"Just do it." – Nike advertisement

--------<>--------

Subject: Where are you?
Date: Thu, 13 Jan 2000 17:11:25
From: Dr. Sara Lyman
To: Jewel Halpern

Hello Jewel,

You have missed two consecutive sessions since our last phone conversation, and I want to be sure everything is all right with you. It seems a risky time for you to be withdrawing from therapy, especially since you were having a relapse with the use of painkiller medication.

I hope you will call my office at your earliest convenience and make an appointment. If not, at least please call and let me know how you are doing. I have never looked at you as just another client. You are an accomplished, intelligent woman with a lot to offer.
Dr. Sara Lyman

--------◇--------

Subject: A thousand times yes!!!
Date: Fri, 14 Jan 2000 16:18:39
From: Jewel Halpern
To: Dakin Caravans

To Dakin, the love of life, forever!

Thank you so much for the roses! All the girls in the office were jealous. I still can't believe you really proposed to me, and that we actually have a wedding date. March 19 can't come fast enough. I love you so much, and I want to make you happy for the rest of your life.

Your Supergirl,
Jewel

--------◇--------

Subject: Hello? Anybody home?
Date: Mon, 14 Feb 2000 23:12:41
From: Vivienne Myers
To: Jewel Halpern

Dear Ms. Jewel Halpern soon-to-be-Caravans:

What's up with this? You get engaged to be married and then drop all your old friends like a bad habit? You haven't called or written me in weeks. If your answering machine is working, I think you'll find I have left three messages in the last four weeks. You remember Vivienne Myers? Your best friend from Vermont? The one who nursed you through all those hard times with your first husband, Red the Jerk? That's ME! Pick up the phone! Talk to me, missy!

Viv

--------◇--------

Subject: Re: Hello? Anybody home?
Date: Fri, 25 Feb 2000 18:14:51
From: Jewel Halpern
To: Vivienne Myers

Hi Viv,

Sorry for the long delay in getting back to you – and the unreturned phone messages. I've been struggling with a lot of things lately, and I wasn't in any shape to be talking to anybody as close to me as you are. Actually, maybe that's exactly what I needed.

I finally got what I wanted in my life: Dakin, who asked me to marry him. Everything was going to be perfect. A fairy tale romance, a dream-come-true life. And at the same time we were getting back together and laying the foundation for all that, I was falling back into an addiction to the painkillers. He never knew, until last Friday night. We had a big blowout, and that's why I'm writing you.

The only real progress I made with my addiction was that I learned how to hide it better. Dakin didn't suspect this time until the final 10 days. Twice he noticed I was a little disoriented. On Friday, I think I wanted to get caught. I really overdosed on the stuff. I got really strung out, crying and saying all kinds of weird things that I can't even remember, and then I started to get sick. I mean really sick, vomiting and wailing and shaking. Dakin almost called the paramedics. I finally started to come down, and I probably only survived because I was able to wretch out everything from my insides. It was not a pretty night.

The next morning, Dakin and I talked everything out. I told him I had hit rock bottom, and there was nowhere to go now but up. I vowed never to take another pain pill, and I mean it. I'm done with that forever. I realize now that I truly had an addiction. I can't just pop a couple of pills to handle one stressful afternoon and expect not to crave that high more and more. It's so insidious the way that feeling takes over your entire mind and body.

Our talk was so brutally honest and deep that I know, I really know I am past this. Dakin is on my side. He didn't judge me as weak and throw me out like last time. He said he still wants to marry me and he will stand by me, no matter what, in sickness and in health. He is crazy, of course, but I love him for that. We're a team, pulling in the same direction. We both want me to be healthy. And I will make it so.

So that's why I haven't called or written lately. I've had a monkey on my back. But the sky is clearing now. We are turning the page. Let's see, can I think of any more clichés? Here comes the sun. Haste makes waste. He who hesitates is lost. Thank you for being a friend.

I'll call you this week.
Jewel

PS: Here is Jewel's new motto:

"Fall seven times, stand up eight." (Japanese proverb)

---------◇---------

Subject: Never again
Date: Sun, 27 Feb 2000 10:32:16
From: Jewel Halpern
To: Dakin Caravans

Dakin, my love,

Consider this another apology for the pain and grief I caused you with my addiction. I believe it will be the final apology of this kind I ever have to make, but as they say in NA, one day at a time.

My heart is heavy for the things I have done. The reason why we only had a few spectacularly great weeks together before things started to go south again is because very quickly I became re-addicted. I think of all the times you knew there was too much pill-popping ... I should have stopped, but I didn't know how. I guess I was afraid to stop. Maybe you wouldn't like the real Jewel ... the one who wasn't a party girl, who didn't travel all over the place, the one who didn't dress in revealing clothes, the one who wasn't a stereotypical California girl ... would you love plain old girl-next-door, Vermont Jewel?

My life now is just like it was in Vermont, except I live in California. I don't take drugs or drink alcohol at all ... no desire at all ... it makes me ill to think of all the damage it caused, and I can't believe I put all that poison into my system. I look forward to a healthy night's sleep. I have a lot of pain and guilt over what I've done to you. ... and us. I treated you so disrespectfully. I didn't guard and protect what I cherished most of all ... our relationship. All over a drug. All of the fights, the disagreements, the tension, the hostility, the unkind words, the loveless nights, all over a drug. Some people have to learn lessons the hard way, and, yes, I'm the ultimate example.

I'm going to be better than the person you found when you tracked me down after 20-some years apart ... We can recapture that magic we felt as teenagers, and that magic that we stirred up again in 1996. Life has many lessons, and I'm learning. If you truly are to become my husband, I want to be my best at being your wife, friend and lover.

I love you,
Jewel

--------<>--------

Subject: Welcome back!
Date: Thu, 09 Mar 2000 08:33:41
From: Spider Juncal
To: Jewel Halpern

Jewel!!!

I KNEW you would come back to us in the Narc Anon group! It was destiny! There is a Higher Power at work here, and your business is unfinished! I look forward to hearing you speak again at our meetings! I anxiously await more of your letters to God, more of your beautiful and blessed presence!

I do have one word of caution, however ... understand, this is just from one friend to another ... I have no ulterior motives ... but your decision to get married to Dakin Caravans may be a mistake! After all these months, I think I know you pretty well now, and I honestly believe it was him, and your messed-up relationship with him, that led you down the path of drug addiction! You are better, healthier and happier on your own! I have seen it! Plus, I truly believe you are destined for bigger and better things, perhaps even world-changing things! You have said that you felt it yourself! Stay with that feeling! Love it! Embrace it! Don't let yourself be trapped in some humdrum, ordinary man-woman relationship, when you could be leading God's flock on its path toward the Promised Land! Did Jesus take a spouse? He did not!

Whatever you decide, I am your loyal friend and disciple,
Spider Juncal

"Beware of false prophets, who come to you in sheep's clothing, but inwardly are ravening wolves." (Matthew 7:15)

"We are as gods, and we might as well get good at it." (Whole Earth Catalog)

--------◇--------

Subject: A new life
Date: Sun, 12 Mar 2000 10:25:39
From: Dakin Caravans
To: Jewel Halpern

My precious Jewel,

I am so excited about how things are coming together for us. The new condo is perfect in every way – size, location, floor plan, etc. We'll be very happy there.

I wanted to write you and say a few words about how I feel as our wedding day approaches. I can't always express myself well when speaking off the top of my head, so I'm more comfortable writing. I hope that doesn't lessen its impact.

I want you to know how I really feel about you. I haven't expressed it much because you and I have been through a lot of turmoil over the last few years, and I could understand if you sometimes doubted my love and commitment to you. Frankly, I doubted it myself for a while. I questioned whether you would ever kick your addiction and get your priorities and life in order. And I believe now that I should have tried harder to help you, rather than threatening to break up with you all the time. It's easier to run than fight, sometimes. I apologize for my running.

I'm with you now. Forever. We'll be married one week from today, and to me, that's a sacred bond. I take it very seriously. I will NOT run away if you ever have problems again. I want you to know that I am your friend as well as your lover and husband-to-be. We are human beings, and that comes with built-in frailties. We crack, and sometimes we break. But we can be put back together again, and as long as we never give up, we can become stronger than ever – especially if we stick together. I'll watch your back. You watch mine. We'll make it through.

I've never known anyone like you. I knew you were special from the first moment I saw your face. It's like there's an aura around you, like you are magical. You are deeper, more complex, more beautiful, more loving, more intuitive, more interesting, more intelligent and more spiritual than any woman I've ever known. Having known you and loved you – and having been loved back by you – has left me hopelessly addicted (sorry if that's a poor choice of words). I can't even conceive of a life without you now. I rejoice that you have accepted my marriage proposal.

I'm happier than I've ever been in my life, and you're the reason.

I love you,
Dakin

--------◇--------

Subject: Dear God letter
Date: Sun, 12 Mar 1999 11:55:20
From: Jewel Halpern
To: Dr. Sara Lyman

Dear God:

Thank you for rescuing me. Thank you for sending me back to Dr. Lyman and back to Narcotics Anonymous. Thank you for showing me the error of my ways and putting me back on track. Thank you, Father, for all you have blessed me with. But most importantly, God, thank you for sending Dakin back into my life.

I've been through so much in my 46 years, it amazes me that I'm still here, still whole, still able to have a positive, healthy and happy future. But I also realize, thanks to you, God, that it's not about me. It should never be about self. My ego has gotten in my way one too many times, and I need to move past that.

In one week, Dakin and I will be married. It will be the final, most blessed and happy chapter in my life. It's a conclusion. It is coming full circle. I was a young girl when I met Dakin, and he became my first love. Now he becomes my last love. Everybody should be so lucky. There is symmetry to this, a kind of perfection. No, our relationship hasn't always been perfect. We've both made mistakes, proving beyond all reasonable doubt that we're both human. But our relationship is forged by fire, and that makes it strong as steel. When you've been to hell and back with someone, they become your friend for life. Nothing can ever tear us apart again. We're two halves of the same whole.

We're talking about quitting our jobs, buying a motor home and spending the rest of our lives traveling around the country. It's sort of symbolic. The destination is not so important as the journey. Maybe that's the answer to those Big Questions Dakin has always pursued. It's the search that matters. The Quest. No matter what you achieve at the other end of your quest, it will always be an anticlimax. Enjoy the journey, because for most of us, that's all you'll ever have.

If you walk with God, your journey will always be blessed.

Your faithful daughter,
Jewel

--------<>--------

Subject: God's letter
Date: Sun, 12 Mar 1999 12:52:55
From: Jewel Halpern
To: Dr. Sara Lyman

Dear Jewel:

Remember in the *Wizard of Oz* when the good witch tells Dorothy that the power to go home was always within her? So it is with you. The power to find peace, harmony, love and serenity is not in some guru, preacher, book or inspirational tape. It is within you. It has always been there. All you have to do is unlock the door and let it free.

You have been your own worst enemy. The path you chose was a difficult and treacherous one, but you negotiated every step and survived. You now stand ready to move to the next level. You would not be prepared for what lies ahead if you hadn't suffered through all that you have. It was a necessary process. No one comes to the Kingdom of Heaven on a free pass. It must be earned. Some find the answers more easily than others, and many never find them at all. But you, Jewel, are on the doorstep. You can be a conduit. You can help others find their way. You're not here to satisfy yourself. It was never about you. It's about love, and love can never exist in a vacuum. You must open your heart enough to love everyone, including and most especially yourself.

God = love ... love = energy ... energy = life ... life = God. It all flows in a circle, replenishing itself forever.

You and Dakin are about to embark on a quest for enlightenment, but remember that enlightenment is not a change, but simply a recognition. What you seek has been there all along. There are no new revelations. You will not find the Holy Grail or a list of commandments that Moses never saw. You won't discover some hidden truth that no human has ever considered before. Don't make that your quest.

Instead, live and love every moment of every day. Keep your mind, heart and eyes wide open. The Christ-mind is simply that of unconditional love. That's it. There are no other lessons to learn. If your journey is a search for any truth beyond that, every mile will weigh heavily, and you will grow weary and frustrated. But if your life is lived every day with unconditional love, you will leave stardust wherever you walk, and from those seeds will grow a new era for mankind.

Watch what happens to the world when you walk through it with unconditional love. You soften and open up like a flower. And the world responds by softening and opening up to you. I speak not only in metaphors, but reality. Your face will change. The muscles will relax, and your worry lines will gradually melt away. Your skin will take on a smooth and healthy shine. You will literally radiate love, and it will become contagious, affecting those around you. Your life will improve, and so will the lives of those you touch. You can, literally, heal the sick. You will perform miracles.

Jewel, your past is over. It can't touch you now. From this moment forward, you are changed. You are filled with unconditional love. Your only purpose is to spread this message not with words, but with deeds. Touch everyone you meet, and touch them with love. Let them see inside your heart. You don't have to force people to see the light. In fact, it can't be done with force. Human nature being what it is, if you show a person something wonderful, he will steal it. So, give him a glimpse of what unconditional love is all about. Then let human nature take over.

May you walk in love and peace,
God

-------◇--------

Chapter Sixteen: Dakin
No education is ever complete

Background: Dr. Corena Bissett felt that Dakin's narrative emails to her played a vital role in helping him keep his mental equilibrium during this period. They served as a personal journal that allowed him to vent the dangerous emotions roiling inside him.

–David Cunningham

---------◇---------

Subject: The beat goes on
Date: Mon, 23 Oct 2000 08:29:58
From: Dakin Caravans
To: Corena Bissett

Good morning, Dr. Doolittle,

I've been doing Internet searches on bipolar and manic disorders, and I suspect you might be right about me...which actually means I'm fine, because a truly insane person doesn't know he is insane. So if I accept your diagnosis, then I must have full command of my faculties and in reality be perfectly sane. Right? But I appreciate your concern. Seriously, Corena, you've been a better friend to me in this last month than anyone else on the planet, and I love you for it.

So return with me now to the Story of Dakin and Jewel, in which our heroes begin their Quest. This is the fun part. We were married on March 19 in the back seat of a white limousine at a drive-thru chapel in Las Vegas. As you drive up to the window, they actually have a sign with a menu – photos $29, roses $15, extra cheese $1. It was a McWedding, with the pastor leaning out of the drive-up window, Bible in hand. After the "service," he told us he appreciated that we took the recitation of our vows seriously. I guess most of his clients are drunk and giggling.

But for us, a quickie wedding just seemed practical. Both of us had been married before and we were in our mid-40s, so we weren't going to have all our family and friends come bearing gifts. The ceremony was just a dividing line between being single and married, and a technical one at that. We had already crossed into being emotionally and spiritually committed to each other. We just needed the government to recognize it, so we got our piece of paper in Nevada and tied the knot at a joint where people often ask, "Can I get fries with that?" and think they're funny.

Back in California, Jewel and I soon decided there was no point in continuing to go to work every day, come home exhausted and live for our weekend "dates," which would consist of dinner and a movie. Hasn't that been done before? Our active years were limited, and since she had the money to make it happen, we decided to buy that motor home and become the Happy Wanderers.

I taught Jewel how to meditate and exposed her to some concepts and Eastern philosophies she wasn't familiar with, and it seemed to open a whole universe of possibilities in her mind. Eventually, she started gravitating toward frothy New-Age stuff and a lot of wild ideas in which I never placed much stock. As far as I'm concerned, if a theory doesn't have any compelling evidence, it doesn't merit more than a passing glance. But Jewel grew fascinated with ESP, psychokinesis, Chakras, the third eye, auras, crystals, pyramids, channeling and even UFOs. Our journey across the country, then, was to be a search for truth.

So we quit our jobs, locked up the condo in Irvine and pointed our luxury motor home toward Giant Rock, a cosmic spot in the Mojave Desert near Yucca Valley. This is where a man named George Van Tassel once channeled with a space alien named "Lo," who I think spoke a kind of broken English through Van Tassel's mouth. Van Tassel presided over conventions of UFO nuts (excuse me, "believers") for 20 years at Giant Rock. I wanted to see the place because of the giant rock that gave the area its name. I've always been interested in geology. Jewel wanted to see if she could detect any mystical vibrations there. The rock is indeed huge and impressive. But there's not much else worth seeing. All that's left of the Giant Rock Café are sand-covered floor tiles. Jewel felt no vibrations. We saw this weird domed building that Van Tassel built and called The Integratron, but it was surrounded by barbed wire, and we couldn't go inside. I heard that the Integratron had become a methamphetamine lab after Van Tassel died, and that two unsolved murders were somehow linked to activities inside the domed building. We left without solving anything.

In a little desert town called Joshua Tree, we sought out something called "The Institute of Metaphysics." We had heard that a Rev. Dingle was running the institute to push a philosophy that mixed various Hindu beliefs with ancient Gnostic Christian heresy. The buildings, which included a round structure with a tall spike, were designed by Lloyd Wright, son of the legendary architect Frank Lloyd Wright. We saw signs indicating a Meditation Center, a Church of Mystic Christianity, and even something called a Caravansary of Joy (that got my attention). But everything was locked up, and nobody answered any of our knocks.

We moved on. I love driving in the desert, especially at dawn and dusk. Way in the back of your mind, you're a little scared, because you know if you break down out there, you could be in serious trouble. You conjure up images of skeletons half-buried in the sand holding dry canteens. But the wide-open spaces are spectacular in their starkness. You look at the jagged rocks and stubborn little cacti and become filled with respect for the tenacity of life.

And at night, the stars! I felt a physical thrill at seeing the nighttime sky in the middle of the desert, far from city lights. I spent hours outside with my telescope, and just as many hours gazing up with the naked eye. I wonder how many people know that you can see our own galaxy, the Milky Way, out there in the desert night? I gaze at the marvelous stardust that looks like a backbone across the sky, realize that I am looking edge-on at our galaxy, and am overwhelmed by the majesty. I'm looking at a structure too impossibly huge for my feeble mind to comprehend.

The distance between any two stars I could choose, no matter how close they appear to me, is so vast as to scramble a brain, and here I was looking at, what, thousands? Tens of thousands of stars? And all I can see from my vantage point is an infinitesimally tiny fraction of the universe. To say that we are bit players on the universal stage is vastly overstating our importance.

We set out to find truth, and for me, a hint of it melted over my consciousness as I looked up at more star systems than I had ever seen before. Einstein said his sense of God was his sense of awe at the universe. I'm not sure I really believe in a traditional God, but I believe if a man wants to get an idea of his true place in the scheme of things, he needs merely to look up.

As far as Jewel was concerned, our search was just beginning. We headed north, stopping briefly in Las Vegas for a second honeymoon two months after our first, then toward Yellowstone. I'd visited the park as a boy and wanted to see if it still could hold my fascination. It did. Have you ever been? When you see a geyser like Old Faithful, it seems like some kind of trick at first. Must be a pump in the ground. Disneyland does stuff like this all the time. What's the big deal, a fountain of water shoots up? Seen it in Vegas. But after a few days in the park, the magic starts to sink in. This is natural. You smell the sulfur and see hot, bubbling pools and beautiful stone formations and realize that truth really is stranger than fiction. What must the first explorers have thought when they wandered into this land and saw nature running amok? In some areas of the park, you feel like you're in the mountains of Anywhere, USA, with prerequisite pine trees, picturesque scenery and the occasional moose, but then the geysers and hot pools and stinky air belching from the earth make you realize the world is a more remarkable place than you ever dreamed possible.

But if my search for meaning took me toward astronomy and geology, Jewel's led her toward people. Wherever we camped, she found new friends. By day, we explored, and by night, we sat around campfires and talked with friends we didn't know the day before. Whether we talked about silly little things or deep philosophy, we loved every minute of it. For Jewel, the purpose of life was to reach out and touch someone. She had so much love in her heart, and she gave it freely to everyone she met. We sat up late and traded ideas with free spirits like ourselves, people who had lived full, rich lives and were happy to share what they had learned. Slowly, I was converting to Jewel-ism. It WAS about people, not things.

Eventually we decided to head toward the heartland, in search of human contact and new ideas. First, we headed down to Boulder, Colorado. This, we had been told, was a very high place, and not just in altitude. We started with a massage that was more than a massage. They called it bodyworking, and it involved a total connection with the mind and body. We did it three times, and each day we walked out of there feeling like our minds and bodies were vibrating on the same frequency as everything good in the world. It was one of the more amazing natural highs I've ever felt.

We also looked into biofeedback in Boulder. We'd heard that it not only helped with achieving consistency in one's pursuit of the alpha state, but it could also cure addictions. It sounded a lot like the same process as hypnosis to me. They wanted to place a trigger response in Jewel's brain so that the ingestion of an addictive painkiller medication such as Vicodin would produce a violent reaction in her stomach and make her instantly vomit. I had no doubt they could do it. I also had no doubt I could do the same thing to her with hypnosis, and it would be a lot cheaper. In any event, Jewel had completely kicked her addiction, so we didn't delve any further into biofeedback.

We headed out of Boulder thinking that it was indeed a very high place, but the most mystical thing about it was that Mork and Mindy used to live there.

We eventually drove through the Texas panhandle and into Oklahoma, where we got caught in a tornado. I told you about this before, but ohmigod, what an experience. We were just outside of a town called Foss and the weather was getting very scary. When the sky turned a yellow-green, I knew we should start looking for funnel clouds. We didn't see it until it was almost on top of us. It came from behind and to the right of our motor home, and it was huge. You know how they say it sounds like a freight train? It does – only louder and sort of unearthly. A scream. It was both beautiful and terrifying. I couldn't tell how far it was from our RV. A hundred yards? A mile? It was hard to judge, because I wasn't sure how big it really was. But it had to be close, because we were being pummeled by a tremendous wind. I stopped for fear of being blown over, and the tornado passed us on the right, illegally, and continued toward a path of destruction ahead. We sat there and stared in silence as it moved away. Jewel was shivering. I had all this adrenaline rushing through my system that had nothing to do, and it hurt.

This, too, was part of our search for meaning. A brush with death gives you remarkable clarity as to what really matters. We waited until we could no longer see the twister, and then proceeded slowly down the road. In Foss, the destruction was frightening. People were still buried in structures that were destroyed. Without one word of discussion between us, we got out of the RV and helped. Jewel and I pulled three people out of a collapsed apartment building and used the first-aid kit in our motor home to dress their wounds. We walked up to a fire captain to offer our help, and he drafted us to become part of a human chain that moved through the swath of destruction looking for victims. Eight people died in Foss that day, and we found one of them. It was a young girl, not more than 11, who was impaled on a tree branch ... a sight one never forgets, no matter how hard one tries. Not even Jewel's training and experience as a police officer could keep back her tears.

We stayed in Foss for a week, doing whatever we could. Sometimes we just helped people sort through their shattered homes for personal belongings, other times we hung out at the impromptu Red Cross shelter and handed out blankets. In the evenings, Jewel entertained the homeless by playing her guitar and singing folk songs of hope and help and humanity. This was as meaningful a week as we ever lived. People needed help, and we offered it. Jewel's sweet songs of comfort brought life to the eyes of some of those people. Whether she knew it or not, Jewel was a godsend to those victims.

What a contrast we found in our next stop – New Orleans. I'd visited the city just once, for one night, and wanted to taste its flavor a little more deeply. What a corrupt place! Maybe we didn't hit the right spots, but for my money, New Orleans and the famous French Quarter are about drinking, throwing up, drinking, hedonistic sex in the alleys, drinking, jazz music and drinking. Oh, and did I mention throwing up? Our scheduled two-week stay lasted three days. I couldn't get out of there fast enough. So now what are we going to do? We're going to Disneyworld!

We had to visit Orlando, because it's the law. The Tourist Center of the Universe may not be as corrupt as New Orleans, but it holds no god before money. Disney and Universal Studios are actually very entertaining and worthwhile excursions, as long as you have about two weeks to do it and a million dollars in the bank. Fortunately, we had both. We had a good time. A street called International Drive is fascinating, too, as an example of what capitalism would be like if it were allowed to breed. The street is tourist hell or tourist paradise, depending on your point of view. One of the buildings on International Drive is upside down. It looks like it was picked up by a giant and dropped. They did that on purpose. The whole area is expensive eye candy.

Once when I was in Las Vegas, I dropped a $10 chip, and almost before it hit the carpet, a casino janitor swept it into his dustpan and escaped into the night. That's what Orlando's International Drive reminded me of. Drop a coin, and you'll never see it again. But it was still fun.

And then, as if the tornado wasn't enough, we experienced a hurricane. We wanted to see the Atlantic Ocean at Daytona Beach, and we rolled into town just as everyone else was rolling out. Adamo was on his way, a relatively small hurricane that was predicted to miss the coast and turn out to sea. Evacuation was voluntary. We stayed, like the California New-Age idiots we were. Hurricane Adamo's eye didn't focus on Daytona Beach, but most of his left side did, and the town was wind-whipped and flooded. The RV was undamaged because we were smart enough to stay away from the storm surge, but it was still a harrowing experience ... unbelievably fierce winds, sideways rain, large pieces of trees flying. So now, I've experienced earthquakes, floods, a tornado and a hurricane. Why go on living? What could possibly top that?

We wanted to stay and help victims in Daytona Beach, but there wasn't much we could do. Nobody was hurt, and damage was limited to flooding along the coast, broken windows and a few homes stripped of their roofs. We moved on.

After experiencing The Finger of God in Oklahoma and Florida, we saw the best in people come out as they grappled with the raw realities of life. But we still hadn't answered those big questions. Why are we here? What's the point if your life could be snuffed out in a millisecond? What really matters? How should the good, fully evolved life be lived?

We would get closer to our answers back in Arizona and California, as we moved nearer to home.

Until I ramble on uncontrollably again, I remain your faithful friend and servant,
Dakin Caravans

--------<>--------

Subject: To the Storm Chaser
Date: Tue, 24 Oct 2000 10:13:22
From: Corena Bissett
To: Dakin Caravans

Hi Dakin,

Wow, I never realized you had so many adventures on the road with Jewel. The few times you mentioned it to me, you always made it sound more like a spiritual journey. What comes next, parachute skiing in the Himalayas? Outrunning lava flows in the Philippines? Lunch with Bigfoot?

Listen, have you thought any more about what I said the other night about manic disorder? I honestly think you should be seeing someone who at least can make a professional judgment of your mental condition. Don't be afraid of it. I think you have some symptoms that are potentially troubling, but I also think it's related to Jewel's death, and that with time and a little professional help, you'll be fine.

I also think you should consider thinking of Lt. Najera as a friend, someone who is committed to resolving any mysteries connected with Jewel's death. If there were drugs involved, his people can find out and clear up any nagging doubts you might have. As long as you had nothing to do with her death (and I believe you when you say you didn't), then you have nothing to fear. Don't resist the police department's efforts to tie up all the loose ends. There's no need for you to add paranoia to your shopping list of disorders.

Just remember my definition of psychopath: "The road nut taken." (I also define a psychopath as "going through California to get to Florida from Vermont, which seems a lot like your travels with Jewel).

And no matter how screwed up you get, you'll never be as bad off as these so-called leaders of society, who actually said these words:

"The police are not here to create disorder. They're here to preserve disorder." – former Chicago mayor Richard Daley.

"It is wonderful to be here in the great state of Chicago." – former Vice President Dan Quayle.

"The Internet is a great way to get on the net." – Republican Presidential candidate Bob Dole.

"Smoking kills, and if you're killed, you've lost a very important part of your life." – anti-smoking spokesperson Brooke Shields.

"The President has kept all of the promises he intended to keep." – Clinton aide George Stephanopolous, speaking on Larry King Live.

"Traditionally, most of Australia's imports come from overseas." – former Australian Cabinet Minister Keppel Enderbery.

"We're going to turn this team around 360 degrees." – Jason Kidd, after being drafted by the Dallas Mavericks.

"I'm not going to have some reporters pawing through our papers. We are the President." – Hillary Clinton commenting on the release of subpoenaed documents.

"China is a big country, inhabited by many Chinese." – former French President, Charles De Gaulle.

And my personal favorite:

"Things are more like they are now than they ever were before." – former President Dwight D. Eisenhower.

Enjoy,
Corena

--------<>--------

Subject: all's well
Date: Tue, 24 Oct 2000 11:16:44
From: Jeri Starrette
To: Dakin Caravans

hey dakin,

don't worry about the other night, i'm not mad. i understand. it's just too soon for you. i can tell you're still dealing with a lot of mental issues, and i want you to know that i'm on your side. i want you to think of me as a friend, and if you want to talk, i'm there for you. if you want anything else ... ;-) ... i'm there for you, too ... i'm home tonight if you want to call ... listen, i got tickets to the bacon brothers concert in anaheim saturday night. two tickets, and no one to go with. are you interested? it's kevin bacon, the actor, and his brother. i've got one of their cds, and they're really good (surprising for an actor, huh?) ...

love,
jeri

```
                    .  $$$$
                    ,  , ( ( ($
                    -        ?
                   \=_      :
                     \     \_
                   _/|T_____//  \_
                _/    (o  o  o  (  |    \
           __./ \    /  \o  o  o\|\     \_
        _/_)-\o__/    \o  o  o|  >/_    \.
       /|/  '           )o  o  o:_     \__o/
                       /o  o  o  o  \       \\
                    _/o  o  o  o  o  \    /  )
                 _/ o/\_o_o  o  o  \   |\\
               ( o / /    /o  o  o )
               '-( (  (.    ( o  o  o(
               /o\ \        )  o  o  o\
               |o  o\ \      |o_o_o/
               '_o  -\ \ |_
                    \_\_T)
                     \ \ |
          _____|/|/_____b'ger
         |||||||||||||||||||||||||||||
```

here i am, waiting on pins and needles for your answer, please say yes...

--------<>--------

Chapter Seventeen: Jewel
There is no limit in the universe

Background: During the time Dakin and Jewel were traveling around the country, Jewel's email address received 22 messages from Spider Juncal, none of which she answered. For the sake of brevity, we reproduce just two of them later in this chapter. Most of them carried the same message – a plaintive plea for Jewel to contact him.
  –David Cunningham

--------◇--------

Subject: Hello from the Road Warriors
Date: Mon, 12 Jun 2000 07:45:18
From: Jewel Halpern-Caravans
To: Vivienne Myers

To my long-lost but forever friend, Viv –

Sorry it's been such a long time, but as I told you on the phone in April, Dakin and I are on the road almost constantly now, and I can't just walk into the den anymore and turn on the computer. We bought this laptop to take on the trip, but we've been so busy with so many adventures that we haven't bothered very often to find a land line and hook up to check our messages. I'm going to try to call you Sunday night, because I have so many stories to tell.

Did you hear about Hurricane Adamo, which grazed through Daytona Beach on Friday? We were right in the middle of it. Well, most of the hurricane was out at sea, but a pretty strong edge of it whipped through the town, and we experienced a lot of wind and driving rain, plus a lot of debris flying through the air. Exciting, but only because we didn't experience any damage to the RV. I can see how a stronger hurricane making a direct hit could be disastrous.

I was more frightened of the tornado we saw in Oklahoma in late April. It was an F3 or F4, which is a powerful twister, and it snuck up behind our RV and raced past us, pelting us with branches and dust. We escaped without damage, but then the tornado ripped through the town ahead of us and killed eight people. Dakin and I stayed a week to help out. It was quite an experience. I'll tell you all about it on Sunday.

We're thinking of heading up the East Coast toward Vermont, so you'll finally get to meet Dakin. Our plans change from day to day, but I'll let you know where we're headed.

Got to run, but I hope you're home when I call. I miss you.

Your forever friend,
Jewel

--------◇--------

Subject: I'll be here
Date: Tue, 13 Jun 2000 20:37:21
From: Vivienne Myers
To: Jewel Halpern-Caravans

So there really IS a Jewel Caravans!

I was beginning to wonder. Thanks for the message. Sounds like you guys are dragging trouble in your wake. You bring a tornado into Oklahoma and then a hurricane to Florida? Please, PLEASE don't come to Vermont. I'm sure the minute you arrive, the Connecticut River will overflow its banks and flood Brattleboro under 10 feet of water. And you'll sit there taking pictures and making stupid tourist comments, then get in your motor home and drive to some other state you can destroy.

Of course I'll be home on Sunday. I look forward to your call. I hope you really do get up to Vermont. I can't wait to meet this middle-aged hunk of yours. He must be an incredibly patient and understanding man to put up with all your shenanigans. We can show him all your old haunts. I think Red Bjerke still works in town, maybe you could ... oh, never mind.
I'm so jealous of your lifestyle. When do I get to retire and drive around the country in an RV?

Talk to you Sunday,
Viv

--------◇--------

Subject: Please write!
Date: Tue, 13 June 2000 18:31:26
From: Spider Juncal
To: Jewel Halpern-Caravans

Dear Jewel,

We miss you at NA, but I'm sure you're having a wonderful time traveling around the country! I have a favor to ask! Could you send us emails from the road and give us a travelogue of your adventures? Man, it would mean a lot to those friends you left behind – most especially me! As beautifully as you write, and with the deep messages you bring, you could do a great service by giving us your insights!

I await your positive response,
Spider Juncal

"And the gospel must first be preached unto all the nations." (Mark 13:10)

"Life, man, is a gas." (Lou Rawls)

--------◇--------

Subject: I beseech thee!
Date: Mon, 07 Aug 2000 18:31:26
From: Spider Juncal
To: Jewel Halpern-Caravans

Jewel!

I know you're out there somewhere!

I don't know how long I can continue writing emails without getting answers! I hope Dakin hasn't driven that RV of yours off a bridge somewhere and robbed the world of its most precious asset! Jewel, I need to discuss something with you, and I really wish you would write me back! I have been reading over my copies of your Dear God letters and your journal, and I think they could be assembled into a GREAT book! Dude, this could be one of those spiritual guidance books that are so big today! But I need your permission to start pursuing it! I don't know what to do if you don't get in touch with me!

Still awaiting some sign that you're alive,

Spider

"Thou hast seen it, O Jehovah; keep not silence: O Lord, be not far from me." (Psalms 35:22)

"At least talk to each other. To communicate is the beginning of understanding." (AT&T advertisement)

--------<>--------

Subject: Dear God letter
Date: Sat, 16 Sept 2000 24:31:34
From: Jewel Halpern-Caravans
To: Dr. Sara Lyman

Dear Sara:

Hi, remember me? It's been a long time, but I'm back in California, after a long, life-changing journey around the country, and last night, I wrote a Dear God letter, my first since before Dakin and I were married. We've been on the road for five months, and our quest has taken us full circle. We were in Laguna Beach today, and next week, we might even head back to the old neighborhood in Greentree to get in touch with our roots. Part of the point of this trip was to find ourselves, and I think it'll help to awaken our youth and bring it into harmony with our adult minds.

After writing the Dear God letter, I thought, why not send it to Dr. Lyman? You helped me so much in those crazy times, and I want you to see where my head is at now. I'm not a finished product, but I've come a long way, and I thank you so much for your role in it. Here's what I wrote:

Dear God,

I recently learned that the word "Buddha" simply means someone who has awakened to his or her true nature.

This is what I have been chasing my whole life. It's what Dakin and I have been pursuing over the last five months as we traveled from coast to coast and from Canada to Mexico. I feel closer to my true nature than ever, and I believe that if I'm not a Buddha yet, I'll be one soon.

I have a calling now, a purpose. I'm here to help others. I'm here to love. To give love. To be love. Dakin and I have done a lot of loving since we hit the road ... loving of each other, and loving of our fellow man. We helped tornado victims in Oklahoma. We filled sandbags to help a neighborhood prepare for a flood in Texas. We gave blood in Mississippi. We helped build a church in Mexico. We gave money to a nonprofit center for the arts in Colorado. We worked the chow line at a homeless shelter in Seattle.

We don't do these things to win points on God's scoreboard. We do them because they must be done, and if not us, then who? There aren't enough hands helping those in need. Heck, who ISN'T in need at some time? Dakin thinks it's kind of pointless to spend so much time at places like the homeless shelter. He says we'll never solve the problem, and all we can do is put a bandage on it. He prefers the work we did with storm victims. He says it's worthwhile if our efforts help one person get back on his feet and become a contributing member of society. That's the conservative in him talking. I don't think about the big picture like that. I see one person who needs help, and I help. Even if my blood just helps a diseased person live one more day, that's good enough for me. I can't help everybody. But maybe I can be an example. If more people took an interest in their neighbors and reached out when help was needed, then maybe it wouldn't seem so hopeless. All we have is each other. There's no one else.

I wonder, God, if you have a negative effect on people sometimes. It seems as if they expect you to solve all their big problems, so they don't really try to solve them on their own. Dakin used to say that religion is a crutch, and maybe some people DO use it to help them limp through life. For me, God, my spiritual awakening hasn't been a crutch at all ... more like a rocket engine that has blasted me into parts of the universe I never dreamed existed.

What I have learned these last five months, God, is that you come in many different flavors. You are everywhere and everything. You are Judaism. You are Catholicism. You are Taoist, Baptist, Muslim. You are Moses, Jesus, Muhammad and Buddha. You are Jewel, and you are Dakin. You are love. Pure and simple.

I don't know if God is in me or I am in God, but we are one. We are love. The only way to spread the word of God is to spread love, and it doesn't matter what flavor you use, as long as the love is genuine. Throughout history, people have committed horrible acts in your name, but that wasn't you. If it's not love, it's not God.

Our journey hasn't taken us just to places. It has taken us to ideas. For this, I have Dakin to thank. He's always searching for answers he knows he'll never find. But the search has been exhilarating.

In Arizona, we connected to nature through the Sedona Vortex Energy and learned how to find our soul-purpose in thoughts, words and deeds. In Big Sur, we visited Esalen and learned about intuitive development and comparative religions. We even took a martial arts course. In Laguna Beach, we studied yoga and how to use Zen in art. From Colorado to Florida to Vermont to New Mexico and California, we explored Buddhism, the power of flow, automatic writing, cosmology and astral projection.

I have A LOT more to say about astral projection, or out-of-body experiences. I'll save that for another letter.

Your devoted daughter,
Jewel

--------<>--------

Subject: hello out there
Date: Sun, 17 Sep 2000 16:07:11
From: Vivienne Myers
To: Jewel Halpern-Caravans

Hey Missy,

It was great to see you again. Hope your trip back to California was less eventful than your first couple months on the road. I can't get over how much you've changed. I don't know if it's Dakin's influence or just living in that far-out, cool-dude, space-cadet state of California, but you're on a different planet now. Not worse, just different. I'm happy to hear you're eating all natural and healthy now, and you look like you're in the best physical shape of your life. Even better than when you got out of the police academy.

You just scared me a little with your, um, "preoccupation" with things like crystals, pyramids and mind trips. You're like a combination of a backwoods nutty-crunchy earth mother and a surf-zombie psychic friend. And I mean that in the nicest possible way.

Dakin seems like a real good guy, and you both looked very happy, so I'm happy for you. Please keep in touch. I want to hear every chapter in Jewel's search for the Lost Ark of the Covenant. (Did you look under the bed?)

Your partner in crime and friend indeed,
Viv

--------<>--------

Subject: Welcome back
Date: Mon, 18 Sep 2000 10:03:48
From: Dr. Sara Lyman
To: Jewel Halpern-Caravans

Hi Jewel,

I was very happy to see your message. I love it when former clients touch base with me. We don't like to send people out into the world and

213

never hear from them again. It sounds like you've had some fascinating adventures. If you're ever in town and want to meet for lunch some day, call my office. Now that you've solved your own problems and are solving those of the rest of the world, maybe you can help me with mine. Shrinks are the looniest people on the planet.

Sincerely,

Sara Lyman

--------<>--------

Subject: can you dig it?
Date: Thu, 21 Sep 2000 22:59:04
From: Jewel Halpern-Caravans
To: Spider Juncal

Hi Spider,

I apologize for not answering all your emails. I got them, but I didn't think it was appropriate to be corresponding with you while Dakin and I were on our "extended honeymoon," for lack of a better term. He's a little peculiar about my contact with other men.

I don't think it's a good idea to publish anything I've written, especially the Dear God letters. Those and my journal entries are very private, and I never intended them to be read by anyone except Dr. Lyman and you. The only reason I gave copies to you was because you seem to understand. Dakin was never as messed up as I was, but since you've been through addiction and recovery and spirituality, you always seemed to get it. That's why I'm writing you now. I have to tell somebody about this.

Have you ever heard of astral projection? They also call it out-of-body experience. Spider, I can do it! I've been taking these incredible trips outside of my body, and it's real! These things are not just in my imagination. Dakin and I learned about this in Sedona, Arizona, which is this highly cool town where anything is possible. The people are just a little more evolved there. We also went to seminars on astral projection in Big Sur and Laguna Beach.

Of all the dimensions, the astral is closest to the physical. I think it's where God lives. In fact, I think it IS God. The astral dimension contains all the thoughts, memories, knowledge, fantasies and dreams of every living thing. They exist like a huge data bank that holds the world's entire collective consciousness.

We're all connected to the astral dimension, but very few realize it. Imagine an umbilical cord coming out of your head and leading to Heaven. This is what joins you to the web of life. Every living thing comes out of that web when it's born, and every living thing goes back to the web when it dies. While our bodies are alive, the invisible umbilical cord keeps us connected to that web, which is in the astral dimension. You can call that web anything you want – Heaven, Nirvana, the circle of life – they're just words. I call it God. From this dimension, all consciousness springs forth.

It explains so many things that people label as paranormal. Think about ESP. How can a mother 3,000 miles away instantly know her son has had an accident and needs help? Because both of them have an open link to the web, and they have a direct line into each other, being of the same blood. This kind of stuff happens all the time. Psychics don't know how or why they get "messages from the other side," they just know they do. It's because their link to the web is a little stronger than anyone else's. But we're all connected, and anyone can learn how to use it.

You can think of the Internet as a model of the astral dimension. All the world's information is hovering out there in cyberspace. Just like the astral dimension, the Internet is everywhere and nowhere. You can't point to it and say, "There's the Internet." Nobody knows how big it is. It's like the universe – infinite, yet still expanding.

Anyone can link with the Internet by opening up a phone connection. Once you're in, you can go anywhere, learn anything, touch anyone. Your mind is no longer limited to the power of one. You are the power of billions. But there's a catch – you have to learn how to use it.

The same is true of the astral dimension. Normally, we connect with it only after we die. Then we remain as part of the collective God-mind until we're reborn in another body (hence, the reincarnation stories). The newborn forms a life-pattern all her own, but in a few rare people, some kind of short-circuit in the umbilical cord can give them a temporary connection to the God-mind, and a "former life" sparks to the surface. People can "remember" being Attila the Hun or Shakespeare or Joan of Arc because they link up with the God-mind, where all those consciousnesses still live, there for the taking.

Who do you want to be today? Where do you want to go today? You don't have to die to join with the God-mind.

Using astral projection, you can actually leave your physical vessel, travel up the umbilical cord as a disembodied soul, and fly through Heaven. You can visit the collective and join with the Almighty, which is in reality everything and everybody.

This is going to sound silly, but remember in *Star Trek*, when Spock uses the Vulcan mind meld and connects his consciousness with another person? That's what astral projection is doing, except instead of connecting with one person, you connect with EVERY person. You can fly through astral planes and see anything, be anybody, understand everything. Words are insufficient. It defies explanation.

I started on this path with meditation and self-hypnosis, but those just scratch the surface of what can be done with your consciousness. Your mind is like a muscle. With exercise and training, you can be stronger, go farther, accomplish more. At first, astral projection was scary. From that first trip, I knew it was different. I wasn't just settling into a comfortable alpha state. I was actually going somewhere.

Dakin asked me how I knew it was real. But what's reality? It's perception. To a bat, reality is total darkness. Its world consists of sound, smell, taste and touch. It has no point of reference for a visual image. If you could surgically give a bat eyesight, the poor thing probably would go insane. Reality to a fly's eyeball is kaleidoscopic images. To a fish, what is the meaning of wet?

Brain researchers have discovered that by electrically stimulating certain parts of your cerebral cortex, they can make you smell scents that aren't there, taste flavors that aren't there, even see things that aren't there. Reality is what your brain tells you is real. How can we ever be sure?

216

But where I went with astral projection – what I saw, what I experienced, what I felt – was real. I couldn't have imagined this. I don't have that fertile an imagination. For instance, when I left my body and joined the God-mind, I could see 360 degrees. Actually, more than that. I could see all around me, plus above and below, all at the same time. It wasn't like a chameleon's eye rotating around. There was no eye to look. I wasn't a physical body, but more like a presence. I could "see" in every direction simultaneously. Try making up something like that in your head! Like the blind bat, you have no point of reference to even imagine what that looks like.

Well, I'm sure this sounds like I have gone off the deep end, huh? I appreciate knowing someone like you, who will take all this in without asking me if I forgot to take my medication today. I couldn't tell my old friend and shrink, Dr. Lyman, about this, and even though Dakin and I have been exploring altered states of consciousness together, I think he might believe I've gone one toke over the line.

Thanks for listening,
Jewel

---------◇---------

Subject: Opportunity knocks!
Date: Fri, 22 Sep 2000 15:44:29
From: TheBigOne
To: Jewel Halpern-Caravans

Get ready. You are about to embark on a journey that will change your life!

My mission is to help you develop your lifelong dream. I can see you are one of those people who are committed to the BIG picture and aren't afraid to work for it.

You must be determined to earn a bare minimum of $10,000 in the next 30 days and to develop a net worth of over 1 Million Dollars Cash in the next 24 months. CLICK HERE for details> Not MLM!

---------◇---------

Chapter Eighteen: Dakin
If you think you're free, no escape is possible

Background: Dakin never put much stock in psychotherapy, at least not for himself. He went to counseling for a brief period after his divorce from Amanda, but he and Dr. Corena Bissett often would engage in verbal fencing matches – always good-natured – over the merits of therapy.

–David Cunningham

--------<>--------

Subject: Thanks a lot
Date: Wed, 25 Oct 2000 11:22:41
From: Dakin Caravans
To: Corena Bissett

Dr. Dr. Jekyll,

Hey, I took your advice and went to see a shrink. It was the partner of the psychotherapist Jewel used to use. I didn't want to go to her shrink, a woman named Dr. Sara Lyman, because she is, as they say in the jury room, prejudiced. She knows everything about me already, but only through the multi-colored lenses of Jewel's stories. I wanted someone who could start fresh with me. So, I chose Dr. Lyman's associate, Dr. Eggers. Big mistake.

He's a kindly old gentleman who probably was once a very fine doctor, but since he passed his 80th birthday, he seems to have lost a step – to put it mildly. Here's how it went:

Dr. Eggers: "So, Dakin, what kind of relationship did you have with your father? My father died when I was nine years old. I miss him very much. I can still see his face. It appears to me in windows. I count. One ... two ... three .... four ... five ...six ..."
"Uh, what are you counting?"
"Faces. My father's faces. I can touch them." (He begins weeping).
"Dr. Eggers, I can come back another time."

"No, this is a good time. This is a great time. I can't think of a better time in my whole life. You know why I feel that way? They changed my medication. I feel worlds better. Worlds."

"I can tell. So how do we do this? Do you ask me questions?"

"Why are you here?"

"A friend of mine, a therapist, thinks I have manic disorder."

"Do YOU think you have manic disorder? Do you drink a lot of coffee? Water? You should drink water. Lots and lots of water. My receptionist spilled a whole pot of hot coffee on my lap. A whole pot! God! No, wait, that was my wife. It was a long time ago. Listen, I don't fool around on my wife. Nosiree! Not anymore. Hmmmm ... one ... two ... three ... four ... five ... six ... seven ..." (He stops and stares out the window).

"Dr. Eggers, are you seeing your father's faces again?"

"No. Why do you ask? I've been in this building for more than 40 years. Seen an awful lot of disturbed people in this office. Crazy people. Why are you here?"

"Manic disorder. I think one of us has it."

The session went downhill from there. It was a total waste of time. Well, maybe not a total waste. I got him to cry two more times, just to see if I could. And at the end of our hour, he thanked me. So I believe I did him some good.

Can't I just change my diet to treat this alleged disorder? Or take drugs? Or drink heavily? Please, please don't send me back to a shrink. I'll do anything but that.

Your desperate fiend,
Charlie Manson

--------◇--------

Subject: Re: Thanks a lot
Date: Wed, 25 Oct 2000 16:13:28
From: Corena Bissett
To: Dakin Caravans

Charlie Manson?

And was your sign-off a typo, or did you mean to sign it, "Your desperate FIEND"?

You're starting to worry me, and I don't care if you ARE a family man. Sorry your session went badly. One bad shrink doesn't spoil the whole profession. If you wanted to come back to Phoenix for a visit, I could see you. Professionally. Or socially. Whatever works best for you.

So how does your Excellent Adventure end? You and Jewel were in Florida, drying out from the hurricane. Then what? How did you end up back in California? Twister pick up your RV and fly it there?

Your pal and confidant,

Corena

--------<>--------

Subject: makin' bacon brothers
Date: Wed, 25 Oct 2000 19:08:10
From: Dakin Caravans
To: Jeri Starrette

Hi Jeri,

Thanks for the invite. I have both Bacon Brothers CDs. Jewel and I went to see them in concert when we were in Orlando. But I have to decline your invitation for another reason ... I appreciate your kindness, but I think I need to be alone for a while to gather myself. I'm adjusting to Jewel's death as well as could be expected, but it will take a while longer for me to adjust to my own place in the world. What do I do now? It's a solitary question, and one I must answer with my eyes closed, looking inward. Jewel and I spent months searching for meaning, and we exposed ourselves to all manner of ideas, some silly and some serious. I have all the data I require. Now I just need to digest it and determine what's best for me.

I'll call you sometime, but for now, please let me sort this out on my own.

Your friend always,

Dakin

--------◇--------

Subject: ready when you are
Date: Thu, 26 Oct 2000 09:31:11
From: Jeri Starrette
To: Dakin Caravans

ok dakin,

i will give you your space ... when you have healed all your wounds and are ready for some good lovin' just give me a call. no matter what you decide, i am your friend.

love,

jeri

ps: here you are, juggling the weights of the world ...

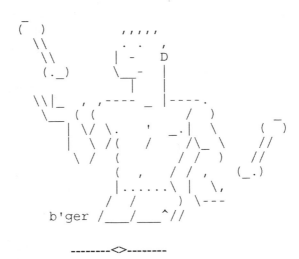

```
--------<>--------
```

Subject: Live long and prosper
Date: Thu, 26 Oct 2000 21:07:34
From: Dakin Caravans
To: Corena Bissett

Dear Dr. Crusher,

I am reminded of a quote from The Next Generation:

"If there's nothing wrong with me, maybe there's something wrong with the universe." – Dr. Beverly C. H. Crusher, Starfleet Commander.

That said, we continue with our saga, The Jewel Trek, in which our heroes regularly cross that thinly drawn line between sanity and madness.

From Florida, we headed quickly up the Atlantic coast to visit Jewel's old friends in Vermont. Being a baseball writer for so many years had taken me to almost every major city in the U.S., but Vermont doesn't have a pro team in any sport, so it was one of five remaining states I hadn't seen. Quaint and very pretty, a nice place to visit. I liked Jewel's best friend from Brattleboro, Vivienne. Obviously, the visit affected Jewel more deeply than I. It put her in a reflective mood, and it changed the focus of the rest of our trip.

We stopped helping other people and started looking for ways to help ourselves. This is where the mind trips really intensified. We were meditating regularly, and I had also taught Jewel self-hypnosis so she could achieve a higher degree of control over her subconscious. I taught her how to regulate pain with her mind, how to program herself for optimum health, how to visualize that her internal organs were all functioning with maximum efficiency, how to "see" her arteries cleaning themselves of blockages, how to energize her white blood cells to attack all invaders with hyper intensity. In short, I taught her how to give herself AIS – Acquired Immunological Strength, the polar opposite of AIDs. I've been doing this to myself for many years, and although I don't pretend it will make me live forever, I'm convinced it will make me healthier and more vital for whatever years I do live. I wanted that for Jewel, too.

In retrospect, I wonder if I killed her by giving her the tools she needed to seize control of her autonomic functions. Maybe things like heartbeat and respiration are supposed to belong solely to the realm of the subconscious.

Jewel used our laptop to hook into the Internet and started downloading all sorts of New Age stuff into her brain. She was thirsty for knowledge of this new frontier and couldn't get enough. Although it was my interest in altered states of consciousness that set her off, I think she was drawn to some of the more bizarre and unproven corridors of thought expressly BECAUSE I was dubious of them. She wanted to be the one who enlightened me. And in the end, she did.

We kept an eye out for lectures or seminars on subjects that Jewel was drawn toward, so as we worked our way back toward Southern California (La-La-Land, birthplace of the New Age), we made it a Magical Mystery Tour.

In New York, we took another look at biofeedback. Jewel seemed to get a lot out of it. I thought it was ridiculously expensive and of very limited value.

We learned about Amish beliefs and lifestyles in Pennsylvania. I thought it was interesting, but out of step with reality. Jewel, at least for a week, thought that a simple, non-technological existence might well be the key to serenity. She liked their devotion to God.

We delved into Buddhism in Chicago. It appealed to both of us. I've dabbled in Buddhism and Zen for years, but ultimately, I grew to suspect that it stifled the advancement of the species. Too much emphasis on renouncement, poverty and begging. Could a Buddhist have invented the silicon chip? Jewel believed that the advancement of the species begins with the individual, and until we can find true inner peace, we'll never move to the next level, whatever that may be.

We also looked into Hinduism at a temple in Aurora, Illinois. I didn't realize this is the second oldest of all world religions, predated only by Judaism. The Hindus have something like 330 million gods, enough for every family to have its own. It seems a gentle, tolerant and undemanding faith. The goal is to become one with the Infinite Being (this, incidentally, is what I believe Jewel liked most about Hinduism. I think in her own way, that's exactly what she eventually did. She left her body to become one with Brahman, which is what Hindus call the ultimate reality). My problem with the Hindus is that they insist that everyone is stuck in a caste system and can't progress from being a peasant or a servant or a pig or a mosquito until the next life. I hope Jewel knew what she was doing. Her karma wasn't always so great.

In Missouri, we found a healer who practiced and taught Reiki, the ancient Japanese art of laying on of hands. Jewel really got into this. The woman talked about Chakras and third eyes, and Jewel studied with her for two weeks. She left there believing that if she had understood Reiki when we were in Oklahoma, she could have done more for some of the tornado victims.

Chakra, as you may or may not know (I don't believe this would be part of your classical training in psychology), is a Sanskrit word for wheel or disk. It also refers to one of seven basic energy centers of the body. Sounds like pseudoscience, but each of the seven Chakras also corresponds to a major nerve ganglia branching forth from the spinal column, so maybe there's something to it.

Chakra is also a variant of chess, invented by Christian Freeling in 1980, so if you can't get in tune with your higher self by connecting with your Chakra system, perhaps you can play a nice board game.

In New Mexico, we learned about flow and the power of crystals and pyramids. Hey, did you know that early in the Twentieth Century, a Frenchman discovered that a dead cat would become mummified if placed in a pyramid? Or that in the 1950s a Czech named Drbal learned that razor blades placed under a cardboard pyramid stayed sharper than other razor blades? Or that food stays fresher when placed in a pyramid? Or that pyramids kill bacteria? Did you know that if you write a wish on a piece of paper and place it in a pyramid, the wish will come true?

I didn't know any of that, either. Jewel thought it was amazing. But after a long talk on the drive to Sedona, I think I convinced her there was at least a chance some of that stuff wasn't true.

Sedona is a very cool place. Well, not when measured in Fahrenheit, at least not in the middle of the summer, when we were there. But on a street called Back O' Beyond Circle there exists a remarkable place run by Archangel Michael, and you'll meet some crazy people there. It's called "Michael's Vision, Home for Creating Health and Aliveness."

We took "an inspiring vortex tour" (basically, a hike to a pretty place) that strengthened our yin-yang balance. Then we rested in hammocks over the murmuring water of Oak Creek, meditating after a relaxing massage, enjoying the sun on a deck beside the creek. We meditated in the "tipi," which was said to be "a very special, almost sacred experience, while connecting with our inner being in the circular pyramid." We felt its healing energy.

Our visit to Archangel Michael's Vision included explorations of aromatherapy, aura healing, Chakra balancing, connecting with angels, vortex meditation, astrology card readings and healing with crystal skulls, which Archangel Michael said "come to us from another dimension." While I left feeling some of it was silly, some of it might be helpful to those who believe. Jewel was completely open-minded.

Then we drove to Big Sur, the highest point in California, as measured in alpha waves. It's home of the Esalen Institute, which has been turning people on for decades. This is my new favorite place in the world. As billed, Esalen is "a convergence of mountains and sea, mind and body, East and West, meditation and action. Esalen is a center for alternative education, a forum for transformational practices, a restorative retreat, a worldwide community of seekers."

We took workshops on spirituality and religious studies, philosophical inquiry and martial arts. Jewel had trained in karate as a teen and also during the police academy in Vermont, so she was way ahead of me, but it felt good to finally incorporate physical activity along with all the mental gymnastics we'd been doing.

We would spar with each other in karate, and she usually won. If I ever got the upper hand, she would resort to another tactic she learned in police academy, known technically as "dirty fighting." It amounts to chopping the throat, kicking in the nuts and poking the eyes – Three Stooges stuff. She would win either by hurting me or making me fall down laughing.

We talked a lot about body-mind duality, but I never felt more together than when I was working out physically. I'm not sure there really IS a duality. Perhaps mind and body are one. The entire organism needs to be fed, not just the head. When the body is healthy and happy, the mind works better (duh!). Actually, it wasn't so much that I felt great WHEN I was working out, but that I felt great AFTER I worked out. The endorphins are still shooting through your brain, and you lie there getting a post-workout Swedish massage (no sadistic Rolfing, please), and you finally understand what Nirvana feels like.

Eventually we headed back down the Pacific coast and came home. Then we made day trips to Laguna Beach, San Diego and other coastal towns, continuing to reach for the outer limits. Just a short drive from our home, we explored the holistic healing power of magnets alongside a koi pond at a place called Nikken.

On three of our mind trips – in Sedona, Big Sur and Laguna Beach – we attended workshops in astral projection. This was the freakiest of all our mind games, because it was real. At least, it felt real. Remember, I told you I had tried this once before, more than 20 years ago. I grew frightened of how intensely real the experience was, and I decided never to go there again. As Jewel and I learned more about it, I gave it a try, and it still frightened me. I never wanted to venture too far from my body. Jewel seemed perfectly comfortable with it and told some amazing stories of her out-of-body experiences.

Hey, it's getting late, and I'm really eating up a lot of your RAM. I'll call you tomorrow night.

Later,

Dakin

--------<>--------

Subject: Real power
Date: Fri, 27 Oct 2000 08:32:48
From: The eMailMan
To: Dakin Caravans

Imagine being able to connect with more than 57 million minds at the speed of light. That's real power!

You can do it – for ONLY $149!!! That's all it costs for 57 million fresh email addresses, with no duplications.

If you can make just one cent from each of theses names, you have a profit of over $500,000. Imagine selling a product for $5 and getting only a 10% response. That's $2,850,000 in your pocket!!!

CLICK HERE FOR DETAILS>

--------<>--------

Subject: Uh oh
Date: Fri, 27 Oct 2000 11:58:14
From: Dakin Caravans
To: Corena Bissett

Hey Corena,

Are you going to be home tonight? Around 8 p.m.? I don't want to spoil your TGIF, but I'd like to call. I have to talk with someone, and you're my first choice.

Lt. Dick (Barnaby Jones) Najera of the Greentree PD just left. He came here to serve me with paperwork that I don't fully understand, but the bottom line is that I must report to the station tomorrow morning. It sounds as if I will be held for questioning, and although Najera actually used the word "arrest," he tried to make it sound like it would be routine, and that I would "probably" be released on my own recognizance later in the afternoon. He also said that if I don't have an attorney, it might be a good idea if I got one. And he said that although he was relying on me to show up of my own free will, I would be considered a fugitive if I didn't appear at exactly 10 a.m., and he would hunt me down and drag me "to justice in a manner that won't be so pleasant." He said he was giving me the option to come in on my own because I have been fully cooperative to this point and the court didn't think I was a "flight risk."

I'm absolutely certain now that he has, or THINKS he has, evidence he can use to charge me with murder in Jewel's death. My conscience is clear, but I wouldn't be the first innocent man to end up behind bars.

I hope you check your emails before going out tonight. If you're not in, I'll leave a message. You can call me back whatever time you get in. I'll be home getting my personal affairs in order. Does one bring a toothbrush to jail, or do they provide that?

Dakin

--------<>--------

Chapter Nineteen: Jewel
A loving person lives in a loving world

Background: On the day before she died, Jewel secretly met with Spider Juncal. As far as I could determine, Dakin never found out about it. Spider told me he and Jewel talked over lunch, but he refused to reveal what they discussed. Lt. Dick Najera said he never asked Juncal about the meeting.

"Juncal isn't a suspect," Najera said. "Jewel Caravans' death is still listed as a probable homicide. We arrested a suspect, her husband, and his death is still listed as a probable suicide. The case isn't closed, but we really don't have any facts to contradict where we stand on that."

–David Cunningham

--------◇--------

Subject: Thank you
Date: Thu, 28 Sep 2000 11:38:56
From: Jewel Halpern-Caravans
To: Spider Juncal

Hello Spider,

It was good to talk with you yesterday after all these months. Dakin doesn't know I went to visit you, and I don't see any reason to get him all worked up over nothing. You know his jealous streak.

Thanks for your encouragement. I'm about to take a huge step, and it's difficult to consider such an adventure without talking with somebody who can give me an unbiased opinion. I couldn't possibly discuss it with Dakin. He's afraid of astral projection and doesn't understand it. We always fear what we don't understand, don't we?

I know my trips have been taking me directly into the God-mind, and it was important to me that you believed me. I'll tell you all about the trip I take tonight in an email sometime in the next day or so. I'm going where no Jewel has gone before. It'll be my longest trip and deepest penetration ever. I'm not going to just be WITH the God-mind, but will actually BE the God-mind. I truly believe it's possible, and I feel close to it already. God is all, and we only feel separated from God because our ego gets in the way. I will transcend that tonight. Maybe I can eventually learn to be the God-mind at all times, in my normal waking state. Maybe this is what separated Jesus and Buddha from ordinary people.

You asked me what an out-of-body experience was really like, so now that I have some time to compose my thoughts, I'll try to tell you.

Generally speaking, it defies explanation. But the feeling at the top, when I've moved all the way up the tunnel and joined with the God-mind, is pure joy. It's unbridled ecstasy, total bliss, rapture, clarity, happiness beyond description and an indescribable sense of freedom.

When you're in the God-mind, you instantly "know" things that you'd have no other way of knowing. But this knowledge isn't linear, like facts you learn from books. It's an all-encompassing sensation that fills you with, well, I guess the word is wisdom. It's like your search is over. There's no reason to look any further.

Dakin and I have spent the last five months searching for an answer to the proverbial Big Question: why are we here? In the God-mind, you instantly understand, and that understanding gives you a feeling of peace, warmth and serenity. You feel at one with everything, and I don't mean just people or life. I mean everything – all matter. You intuitively realize that everything in the entire universe is made up of the same starstuff. We're all just colonies of elementary particles, and those particles are the same whether we're a piece of granite, a flickering fire, an elephant, or a human.

Have you ever heard of the Gaia theory? That the entire planet is one giant living organism? That humans are to the earth what stomach enzymes are to humans? Not only is that theory true, but on an infinitely larger scale, the entire UNIVERSE is one big organism. It has cosmic structure and a purpose, and that purpose is to thrive.

We're here to help the organism thrive. We're all part of this organism, which can be called the God-mind. By helping it thrive, we help ourselves. We really ARE all one.

So how do we do it? Simply by loving – loving others, loving ourselves, loving all that exists. Love is the answer. Any act that comes from love will serve. Any act that's not loving defeats the purpose.

So the real answer to "Why are we here?" is simply this: to love. That's why we were created. All things great and beautiful flow out of love. If we aren't loving, we aren't fulfilling our mission.

The sense of purpose, unity and beauty you feel when you join with the God-mind can't be put into words, at least not by me. This knowledge that floods into your soul seems to come from being joined with all the souls of everyone and everything that has ever lived. Actually, it feels like just one soul, the God-mind, and everything connects to it. We're tiny leaves on a giant tree.

So, that's the magic happy place. How do you get there? It helps to have some training in self-hypnosis and meditation. You have to put yourself into a "trance" (I hate that word; it sounds so fake). You put your body and most of your conscious mind to sleep while keeping a line open into your subconscious. This is a process that takes practice, and like anything else, the more you do it, the easier it becomes.

I can't give you a complete "how-to" manual here, but you start with tiny trips, like 20 feet away from your body, then into another room, then outside. At first, you're not sure if you're really moving your spirit outside of your body or if you're just imagining things. But we did tests. Dakin would place a deck of cards on the front seat of the RV, turning one random card face-up on the top. I'd lie in the back of the RV and begin astral projection. I floated up to the front of the motor home, saw the card, then came back into my body and told Dakin which card it was. We did it 10 times, and I got it right 10 times! I had seen it!

Gradually you work up to longer flights. For me, it was unprogrammed. I had no idea where astral projection would take me on any given trip. I came to realize that I truly was leaving my body and could do it at will. I was tapping into a universal pool of knowledge I couldn't otherwise have realized.

Not every trip goes to the God-mind. That's something I've experienced only recently. At first, you seem to float up above your body. You look at yourself from above, with "eyes" you've never used before. Everything looks different. Because you don't really have eyes and can see in all directions at once, you look toward a door and see it behind you and on both sides, as well as in front of you. It's very disorienting until you learn how to navigate in the astral plane. If you go through the door in front of you, where it's actually located, you'll enter the next room, and everything appears similar to the way it really is. If you go through one of the doors that isn't there, you'll enter unfamiliar territory, sort of like an Alice in Wonderland effect. That's when you realize you really have become a spirit and can travel through planes that don't exist in our three-dimensional world.

I know this sounds totally bizarre, but there are actually very well thought-out theories in quantum physics that account for dimensions of existence beyond those we experience. The theories have been called highly speculative and not provable because a human couldn't experience any other dimension and still remain a three-dimensional being. But those theories don't consider the possibility of visiting other dimensions while traveling outside your physical body as a spirit or soul made of – what? I don't know. Maybe pure energy.

I wish they could do experiments on out-of-body travelers and prove it's real. But if you hook up electrodes to a person's brain, they would just record brain waves of the physical being. There's no way I know of to track a person's soul as it travels out of the body and into other dimensions. How can science measure something that has no height, weight, density or substance?

The trips to God-mind will sound familiar to you if you've ever heard about near-death experiences. You know how people say that when they feel they're dying, they move upward through a tunnel, toward a bright light? And they feel all warm and fuzzy and peaceful? That's EXACTLY how it feels to enter the God-mind through astral projection. Until I did it, I had no reason to believe near-death experiences were real. Frankly, I suspected that the brain just produced that kind of sensation as it died. I figured it was a near-death hallucination. But now that I've gone through that tunnel and come back, I know it's real. My first trip was purely accidental. I was on one of my non-programmed flights, and something was pulling me in an upward direction. I moved up through the roof of our motor home and out into the night sky. I continued moving toward the stars, faster and faster, and while I could see the countryside and distant city lights shining below me, I could at the same time sense a bright light high above, gradually growing larger. I accelerated into a tunnel that closed around me, leaving the Earth behind. There was just the tunnel, the ever-growing light, and a sense of peace. I felt no fear. This seemed so natural, like I'd done it a thousand times before. Whatever lay ahead, I knew it was good.

I don't think I can describe what it's like to come out of the tunnel and into the light. You don't really "see" anything. You sense things. You understand. You become totally fulfilled. Instead of being "told" anything, you just spontaneously fill up with wisdom. Everything makes sense. You're not alone. You're with an infinite number of other souls and, simultaneously, with just one all-encompassing God soul. I was very clear, however, that I was "with" this God-mind, not inside of it. I was just visiting.

The only bad part is that when you voluntarily break with the God-mind, travel back down the tunnel and rejoin your body, almost all that wisdom and feeling of fulfillment stays behind. It's as if it can only exist on the astral plane. It would be great for all the scientists and world religious leaders if I could take a camera and tape recorder with me and document all I know when I reach the God-mind, but three-dimensional matter doesn't exist there. And when I return, all I'm left with is a general sense of what I've seen and experienced. I wish I could describe it more clearly, but I can't. I think you can understand why I want to go back there again and again. I feel like each time I go, I return with a little more of the God-mind inside my physical, three-dimensional brain. It's like an addictive drug. I can't get enough.

Maybe someday, I'll take enough of the God-mind back with me so you and I can collaborate on a book or a seminar and teach others how to do it. Maybe the next step in our evolution is to become spirit-beings infused with love for the entire universe-organism in which we serve.

I'll write again soon,

Jewel

PS: Thanks for the special tea. I'll try it before I enter my astral projection session tonight. You say it enhances concentration, right?

--------<>--------

Subject: Godspeed!
Date: Thu, 28 Sep 2000 14:22:33
From: Spider Juncal
To: Jewel Halpern-Caravans

To the new Messiah!

I will follow you anywhere! Trip safely, and Godspeed.

Love,
Spider

"The whole universe can be your home if you can get big enough to live in it." (David Crosby)

--------◇--------

Subject: Dear God letter
Date: Thu, 28 Sep 2000 16:01:27
From: Jewel Halpern-Caravans
To: Spider Juncal

Hello again Spider,

I'm almost ready for my flight. Pass this message along to God if you see him sometime.

Dear God:

I am about to become a star-child. I want to join with you now, and I feel you have given me the ability to do so because it is exactly what you want me to do.

I have no fear. I realize that someday, I'll have to leave my physical body behind forever and become pure consciousness. I will be ready for this step. I believe we are not fully evolved, that our bodies are just vessels transporting us from one life to another until our spirits can finally progress to a permanent union with the God-mind. I hear your call. I believe you have chosen me for a reason, and I will learn this reason when I finally join with you.

When the day comes that I must leave my physical body forever, I'll leave with joy and fulfillment. I have no regrets. You have treated me well. I know that when the soul releases its body, it moves to a higher plane of existence. There's no such thing as death. Matter cannot be destroyed, only changed. This knowledge, acquired while visiting you in the God-mind, gives me complete serenity. I trust that my God will care for me, as you care for all your creations.

I ask only that you touch Dakin as you have touched me. Open your doors to him. His earthly mind is filled with prejudices and doubts, and if you don't give him the keys he needs, he'll never accept what's happening to me and what can happen to us all. I know I will be with Dakin for eternity, that we are soulmates who will never be separated. I could never take the next step without that realization. I love him more than I love life itself. I won't leave him behind.

Sometimes our spirits become distracted by weaknesses of the body. Addictions to drugs, alcohol, nicotine, caffeine, pornography, gambling and other vices lure us away from your Light. We are tested daily. Most of us fail. You keep giving us chances, and we keep screwing up. I believe you have opened your doors so that Dakin and I can walk through them, learn your message, and come back to spread it to all mankind. It is time for new messengers.

As I sit here tonight, shortly before I make my most important trip ever, I think back on my life and wonder if you were grooming me for this day all along. It seems like every step of the way was designed to take me to the threshold at which I find myself tonight, here in the hills where I grew up.

Just a few miles from where I sit at this very moment is the street corner where Dakin and I met on that cool Halloween night. All around us are the places where Dakin and I played and fell in love as teenagers. We've spent the last few days visiting them and reminiscing. We walked in the woods where we shared our first kiss. As we came to that exact spot yesterday, Dakin wrapped an arm around my waist, gently pulled me toward him, caressed my face as he looked into my eyes, then kissed me. It was just as exciting as the first time.

We went to the movie theater where we had our first real date. The name has changed and it's been remodeled, but it's still there. We sat in the back row and made out, just as we did 30 years ago. Dakin, always the goofball, acted like the shy schoolboy he was the first time we sat in those seats. He pretended to be real nervous as he slowly slid his hand down from my shoulder and gently cupped my left breast. In 1969, I was silently thrilled. This time, I giggled, turned and gave him a deep kiss.

We went down to the beach with a blanket and a picnic basket, as we did one Saturday evening in 1969. We walked along the sand, found the same secluded cove we visited 30 years ago, and laid down. Back then, we just kissed. This time, we made love.

God, you created us as soulmates, Dakin and I. We've both known it from that first glance. Some might call it a miracle that, after all these years apart, we found each other again. I call it destiny. It had to happen. There could be no other fate for us.

And now, I believe the same is true as I embark on a union with the God-mind. This is our destiny. We will be together with you.

Oh, God, I hope and pray I'm making the right decision. I'm following signs written in a different language. How can I be sure? How can we ever be sure when we come to life-changing decisions? I guess we have to follow our hearts. Mine is drawn toward the light.

Dakin and I have found a beautiful, fairy-tale life together, and it's so hard to consider taking a step that might mean changing that. But I believe we are standing in the doorway to a new era, and it would be small and foolish of me to turn my back on that for the sake of selfish pleasures. Dakin and I started this journey together, and we'll finish it the same way. He resists taking that final step, but that's simply because of fear. I'll take the step for both of us, and then I'll come back to show him the way.

We'll be pioneers. Dakin and I will explore previously uncharted realms of existence and open the door for mankind to follow us and evolve.

I am your humble servant, God.
Jewel

--------◇--------

Subject: Think a second time
Date: Thu, 28 Sep 2000 16:28:46
From: Vivienne Myers
To: Jewel Halpern-Caravans

Hi Jewel,

I just got this from a friend on the net. She said it was written by a student from Columbine High, where they had those shootings. I think it's too good for a high school kid to have written, but I loved it anyway, and I thought you would, too:

"The paradox of our time in history is that we have taller buildings, but shorter tempers; wider freeways, but narrower viewpoints; we spend more but have less; we buy more but enjoy it less. We have bigger houses and smaller families; more conveniences but less time; we have more degrees but less sense; more knowledge but less judgment; more experts but more problems; more medicine but less wellness.

"We have multiplied our possessions but reduced our values. We talk too much, love too seldom, and hate too often. We've learned how to make a living but not a life; we've added years to life, not life to years. We've been all the way to the moon and back but have trouble crossing the street to meet the new neighbor. We've conquered outer space but not inner space; we've cleaned up the air but polluted the soul; we've split the atom but not our prejudice. We have higher incomes but lower morals; we've become long on quantity but short on quality. These are the times of tall men and short character; steep profits and shallow relationships. These are the times of world peace but domestic warfare; more leisure but less fun; more kinds of food but less nutrition. These are days of two incomes but more divorce; of fancier houses but broken homes.

"It is a time when there is much in the show window and nothing in the stockroom; a time when technology can bring this letter to you, and a time when you can choose to make a difference ... or just hit delete."

Talk to you soon,
Love, Viv

--------<>--------

Subject: I love you
Date: Thu, 28 Sep 2000 16:54:22
From: Jewel Halpern-Caravans
To: Dakin Caravans

My beloved Dakin,

Remember those emails we used to send each other before we were married, when you were in Arizona and I was in California? I thought it was a wonderful way to communicate, so tonight I figured I'd send you one more. Consider it a love letter for old time's sake. It goes from this laptop, out into cyberspace, and when you sign onto the Net with your own profile, it will magically reappear, coming back to the same machine from which it was sent.

That's what you did for me, Dakin – magically reappeared – and I wish I could do something as wonderful for you. You were a fond memory for me for all those years I was in Vermont, and then you popped back into my life like magic, out of thin air. You were a message from God, appearing to tell me that my destiny was yet to be fulfilled.

Thanks to you, I'm finally fulfilling that destiny. I love you so much. You have taken my ordinary life and given it meaning. Together, we seized this world and made it ours. So many people bounce around from day to day, letting things happen to them, feeling like they're powerless against the crush of fate. They live only for their little escapes – their Budweiser weekends or sitcoms or bowling leagues or Internet porn. Except for those happy-sad moments, they lead lives of silent-scream desperation.

Together, you and I found another way. We opened our minds and hearts to the world. We've lived each day like it was our first. With the eyes of children, we embraced this place and all its inhabitants. We found the meaning of love. One size fits all. And we also found the meaning of Heaven. It is here and now, if only you choose to live it.

You became my Heaven, Dakin, and your love opened me to possibilities I never could have imagined. I honestly didn't think unconditional love was possible until you came back into my life. I would always hold back, waiting for the other person to do something to violate my trust and render himself undeserving of my love. I never realized how much I was hurting myself with that attitude. I was emotionally barren.

But now, I see that love is meant to be unconditional not only between two lovers, but also between all living things. It's the secret to creating Heaven on earth. Will it ever actually happen? You probably don't believe it will, Dakin, but I do. I can imagine a world where everyone is in love with everyone else, where there is no oppression, no violence, no sorrow. I can imagine a world where we are all God. The all-encompassing divine spirit can fill each and every one of us. It's not just pie in the sky.

But before that can happen, someone has to make a sacrifice. Someone has to risk all they have and cross the line into God-mind. Maybe we're the ones who are supposed to take that risk, Dakin. Maybe that's our destiny. Maybe that's why I was available when you came looking for me. Maybe our love and our quest for meaning have a larger purpose.

"The road to greatness is a dark and lonely one," said Theodore Roosevelt, "and I find no fault in those who choose not to take it." But if you will stand by my side, Dakin, I will choose that road. Standing together with hearts full of love, we can make a difference.

I will love you forever,

Your Jewel

--------◇--------

Chapter Twenty: Dakin
The only immutable law in the universe is change

Background: These are the last emails found on Dakin's computer. Note that the final message, sent by Spider Juncal, was sent shortly before noon on Sept. 28. Dakin never saw it. He had already been arrested.

–David Cunningham

--------◇--------

Subject: The end
Date: Sat, 28 Oct 2000 07:10:19
From: Dakin Caravans
To: Corena Bissett

Good morning, Dr. Bissett,

On my last day of freedom, I finally get your name right. It's about time I got SOMETHING right. Thanks for spending all that time on the phone with me last night. I can't tell you how much it meant to me. I'm sure you're sleeping in this morning, considering how late we were talking, but I have to get ready for jail, and I can always sleep when I'm dead. So here I am. I doubt they'll let me send emails from the brig, so I thought I'd dash off one final message.

Hey, you know that website I told you about, the one where Spider Juncal was going to turn Jewel into The Messiah? It's finally up and running. I checked it out last night after we got off the phone. So you can click there now and see just what a fruit loop I've been dealing with. I was right about him having all of Jewel's diaries and letters. They're all posted there. He sets her up as the Second Coming of Jesus. The daughter of God has risen! Everything has exclamation points! He's a f***ing looney-toon!

Actually, some of the website is pretty interesting. He may be a Jesus freak, but the guy sounds reasonably well read and intelligent, and the site has lots of graphics and pictures and special effects. He makes a pretty convincing case for Jewel. They were close friends when she was going through Narcotics Anonymous, and I believe he helped her a lot. He got to know her mind and personality, and she shared a lot of her innermost thoughts with him, so he got to glimpse some of that wide-eyed and innocent beauty that so attracted me to her. I can see how someone like Juncal could mistake her for the Messiah. She became a very spiritual person in the last few years of her life, and some of the head trips we were taking in those final five months were intense enough to convince anybody she was a mystical being.

Among the pictures you'll see on the site is a photograph of Jewel and me, taken on our wedding night. I'm dressed all in black (the bad guy) while Jewel wears a beautiful, white, flowing, non-traditional dress that looks (coincidentally) almost like Jesus' robes. That photo was stolen from my condo in the burglary. So now the case is closed. Juncal is a common thief, and shameless enough to put his plunder right there on the Internet for the entire world to see.

But while I go directly to jail and do not pass Go and do not collect $200, Spider Juncal is making a fortune off the legacy of my late wife. His website has advertising. Lots of it. Very lucrative-looking ads with pop-up screens and animation. Jewel the Messiah is big business now. So how do you suppose history will record Dakin Caravans when the "New Age Gospel" of Jewel is written and ministries spring up all over the world for the "Precious Jewel of Our Father Church and Sunday School?" Will I be the benign new-age Joseph, symbolically sterile and ineffectual? Or will Spider join forces with the evil Lt. Dick Najera and paint me as the Anti-Jewel, a modern Judas who spiked her Kool-Aid?

But enough frivolity. I have graver issues to address today. An innocent man (me) is about to be incarcerated. I thought long and hard about retaining an attorney, but Johnnie Cochran was busy. Then I considered renting a white Bronco and leading police on a low-speed chase through the freeways of Southern California. Or hiring a paranoid-schizophrenic South American maid to testify she saw me eating a McDonald's cheeseburger and practicing with an imaginary golf club while the alleged murder took place. But then I realized that the only place for a just man in an unjust society is the slammer.

Sssssshhhhh. Don't tell anybody, but the lockup that can hold Dakin Caravans hasn't been built yet. I'm busting out tonight. Tunneling through the

244

wall with a rock hammer. I have a million dollars stashed in a suitcase buried under a tree. You'll find me in Mexico running a charter boat service.

All seriousness aside, I believe that after another round of inane questions from Lt. Dick (Inspector Gadget) Najera, I will be released with nothing more than a spanking and stern lecture. They have nothing. It's impossible. How could any evidence point to me as a murderer when I'm not one? I'm being naive, you say? Lots of innocent men have hanged, especially in the name of religion? I suppose you're right.

But they'll never take me alive.

Hasta la vista, or who knows when,
Dakin

--------◇--------

Subject: Angels
Date: Sat, 28 Oct 2000 08:31:18
From: Dakin Caravans
To: Jewel Halpern-Caravans

Hello Supergirl,

This may be the last email I ever send you. OK, you've heard that before. This time I'm serious. Something has gone seriously wrong with the world, and I don't think I can stay here anymore. Move over, Jewel, I'm coming to join you!

You know my old philosophy that the world is full of incompetent and bad people, but all we need to do is avoid them? That isn't working for me anymore. Somehow, I've been backed into a corner. But I remain the eternal optimist. I will never complain that there is no way out. There is ALWAYS a way out, and this time, I have you to thank for showing me the path.

I'm not talking suicide. That's the ultimate in bad karma. I think it was the Hindus who said that people who commit suicide come back as excrement-eating maggots or those ugly black birds that feed off road kill.

They're doomed to spend their next several lives cleaning up other's messes until they repent for rejecting the most precious gift God can give – life.

No, there's another alternative, and I think you tapped into it, Jewel. I think it might be possible to join with God and evolve into a HIGHER being, rather than going backward by killing yourself. I think we can voluntarily rise above the confines of the body and live freely and with peace, sitting at the feet of God and carrying out Her will.

I'm writing this to you, my dearly departed Jewel, because no one on this side of existence could listen to these ideas and consider me sane. For all I know, you're the only person in the history of the world who believed this stuff. Well, maybe Spider Juncal would believe, too, but he's certifiable.

I don't know if you were the Second Coming, but I do believe you were the daughter of God. I spent a lot of time mulling over the website that worships you as a deity, and I've come to the conclusion that Spider Juncal is right. There was divinity in your soul. You lived in a different realm from the rest of us. I could meditate, but you could soar. I could think, but you could feel. I saw stars, but you experienced the entire universe.

You moved through life intuitively, and your instincts were almost always right. If God is life, then you were always plugged directly into the Supreme Being. You knew things the rest of us had to learn. I wish I understood how you did it. I hope that my male, rational brain is capable of making the leap that your multi-tasking, omnipresent, female mind executed so naturally. I will try.

If I'm required to remain locked up for more than a few hours today, I will try to reach you through astral projection. Am I scared? Maybe a little. Every time I tried it before, I got frightened. I knew it was something different from meditation, something much more powerful. I could feel my spirit, my sense of self, rising completely out of my body. I could see myself from above. I knew it was no trick of the imagination.

But if what you said is true – if we can travel as spirits and join with this thing you called God-mind – then I want to see it. I want to see you again, Jewel. I need to touch you, kiss you, hold you. Can I do that on the astral plane? Maybe you can show me how to come back with a way to prove to the police that I didn't murder you. Maybe you or your new friend, God, can show me how I'm supposed to live my life now. If you were indeed a New Age messenger, I'd be happy to come back and spread your message to all the world, in the name of God and Jewel. All I'm looking for is a little guidance. As always, I'm searching for an answer.

I've spent so many years on this search. I'm tired and lonely. But I'm now beginning to realize the answer isn't "out there." It isn't hidden in Area 51. It isn't in the Torah or the Koran or the Bible. It isn't inside a secret mantra that only the Maharishi Mahesh Yogi knows. You can't find it on a mountaintop or in a cave. It wasn't written between the lines of Shakespeare or a printout of your brain waves. The answer isn't inside a hallucinogenic drug or a book on quantum physics theory.

Carl Sagan didn't have it, and neither did Carl Jung. Baba Ram Dass didn't know, and neither did Babe Ruth. The answer didn't come from John Lennon or Johann Sebastian Bach. You won't find it with Anthony Robbins, J. Krishnamurti, Steven Spielberg or Sigmund Freud.

Maybe you can find HINTS from all those sources, but not "The Answer." If there is such a thing, I believe that you have found it, Jewel. If you are not just fertilizer in the earth ... if there really IS a soul ... if there really IS a God ... if there really IS an answer ... then I think you must have found it. Please share it with me if I see you later tonight.

Searching is good. Enlightenment comes gradually, and we have to keep growing. If you don't find THE Answer, you can always find AN answer. Almost any will do. The world is a fascinating and wonderful place. Life is not only worth living, but it is imperative that we do so, and do it well. We are all we have, and we need to help each other. As I have learned in the last month, nobody can do it alone.

I love you.
Dakin

--------◇--------

Subject: It's a miracle!
Date: Sat, 28 Oct 2000 09:42:10
From: TheSage0411
To: Dakin Caravans

Here is The Answer you have been looking for. A better life awaits you!

The new FAT-BLOCKING DRUG – Xenical – is available through the Internet. Are you ready for a whole new you? Now approved by the FDA. Click Here!>

--------◇--------

Subject: Let me help!
Date: Sat, 28 Oct 2000 11:55:32
From: Spider Juncal
To: Dakin Caravans

Brother Dakin!

I have learned that since the police finally sobered up and realized I had nothing to do with Jewel's death, they have started coming after you! You don't deserve that, man! They don't realize that Jewel was a being of a higher order! No one can be responsible for her murder, for she did not truly die! She lives, as her brother Jesus lives! Listen, I want to help you! Ask, and you shall receive! I will testify for you! I will give the police access to everything that I have from the Blessed Life of Jewel!

We may have had our differences, but that is the past, and nothing can be more meaningless than the past! It doesn't even exist! We are brothers in peace, and we both share a love of truth, God and Jewel! I have powers you don't understand, and I can help save you from the Nazi state! Trust me! All you need to do is call or write, and I will be there! I have legions of brothers and sisters who will rally to your side! All I have to do is say the word! We must stand together to protect and honor the name of Jewel!

I await your command,

Spider Juncal

"Do unto others as you would have them do unto you." (Luke 6:31)

"Life has no boundaries, and death is only an illusion." (Susan Atkins)

--------◇--------

This article, appearing in the Greentree News on Oct. 29, 2000, first brought the strange story of Dakin and Jewel Caravans to the public's attention.
– David Cunningham

--------◇--------

**Murder suspect, ex-reporter
dies mysteriously in jail cell**
By Joel Knopken
Staff writer

GREENTREE – A former newspaper reporter who was arrested on suspicion of murdering his wife was found dead in his Greentree jail cell Saturday night. Police are calling his death a possible suicide, although the cause of death is still unknown.

It marks the first jail-cell death of a suspect in the 45-year history of the Greentree Police Department.

Dakin Caravans, 47, was booked into the Greentree jail Saturday morning and questioned by Lt. Dick Najera, who has been investigating the Sept. 28 death of Caravans' wife. At 10:35 p.m., Sgt. Berk Bussiere walked through the jail area and found Caravans lying motionless on the floor of his cell.

Within minutes, paramedics from the fire station adjacent to police headquarters arrived on the scene, but they could detect no heartbeat or breathing from the prisoner. Caravans was transported to Torrance Memorial Hospital where he was pronounced dead on arrival.

"The guy had no wounds, no sign of trauma of any kind. There was no bleeding," Bussiere said. "Maybe he had a heart attack. But our department had reason to believe that he might be suicidal. That's why I was checking up on him."

Caravans had been alone in the cell for about 12 hours, excluding the period when Najera questioned him earlier in the afternoon. Police found no weapon or any means by which the suspect might have killed himself, but Najera said he had been informed that Caravans "was suffering from a manic disorder," a condition that often leads to suicidal tendencies.

Najera said evidence that linked Caravans to the mysterious death of his wife, Jewel Caravans, led to his arrest. Although Najera wouldn't elaborate, he did say that an autopsy report on Jewel Caravans' body had revealed traces of jimson weed, a poisonous and hallucinogenic plant that has been known to cause cardiac arrest and respiratory failure.

Jewel Caravans died inside the couple's motor home, parked on Moonlight Bluff, sometime during the evening of Sept. 28. Dakin Caravans admitted he was the only person with her that night, according to Najera.

Police earlier had questioned and released a 48-year-old Laguna Beach man, Erasmus Timothy "Spider" Juncal III, in connection with the woman's death. Juncal runs a website "shrine" to Jewel Caravans in which he proclaims her to be the Messiah. The site includes diaries and "Dear God" letters allegedly written by Mrs. Caravans, as well as letters that Juncal claims were written to her by God.

Caravans and his wife died in eerily similar fashions. Exactly one month apart, each seemed to simply stop living. Neither had visible injuries or an obvious cause of death. Both seemed to have been in unusually good health.

Jewel Caravans worked as an artist for Tosh Greeting Cards and was a former police officer in Brattleboro, Vermont. The former Jewel Halpern, she and Dakin Caravans both grew up in Greentree and were graduated from Greentree High School in the early 1970s.

Dakin Caravans worked at the Long Beach Press-Telegram for 18 years, covering major league baseball for more than a decade. He also covered the Los Angeles Rams, Raiders and Lakers and was a former Chapter Chairman of the Baseball Writers Association of America. More recently, he covered the Arizona Diamondbacks for the Arizona Republic.

After leaving the newspaper business in 1999, Caravans played drums for a rock group called the Bug Burnett Band and painted portraits.

Eyewitness Records is planning to release a Bug Burnett Band single in November that tells the story of a woman who is murdered, according to Najera. Caravans is believed to be the drummer on that song, entitled "Not That There's Anything Wrong With That."

Caravans is survived by a daughter, Heather, 21, and a son, Casey, 18, both from a previous marriage.

--------◇--------

Epilogue

Here's what the police don't know.

I interviewed Casey Caravans, Dakin's son, during research for this book. He showed me one unbelievable email message that he never provided to the police. It arrived on his own computer four days after his dad died, and he said he decided to conceal its existence for two reasons: (1) he was afraid the police would confiscate his own computer, as they had done with the computers owned by his dad and Jewel Caravans, and (2) he figured nobody would believe him, anyway.

With Casey's permission, I hired an independent software expert to examine his computer and also the server through which his email is processed. That expert was Dean Faust, President and founder of Cybermessages, Inc. in San Jose, California. Faust was one of the first email system designers and continues to work in the field of network and Internet messaging. If anyone can detect email fraud or track down the original source of an email message, it is Faust.

His conclusion, after spending nearly a week exhausting all possibilities for the mysterious email message, follows:

"I'm stumped. The source of the email doesn't exist. It wasn't sent anonymously, but there's no computer or sender address that matches its stated origination. It wasn't created on the computer it arrived at, and if it's a hoax, I can't figure out how it possibly could have been done. If you try to reply to the email, you get the automated return message that says the email address doesn't exist. In fact, there's no record that particular email address has ever existed.

"The time that the email was sent is 00:00:00, and that's a designation no computer server would ever generate. It doesn't correspond to any time on the military clock. The email arrived in the receiver's server, but there's no server for the sender. There simply isn't one. You can't track it.

"You see, all email includes an electronic code that can be used to trace the originating site, but this message doesn't have one. This email seems to have been spontaneously generated in cyberspace, like it came from a ghost."

Here is a copy of that mysterious ghost email:

--------<>--------

Subject: Unknown
Date: Wed, 01 Nov 2000 00:00:00
From: Dakin Caravans
To: Casey Caravans

Hi Casey,

Please don't get freaked by this message. I'm able to communicate with you with email because it's just digital code that can be transmitted through the air and easily fed into phone lines. Not a difficult trick for someone in my situation.

I live. Jewel and I both do. We're together in a place you can't understand. Neither of us understood it ourselves until we came here. Our bodies no longer exist, but the essence that one would call "us" didn't die. I don't think I can explain in words what happened to us and where we are. It's a place beyond words. I'm sure in your church, they'd call it Heaven. That's a good name.

When most people die, they come back here involuntarily. It just happens. Every soul originates here, and every soul returns here. They rejoin a sort of cosmic consciousness. They're absorbed into the whole. But Jewel came here by choice, through a mental process sometimes called an "out-of-body experience." Her position here is a little different from a person who dies a more typical death. She stayed here too long and went too deep, and her body stopped functioning. She couldn't go back. But she didn't mind, because this is a place where everything is right, where all questions are answered. I didn't know any of this until I got here myself.

While I was at the jail, I decided to try the same kind of out-of-body experience. The process begins like meditation, with a progressive relaxation of the muscles and mind, like putting your body and consciousness to sleep while the subconscious mind remains awake.

Sitting on the floor of the cell, I began with the mental imagery of my mind slowly lifting outside of my skull. What starts as a flight of imagination, with the help of the proper brain-wave pattern, soon becomes real. My soul actually arose and hovered above my body, observing. I was in just the right state of mind to travel. Fear can inhibit out-of-body travel, but I had nothing

252

to lose, and fear no longer meant anything to me. I simply cut myself free from the body and drifted aimlessly. I felt myself merge with strange pools that weren't quite liquid, nor quite solid. I was no longer in jail. I wasn't even in the real world. It was a different dimension, where matter didn't exist. Time and space were skewed. I was flying, exploring, soaring for days, while only seconds passed to my still-living body. I was learning about realms a three-dimensional brain could never understand.

Light, color, sound, sensations, knowledge, wonder, fascination – they were all fused into one all-encompassing revelation. I was finding my way to Heaven. I didn't just learn or understand the meaning of God and the universe – I WAS the meaning. Always have been, just never realized it before. And so are you.

You, God and the universe are one. There's no difference. Even the boundary of your skin is imaginary. Nothing is solid. All is fluid, infinite and ever changing. The God-mind flows through you always, opening you to love. All we have to do is learn to get out of our own way and let it guide us.

As I surrendered, I moved up a long tunnel toward a light, and in that tunnel, I touched Jewel. I didn't really "see" her – we don't see things here as much as feel them and sense them. But I literally ran into her, and the touch was an absolutely exquisite experience. It was like two souls meant to be together, and instead of being separated by skin and bones, we could actually merge with one another and become two parts of a single whole. We knew each other in totality. After that, I could never leave her. I had to stay. I only wish we could've absorbed these truths in the living world, because we know now that people, even in the flesh, can live in total love all the time. That's where we're all headed. It's our destiny. It will happen, and when it does, there will be Heaven on earth.

I'm sorry, Casey. When we die, we leave behind sorrow and pain, but I thought that by communicating with you this way, I could ease that pain. Now you know that the only thing that ceased to exist was my body. The essence of what was me is still here.

I'll always be there in your heart and mind, where I left my mark. That will live as long as you do, and in many ways, I will live even in your children and grandchildren, just as you, too, will outlive your body. Your challenge is to survive and thrive and move always toward love and the light, no matter what happens in your life.

Speaking of light, I want to shed some on what happened to Jewel. On the night she died, she drank some jimson weed tea given to her by a friend named Spider Juncal. He told her it would heighten her ability to concentrate and intensify her experience, which it did. He didn't tell her it was also hallucinogenic, poisonous, and known to cause heart attacks.

After Jewel's spirit began its journey to this place, she sensed her body was in trouble. She came back. And then she used the power of her mind to fight the effects of the drug. She was able to return her heartbeat to a smooth, steady rhythm. She neutralized the drug and stabilized her body from within. The episode gave her a burst of confidence that she could master almost anything. Comfortable that the physical crisis was past, she continued with her out-of-body experience, filled with a conviction that she could go as deep into this heaven as she wanted. She was right. What she didn't realize was that once a spirit passes a certain point and joins with this cosmic God-mind, it can't return. It must live in this different dimension until reincarnated as another living being with a new consciousness.

But don't grieve for her. She wasn't murdered. She's fine.

Because I came here through a self-made portal, I'm like Jewel – a soul not yet ready to be re-absorbed by the whole. We came here too soon. Someday humans will evolve into pure consciousness and live entirely as Jewel and I exist today, but our species isn't ready yet.

Jewel and I are free to stay with each other for a while. We won't be taken back fully into the cosmic consciousness until our natural lives would have ended. In the meantime, we have the ability to reach out to you in certain ways. We can still watch over our loved ones.

Have you ever heard of guardian angels? You and your sister Heather now have a couple of them.

We love you both.
Dad

--------<>--------

That was the last anybody ever heard from Dakin or Jewel Caravans. But Jewel may have foretold her own fate when she quoted the following from "A Course in Miracles." This was the final entry in her personal journal:

> *"On this side of the bridge to timelessness*
> *You understand nothing.*
> *But as you step lightly across it, upheld by timelessness,*
> *You are directed straight to the Heart of God.*
> *At its center, and only there, you are safe forever,*
> *Because you are complete forever."*

--------<>--------